SK

IN THE HILLS OF MONTEREY

Other Five Star Westerns by Max Brand:

Sixteen in Nome
Outlaws All: A Western Trio
The Lightning Warrior
The Wolf Strain: A Western Trio
The Stone that Shines
Men Beyond the Law: A Western Trio
Beyond the Outposts
The Fugitive's Mission: A Western Trio

IN THE HILLS OF MONTEREY

A Western Story

MAX BRAND™

Five Star
Unity, Maine

Five Star Western
Published in conjunction with Golden West Literary Agency.

February 1998

First Edition

Five Star Standard Print Western Series.

The text of this edition is unabridged.

Set in 11 pt. Plantin by Al Chase.

Printed in the United States on permanent paper.

Library of Congress Cataloging in Publication Data

Brand, Max, 1892–1944.
    In the hills of Monterey : a western story / by Max Brand. —
1st ed.
    p. cm.
    ISBN 0-7862-0988-7 (hc : alk. paper)
    I. Title.
PS3511.A87I5   1998
   813´.52—dc21
                                             97-38421

IN THE HILLS OF MONTEREY

Chapter One

"LA CANTANTE"

As for the hilt, it was plain as could be. To be sure, it was of good steel at the guard and so put together as to combine the greatest safety with the least weight. But the hilt was negligible. What their eyes lingered over was the blade, for it was the finest Damascus steel, and over the wavy markings of its surface the light quivered until it seemed to be burning with blue fire, pooled at the broader base, or spilling off the taper point of the rapier. And the blue light continued to ebb and slowly flow along the narrow sword, because the brig was rocking in a soft cradle of waves, completely becalmed.

Due east, the California coast was piled blue, and an hour's fair breeze would bring them into Monterey harbor. But, just as they had grown eager for the ending of the trip, just as their eyes were beginning to brighten, and their hearts to stir at the thought of firm ground underfoot, with all the sweet earth's odors in their nostrils — just at that moment the wind dropped down, and, though the clouds continued to tumble across the sky, rolling landwards and to the north, there was not a breath to shake the sails. If, from time to time, the anxious eye of the helmsman detected a quiver on the fore royal or the main royal, or if the spanker shuddered, yet he knew well enough that it was only the gentle swing of the ship in the waves that caused the life in the canvas. In the meantime, the silence in the cabin continued, with each man leaning forward, until Francisco Valdez picked up the small sword.

"As for its name," he said, "you yourselves may hear it

sing." So saying, he flourished it, and the supple blade cut the air with a murmur of music. "And on this account," he added, as the listeners sat back in their chairs, "it was called *La Cantante*, which, as you know," he continued, turning particularly to the captain, "means The Singer."

The captain was a bluff Bostonian, who was christened Seth Wundy, but this title had long since been forgotten in favor of a sea-going nickname given him before he first crossed the line. In seven seas men knew old South Wind, but Seth Wundy was a name without a body. South Wind now turned upon the graceful young Spaniard who was resting the point of the sword on the deck and passing sensitive fingers over his waved and curling black hair.

"Port your helm, Mister Valdez," said the captain. "You're tacking close on shore. I ain't had the time nor the liking to learn more'n one language, as I've told you before. As for names, I save those for men and dogs, and I call a sword a sword, laying one good downright swing of a cutlass against a dozen of those long hatpins."

And, making a gesture almost as violent as though a cutlass were actually in his brown fist, he banished all thought of *La Cantante* and washed down the conclusion with a hearty pull at his tankard of grog. But the third occupant of the cabin paid no attention to the words or to the manner of the captain. His eyes had not left the beauty of the sword since it was first drawn from its scabbard, and though, out of courtesy to the captain, he spoke in English, his entire attention was for Valdez and the blade.

"May I take the rapier, *señor?*" he asked.

"I shall be too happy, *monsieur*," answered Valdez, with a glance towards South Wind, "to have the opinion of a master."

Monsieur Louis Auguste Mortier acknowledged the compliment with a deprecatory lifting of his brows, and then, taking

8

the weapon in both hands, he examined it with as much care as a jeweler who stares into the lights and colors of a ruby. He tried its flexibility, taking it near the point and bending it almost double. He tried its balance by resting it on the tip of his forefinger near the guard. Having studied it for some time in profound silence, while Valdez beamed and the captain scowled at his grog, the Frenchman at length caught it by the hilt and, leaping to his feet, came on guard with a violence that made the blade quiver from hilt to point. He passed through half a dozen movements, executed with such fire that it was plain he was engaging an imaginary foeman, and it was easy to note thrust and parry, lunge, parry, riposte, and lastly deadly flanconnade pushed home with such finality that the wide eyes of the captain seemed to see the fall of a dead man on the deck of his cabin.

He was mortified by the interest that had been wakened in him, however, and at once concealed his face behind his tilting flagon, while Mortier, quivering with excitement, returned the rapier to its owner.

"It is not a sword, *Señor* Valdez!" he cried. "It is a floating feather . . . it is all foible and point . . . and yet it has the strength of a stubborn woman. With such a sword one could kill a man with a thought." And he blew out his breath, as though he were wafting sharp death into the bosom of an enemy. "Do not sheathe it," he protested, as Valdez was about to put it up. "For, while I look at it, I think of the fighting after Waterloo. If I had had such a sword as that. . . ."

"The fighting *after* Waterloo?" queried South Wind in his great, gruff voice. "I thought that the fighting ended there. I thought you Frenchmen had your fill of smoke and blood that day."

Monsieur Mortier turned upon him with anger and with pride, summed up in a smile as cold as the steel of *La Cantante.*

"You were not in Paris, my captain," he said, "after that black day. But there were things to see even after the swine rolled their guns and marched their men through the streets where formerly. . . ."

Emotion choked him. He bowed his head, and the captain bit his lip and frowned again at his grog, perhaps from shame that any mature man should show such emotion, perhaps because a twinge of sympathy had touched him unawares.

"But afterward," went on Mortier, "we hunted them in the streets, and in the restaurant I sat with a friend, until a great beef-eater comes in with his spurs clanking and his cheeks red with good French wine he had swilled down . . . I watch him . . . my friend and I . . . I stare, and I smile . . . so!"

Here an expression of supercilious contempt crossed his face, a very devil of grinning malice.

"These English are slow to rise," he said, "but when they begin, they thunder at once. Presently the man leaps up and strides across the room. He bellows a curse out of his bull throat. He strikes me across the face."

He paused, breathing heavily, but with his eyes rapt upon space.

"What do I do? I wipe the blood from my mouth with my handkerchief. I draw out my card. I stand up and present it. If he will favor me with his name, my friend will call upon him and arrange the necessary details."

"Faugh!" grunted South Wind. "If he gave you a blow, why not give it him back and be done?"

"Ah," said Mortier, "that is your Saxon way. I have another touch . . . quite another touch. At dawn of the next morning we stand in the cool, his seconds behind him, my seconds behind me. He stands like one of his bayonets, stiff and still. He salutes, like the fan of a windmill swinging. In a moment, we are at it. Ah, and they fight with much heart, these English.

10

But not like those who followed the emperor from Moscow to Madrid, from Friedland to Cairo . . . their hearts and their hands are strong, but they do not know the soul of the sword. So, a little play, a touch here, a touch there . . . I let him come at me, raging like a bull . . . I seem winded . . . I stagger . . . my guard is down and wide . . . he presses wildly in to finish . . . and then a quick thrust under and up . . . *ha!* . . . there he falls. No need of the doctor. I know anatomy as well as any of that breed. The fellow's done for. And that, *Señor* Valdez, was how we fought after Waterloo. They had stolen away our emperor, but they had left us our swords and our hearts, and still we fought for his glory."

Here the captain was heard to mutter something about "murder," but the enthusiasm of Valdez drowned out all murmured comments. Those must have been glorious days, he declared, and, had he been in Paris, he would have joined in the sport. This brought another growl from the captain, to the effect that honest fists were the only weapons to settle a quarrel, but he was now out of the current of the conversation that was bandied back and forth between the Spaniard and the Frenchman alone.

"Ah," cried Mortier, "I see it in your face . . . the love of the sword. But who could keep from it, with such a blade! There is a story behind it . . . there is a tale for every inch of the steel, eh, *mon ami?*"

"Ten tales for every inch," replied Valdez. "A Valdez rode in the Second Crusade. He brought back a Saracen scimitar that cut steel as other swords cut cloth. It passed through a dozen forms. It was drawn out once to the length of a great estoc. It was made a cut-and-thrust rapier in my grandfather's day. And at last it was whittled away, as men's hands grew lighter, and their wits grew sharper, until you see it as it is . . . as old as a song and as new as a song. And, therefore, is it not right to call it *La Cantante*?"

Mortier was delighted. He half closed his eyes, as he answered: "I knew it by the light on it, for that light was telling of its hundred men . . . a hundred dead men, *señor*. I would give a year of life for a dozen passes. A year of life, *Señor* Valdez, but I have no foils with me."

Enthusiasm carried Valdez away. He clapped his hands together twice, and instantly there appeared at the open door of the cabin a figure that was like a breath from an Oriental story. He was of not more than the middle height, but his strange costume made him seem tall. About his head was wrapped a turban of the snowiest white; his body was closely fitted by a brocaded jacket of blue velvet, out of which flowed wide sleeves of white muslin, of elbow length, exposing brawny forearms. A crimson sash girt his waist. His pantaloons, of the same white stuff of which the sleeves were made, dropped below the knee and were secured halfway to the ankle by a tight band, beneath which were bare legs, disappearing into red slippers of soft leather. His skin was, wherever it was exposed, of the swarthiest complexion. Yet his eyes were blue, and apparently the rich bronze had been the result of exposure to many a sun, where the sun bites strongest. Why he should have been so arrayed would have been hard to tell, unless the vanity of Valdez expressed itself less in his own costume than in the garb of his servant. He now fixed his eyes upon the deck and bowed to his master.

"I'll play at the foils with you, *Monsieur* Mortier," said Valdez. "El Rojo, bring a pair into the waist of the ship. That will give us room enough, my friend?"

"Room enough," answered Mortier, with shining eyes, "for close work is the best work." And he threw off his coat, as though swept away with eagerness for the test. "But where," he continued, "did you get a Moorish servant with blue eyes?

I never noticed them until this moment. He looked up when you mentioned the foils, and the sun glinted in them."

"There are stranger things about him than the blue of his eyes," nodded Valdez, as the two went toward the waist of the brig, where there was an open space on the deck. The captain reluctantly followed them, as though he could not miss the athletic contest, even if he despised the tools with which it was conducted. "My father got him two years or more ago. I've heard him tell the story twenty times. My father was a passenger on a merchant vessel bound for Alexandria, and, as they lay near the port of Tunis, they made out a sail bearing swiftly down on them, with a strong shore breeze bringing it along. It came faster than the wind could have carried it, however, and presently the lookout called that it was a galley with oars to help the wind. The captain put on all sail, but, as a matter of fact, he had no wish to escape. He carried ten twenty-four-pounder carronades, and his ship was heavily manned, for he was taking out a full extra crew to sail back another brig. And merchantmen sailing the Mediterranean in those days drilled their crews at the guns and cutlass work.

"He put on all sail, therefore, but he dropped a drag behind that kept down his speed. The galley came up quickly, furled its sail, and stood in, with the force of the oars alone. At the same time it began to open with a brace of long eighteen-pounders. The aim was bad, however, and the captain let a few shots plow through the rigging, without making any response. In the meantime, he had sent three-fourths of his crew and passengers below to make everything ready between decks and to get out their weapons . . . so that the lookout from the galley could see nothing more than a dozen men, scurrying about . . . the ordinary crew of merchantmen for that size. But when the pirate came into point-blank range, the captain wore his ship, knocked the covers from the ports, and gave the Moors a

13

broadside that raked them fore and aft. Think of it, *Monsieur* Mortier . . . think of those solid shots, plowing aft through the bodies of the men at the oars . . . my father used to say that the shrieks often wakened him at night.

"The pirate saw he had caught a Tartar, and he tried to get away, but everything was in confusion. There was hardly an oar on his boat that did not have a dead man tied to it. Besides, one of the shots had hulled it fairly between wind and water, and it was filling fast. Our ship stood away, tacked, and, coming about, stood down at the galley, with the intention of running it down, since it lay so low in the sea.

"It succeeded perfectly. The wind was strong. Our ship bowled the pirate brig along at a brisk rate, and the bows struck heavily on the side of the pirate brig. It careened far over, the water rushed in over the side, and the galley went down in a trice. The rowers were dead men, tied in their places, and the waves lashed their bodies. However, nearly a score of the fighting force had leaped from the deck of the galley into the rigging of our brig, and now they poured down onto the deck, all fighting madmen who knew it was better to die at once than to rot in a Spanish prison, or be strung up at the yardarms. The pirate captain was one of them. He was a man of mark, covered with gold and jewels, with enough pearls on the butt of one of his pistols to ransom a duchess. He led the battle with his tigers beside him. In the rear came El Rojo, taking no part.

"Their first assault swept back the crew, but the captain rallied a dozen men from the stern and brought them forward with muskets. A volley at close range dropped half of the pirates, and their leader was among those who fell. Then the crew took to their cutlasses and went in to finish the work. It was not so hard. The Moors were disheartened and gave back, except for a raging devil who stood over the pirate captain, naked to the waist, with long, red hair flying in the wind, his bare feet giving him a perfect grip on the deck. He fought with no cutlass, but with a rapier that danced like a will-o'-the-wisp and brought men down as fast as they came within the touch of it. Finally an old soldier, who happened to be in the crew, ran in, took a thrust of the rapier through his left shoulder, and cut down the red-headed devil with his cutlass.

"That was El Rojo. The merchant captain wanted to throw him overboard with the rest, but my father pointed out that he was only a slave, and therefore not accountable . . . the collar was around his throat."

"Collar?" broke in South Wind.

"It's still there. Come here, El Rojo."

The slave was approaching, carrying the foils over his arm, and Valdez tore open the jacket at his throat. He exposed in this fashion a thin bronze collar that fitted around El Rojo's neck and upon which were inscribed Arabic letters.

"My father bought him," continued Valdez, as El Rojo calmly stepped back and buttoned his jacket once more. "And, after it was decided that I should come to the end of the world . . . to this California . . . El Rojo dropped on his knees and begged to be allowed to come with me. Yes, El Rojo?"

The servant crossed his arms on his breast and bowed low.

"A faithful devil, eh?" murmured Mortier.

"A cursed pirate!" snorted South Wind.

"Not faithful to me," answered Valdez, "but faithful to Sanduval."

Here he was interrupted by a neigh and a stamping of a horse's hoofs between decks that caused El Rojo to turn and flee across the top deck. He had disappeared only a moment when the disturbance ceased.

"You see?" said Valdez, smiling. "A word from El Rojo quiets Sanduval. They know each other. And when my father gave me his finest stallion to take on the voyage, and to stock the *hacienda* with blooded horses, El Rojo begged that he might come, also. And so you see him."

South Wind had hung upon this narrative with a profound interest, and so had several of the sailors who were working nearby to fit the ship for port. But *Monsieur* Mortier had only vaguely heard the last words. He was too busy trying out the foils, and, when Valdez perceived this, he threw off his coat in turn and made ready for the play.

Chapter Two

A SLAVE WITH A SWORD

The mate of the good brig, *Fortune*, was as stern a man as ever furled an ice-sheeted sail in a storm off the Horn and rose from the forecastle by the strength of his hand, the courage in his heart, and the iron in his soul. The crew of the ship on which he sailed became slaves, whom he drove with curses, from dawn to dark and from dark to dawn again, but foil play on a ship at sea was so unusual a spectacle that even he relented and allowed all hands to gather for the fun. Half guiltily, as though they knew that they were stealing time that should have been spent upon the rigging to make all shipshape for the port, they gathered, with grins on their brown faces, and saw the deck cleared, while the two antagonists stood forth.

Physically the combatants were not unevenly matched. They were of a height, and the greater experience of the French soldier might be supposed to be counter-balanced by the greater ability of the young Spaniard. But, after the first crossing of the swords, it was seen at once that appearances had little to do with the matter in hand. For, the instant he raised his foil, there was a total change in the bearing of Mortier. From being rather stodgy in build, he became at once as tapering as a youth, his arms seemed to grow longer, and the movements of his feet were swifter and more subtle than the most intricate dance steps. He drifted lightly here and there, engaging, separating, engaging again. But, after the first touch of the foils, there was an even greater alteration in Valdez. He had stepped lightly to the encounter, with his lips slightly compressed, as though to keep back a smile of conscious superiority. But after steel had chimed on steel, the incipient smile disappeared. The color left his face, and behind his lips it was plainly to be seen that he was gritting his teeth. He had met a master, and to be disgraced before so many eyes was the bitterest of poisons.

Not that he gave in easily. He pressed an attack at once and showed that he had been at least well taught. His lunges were fierce, but, though he was well extended in them, he did not throw himself off balance, and his recoveries were smooth and swift. He advanced and retreated without diminishing his readiness to thrust or parry. And if, as the captain was doing, one watched his movements alone, it seemed quite impossible that another could avoid the button at the taper tip of the foil.

That, however, was exactly what the Frenchman was doing. The blade in his hand was a phantom thing. He turned the most severe lunge with a light, quick tap of his own foil, and he sent a riposte in return that leaped like the head of a striking snake. Yet, after a minute or two of the engagement, he had not yet touched Valdez, and the latter suddenly lowered his foil.

"Monsieur," he said, panting with his exertions and with shame as well, "if you can touch me, do it now. I am past the days when I was willing to be made a fool of."

Mortier was instantly eloquent with praise. He had rarely fenced, he swore, with a better man. He had been doing his best, but his best had not been good enough. However, since *Señor* Valdez wished to end the bout, he would redouble his efforts to make a hit.

His actions, however, entirely belied his words. They had hardly engaged again before his button lodged against the breast of Valdez, a touch made with such perfect ease that Valdez allowed an exclamation of rage to escape him, and, hurriedly saluting, he attacked again. It was as though he had dropped his foil and rushed blindly against the button. Again he was touched, and again. And finally he stepped back and lowered his point. It was a tribute to him that, although his lips were white with shame, he was able to force a smile.

"I see, *monsieur,*" he said, "that I am not yet past my pupil days. I shall remember this lesson."

"You are wrong," protested Mortier. "Luck helped me. Besides, *señor,* I have lived twice the number of your years. It is not I who have touched you but time . . . which teaches men a thousand tricks."

It was said with a manner that gave a double weight to the words, but the pride of Valdez had been wounded to the quick. He could not help but see the broad grins on the faces of the sailors, and a spot of red color leaped into either cheek.

"For my part," he said, "I am winded. But if you still wish exercise, my servant has at least a strong wrist, *monsieur.* And if you care to use him, he is entirely at your disposal."

Louis Mortier bowed. "A slave with a sword," he said, "is at least a man. I shall be too happy."

Valdez clapped his hands together and called. There was a light, swift scuffing across the deck, and El Rojo stood before him. The order of Valdez was a mere gesture that explained everything. For, passing his foil to the slave, he waved toward Mortier. The reply of El Rojo was a low bow, after which he laid his foil on the deck, removed his brocaded jacket, folded it carefully, placed it apart where it would not be apt to come under trampling feet, then raised the foil and, with another low inclination to Mortier, as though asking his pardon for raising a hand against him, came on guard. All of this he performed with such perfect gravity and deliberateness that the smiles of the sailors changed to a low chuckle, barely audible. Indeed, the encounter promised to be ridiculous in the extreme, for yonder was Mortier, obviously a master of fence and now on fire with enthusiasm for his work. As for El Rojo, in his turban and outlandish costume, a great scimitar would have been more in keeping. Nevertheless, Valdez, leaning against the rail, called out: "Ten *pesos* on the first touch, *monsieur*."

In spite of himself, the brows of Mortier raised a trifle. "Very well," he answered. "Ten *pesos* on it, *señor. Monsieur* El Rojo, with your permission."

Instantly he engaged, twice lunging low and following with a high thrust, lightning fast. These attempts were frustrated, not so much by the parries of El Rojo, as by the speed with which he gave ground. But the instant the engagement commenced, his great length of arm was noticed. Ordinarily this feature was masked by the flowing nature of his garments, but now, as he was extended, one noticed a great reach. Indeed, with his sword arm held rather stiffly out, after the Italian fashion, and with his left arm thrown behind him, his size seemed to be redoubled, for his shoulders were very broad, and with his arms extended he became as impressive as the eagle when it drops from the branch and spreads its wings to shoot across the valley. He was in all things a direct contrast with Mortier, for, whereas the steps of the Frenchman were like intricate dancing, the footwork of the slave was like the smooth flowing of water that carried him gliding back and forth. In a moment Mortier was breathing hard, but the lips of the slave had not parted, and not a muscle of his facial expression had altered.

Here the Frenchman drew back for an instant, as if at once to draw his breath and consider a new plan of assault, but he was given no intermission. For El Rojo, gliding forward at once, engaged him again. Yet there was this peculiarity in his fence, that, while he pressed close to Mortier, he seemed rather on the defensive than the offensive. His point drifted easily toward the breast of the Frenchman, but most of his work

20

consisted in parries of the volleyed lunges and thrusts of the other.

Yet, gentle though his movements seemed, they brought the sweat dripping from the face of Mortier. His breath began to come in gasps, and his lips grinned from his teeth, with the venomous force of his attack. The chuckling of the sailors had ceased some time before, and now they noticed with the most intense amazement that the Moor had not yet altered his expression. Indeed, with his head poised high and easily, the lids drooping a little over his eyes, he was as calm as any wearied traveler, sitting upon the deck and watching for land. So this perfect calm began to have a new meaning. There was a satirical meaning in it, and behind the eyes they began to guess at a mocking sneer. Their sympathies were instantly with Mortier. Like most Anglo-Saxons, they were opposed to the French, but here was a case of the honor of a Christian against a Moslem, of the white against the dark, and they began to mutter to one another and invoke good fortune for Mortier. Moreover, they were antagonized by the enthusiasm of Valdez who had earlier become disliked because of his cold and supercilious manner. A Yankee crew is apt to consider all men equal, with the exception of their captain who may be endowed with Satanic qualities. Therefore, the aristocratic presumptions of Francisco Valdez met with no favor on the *Fortune*, and, when the men before the mast marked him clapping his hands and laughing, they scowled upon El Rojo and wished him double misfortune. But bad luck did not seem destined for the slave. In the very midst of a fierce attack by Louis Mortier, between two final motions of the attack, a sudden thrust nailed him fairly over the heart with such force that the foil almost doubled in the hand of El Rojo.

"Diable!" gasped Mortier, his sword suspended in air, quivering with the ferocity with which he had intended to drive

home his attack. And he added, a word wrung from him on the spur of the moment: "Magic!"

"Magic?" echoed Valdez, reducing his laughter to a smile. "Not magic, but ten *pesos, monsieur.*"

Mortier paid with perfect good grace, for a single instant had been time enough for him to recover his poise.

"And twenty *pesos* on the next touch," continued Valdez.

The French soldier turned his glance upon the slave. The latter had lowered his foil and stood apart, with his glance directed toward the blue California shore, as though his interest were far beyond the deck of the staunch brig. The very sailors marked in his face an expression they had more than once noticed, whether in gale or sunshine, on the long voyage from Boston where they had picked up their strange passengers — the stallion and the two men.

"Bras de fer," Mortier muttered to himself, as he regarded the calm unconcern of his late antagonist. And he added aloud to his companion of the voyage: "Where did he get his strength, *Señor* Valdez?"

"From the galleys," answered Valdez. "He pulled at an oar in a Tunis ship for many a day. And that, perhaps, is where he got his long arms also. But twenty *pesos, monsieur,* that the slave will touch the soldier of Napoleon again."

The mention of that sacred name caused Mortier to stiffen and raise his head. But, the next instant, he looked again to the immobile face of El Rojo and shook his head ever so lightly.

"Under what masters did he learn?"

"I can tell you that also," answered Valdez. "When the pirates from Tunis brought in ship after ship, there were some great men with the sword among the captives. Now the first master of El Rojo was a great man in Tunis. When he asked it, El Rojo was given to him at once. And when he begged that the best fighters of the captive crews be given to him for a month, it was granted, too. So he took the chosen men and amused himself with letting them engage El Rojo. Their freedom, if they touched him . . . if they only grazed him with their weapons. Mind you, those battles were not with foils. But sometimes there was an Englishman, wonderfully dexterous with a blade. If that were the case, he was set loose against the long arms of El Rojo . . . if he touched the slave, it was freedom for the beef-eater. And there were gentlemen of Italy who knew the rapier as a priest knows his breviary. They were pitted against El Rojo with the naked point. Mind you, if the slave did not win, he got the point through an arm or a leg, or through the body. So it paid him to learn. Or perhaps among the prisoners was some Pole, and the Poles are born to the saber, as we are born to the taste of milk and bread. It made no difference to the great man. He gave them their own weapons and pitted them against El Rojo, and the slave had to protect himself or die, for the edge of a saber is not to be jested with."

"A work of hell," breathed *Monsieur* Mortier.

"You have not seen," answered Valdez. "El Rojo!"

He who was called "The Red" turned with his accustomed profound bow to his master.

"Take off your shirt!"

Beneath the bronzed skin of El Rojo a flush appeared.

"Look!" laughed Valdez. "He is as modest as a maiden. I said off with the shirt, El Rojo. Let them see your skin!"

Slowly, with eyes on the deck, the slave obeyed. He drew off the white tunic with the flowing sleeves and exposed his body. There was a drawn breath of excitement from the sailors, and from Captain South Wind a deep, muffled growl. For the skin of El Rojo was as dazzlingly white as the skin of any Christian, and the place where his body had not been protected either by the sleeves or the neck of his tunic was marked with a sharp line of tan. No matter what his nationality or his name; no matter if he had been a pirate of Tunis, blood speaks, and the blood of this man was not the blood of one whose forefathers had been raised under the sun of the tropics. For the skin was milky white, and it added luster and meaning suddenly to the blue of his eyes. There was a little stir among the honest sailors, because one of them had been forced to strip and show himself before strangers from a strange land. And the spot of color that leaped into the cheeks of El Rojo was easily understandable. But silence followed. They were too filled with interest by the sight that was revealed to their eyes. The body of El Rojo was spotted with scars as thick as the body of one who has lain near to death with smallpox. Here was a round scar a coin could have covered. There was a long mark, as though a knife had run over the skin. And now that eyes began to look for them, it was possible to see other marks, like thin shadows through the white sheath of his skin. Literally the body of El Rojo had been marked by war.

The Frenchman voiced the thought of all. "He's been though a tiger's claws, *Señor* Valdez."

"Through the swords of men," answered the young Spaniard. "You are wrong, *monsieur.*"

"In the word . . . ," said Mortier, as the slave put on his tunic again, "in the word, but not in the thought. And you have taken the shame of my defeat from me, *señor.* We Christians learn to thrust and parry with blunt weapons. This poor devil has been made to do his practice with death staring him in the face. It is small wonder to me that I was touched. *Señor* Valdez, I shall not wager my skill against him for twenty *pesos.*"

"Why, then," exclaimed Valdez, "to save the bet, *monsieur,* I wager the twenty pesos that he disarms you without being touched."

The Frenchman laughed. "I have been in a hundred frays,

my friend," he said, "and I have never yet lost my sword. You give me odds that are too great."

"The bet," answered Valdez.

"It would be stolen money," answered Mortier.

"The bet," repeated the owner of the slave.

"Why, then, if you force me, I accept your money, *monsieur*."

And, perceptibly tightening his grip upon the foil, Mortier faced El Rojo again. But there was a change in the latter. Whereas he had formerly been the perfect blank of disinterest, he now engaged the sword of the Frenchman with a certain eagerness, not so much perceptible in the mask of his face as in the motions of his hand and body. There was still no approximation to the staccato dancing steps of Mortier. But he seemed to flow upon the Frenchman with his attack. Where the other danced, he stepped, but his steps were the strides of a panther, slipping back and forth, working irresistibly in upon his foe. Once, twice, and again his button touched the body of the other in a vital place, and still he came, with lips closed, with breath easy, with eye composed. And Mortier fought back with all the strength of his body, with all the wits and tricks he had learned in a score of campaigns. He was no school fencer, this warrior of Napoleon's. He had the speed of a cornered rat — and the wiles. It mattered not that he was fighting to win a bet, and that the bet was merely to keep the sword in his hand.

For the constant touch of the other's foil against his body maddened him. Perhaps he saw, in that moment, not the circling faces of the ignorant sailors before the mast, but all the eyes of the great men of his past looked in upon him, and in the eyes of each was scorn and wonder. He fought as one possessed, but even as he thrust and lunged a slight touch put his foil aside, and the button of El Rojo was at his heart again.

Yet when the climax came, it came by surprise. The sailors had lost their sympathies. The shining white skin of the slave had not left their memories, and, though they appreciated the desperate efforts of the Frenchman, yet they also appreciated the efforts of El Rojo. Even South Wind bent forward and swayed from side to side, as the fortunes of the battle seemed to sway. And then, as El Rojo slipped back before a violent attack, his foil darted out, as the pronged tongue of a snake darts, and no doubt the motion was as swift as the dart of a snake's tongue. Yet, judged by the calm face of the slave, it seemed a slow and deliberate thing. His blade wrapped like a living thing around the blade of Louis Mortier, and the sword of the Frenchman was torn from his hands. It flew back across the railing and darted down beneath the blue of the slowly moving waters.

Chapter Three

A NEW GOVERNOR

It mattered not that behind him marched fifty soldiers with muskets upon their shoulders. It mattered not that behind the soldiers straggled the baggage train that bore food for the men and weapons for the soldiers and finery for the women of Alta California. It mattered not that he carried with him those documents that gave him authority as the governor of the province. What was of chief concern to José Bernardo Pyndero was that the weight of a rapier tugged at the belt around him and in that scabbard lay the sword that had won him his fame.

There are degrees of greatness. But when a man has never met defeat, surely here is excuse for pride. He was proud of the high fortune that had been with him all his life. He was proud of the new title he had won, for to be a governor was no idle thing. He was proud of the record behind him that told how, as a leader of Spanish brigands, he had fought against the marshals of Napoleon. But he was most of all proud of the sword that had never failed him in a hundred encounters. It was nothing that he had taken his wounds and his scars in battle, but it was very much that the king of Spain had himself seen Pyndero at work, foil in hand.

So, as he came in view of the seat of his government, what was more natural than that he should halt his good horse and drop his hand upon his hilt? Yonder lay the town of Monterey, red roofs and white walls, set out upon a spreading lawn of green. And over the vast district to the south, that he had traversed, his word was the law, and over the vast district to the north his word was law also, even to that bay Sir Francis Drake had seen and where the mission of San Francisco had been established. This was a domain worthy of a king, and like a king he resolved to write his name into history. Much should be done under the rule of José Bernardo Pyndero.

He looked back upon his men. They were not such soldiers as he was wont to lead. The brigands who had obeyed his order in battle in Spain had been a ragged crew enough, but these fellows, half Spanish and the more important half Indian, were a different matter. To handle them was like handling raw coals from a fire. No matter as to that! He had taught them what the hand of a master might be, and they had learned to shrink and bow to him. And if he scowled upon their ragged clothes, he smiled upon their guns. The Little Corporal had taught the whole world that a gun is a gun, no matter in what indifferent hands. And the fifty behind him were not to be scoffed at. When he thought of the infinite pains he had been at to bring this handful from far south in the old province to this new land, he was half in despair. But he recalled that in this country fifty were as many as fifty thousand in that blood-drenched peninsula over which the English and the French had fought.

Therefore, considering all these things, José Pyndero thrust out his chest and rode down bravely into the streets of Monterey. For he knew that no matter how many eyes marked the poor array of his followers, just as many would mark the array of the new governor and the orders and the medals upon his breast. He could have wished that his horse was of better blood. But who of generous mind will not admit that the horse is nothing, and that the rider is everything?

On the outskirts of the town they came to meet him. They had had news of his coming, and the whole populace turned out to give him the proper greeting. They shouted till their throats were hoarse. They shouted as they looked upon the soldiers. They shouted still more as they looked upon the mules, prodded forward by the lazy Indians. But they shouted most of all when they beheld the new governor.

Wax was not needed to make his mustache stand straight out. Pride accomplished that much. And pride also made the soldiers stand straighter under their guns than he had ever been able to make them stand during the long march. He had drilled and cursed and shouted at them for a long hour every day, no matter in what desert they were marching. But curses and shouts could not do what the glimpses of peaceful townsfolk accomplished. And, as the latter called their welcome and their praises, the soldiers stepped out in a truer rhythm. There was not even need of the drum to make them step in time. They bore themselves with a grand manner that was an ample recompense for the tattered state of their garments and the dust upon their faces. They were like a band of heroes, descending into a conquered town.

In this wise they reached the *presidio*. In this wise they appeared before the stiff, straight lines of the soldiers who were drawn up to receive them. In this wise they were shown to their quarters in the new land.

So, when all was over, the governor found himself introduced to his residence. It was far better than one could have expected in such a land, after the march over the parched interior. It was built of the universally used adobe, but it had been newly constructed, so that all the edges and lines of the building were crisp and clean. The patio, in which at least half of the social life of the house would revolve, was spacious and well walled. There was a garden of twenty varieties of blossoms. Best of all, the whole building had been put in order by the good townsfolk. The government had furnished the house and its equipment, and the women of the town had made ready for their new governor by sending their own servants and hiring others to make all ready for his excellency.

José Bernardo Pyndero was enchanted. He had thought himself bound for the ends of the world to take the rule over a mass of savages. Instead, he began to believe that he had fallen in with the most pleasant people in the world. Moreover, this was the first fragrance of admiration and obedience and respect, so that he saw he was, indeed, to rule this domain like a king. Therefore, let us look in upon José Bernardo Pyndero, after he has retired to his room and been dressed and bathed, so that the dust of the journey is removed from his body, and the weariness of the journey is rubbed out of his brain. Let us see the great swordsman as he steps out into the patio that is the universal hall of the house. There he finds that people are already gathering to bid him welcome, and, as it is dusk and lights are beginning to be lighted here and there about the patio, he advances upon his visitors both to see and to be seen.

His bearing is at once worthy of the sole representative of an ancient and famous family, the governor of a great province, a man of fashion, and the first swordsman in all Spain. As for his carriage and figure, all that need be said is it was all that could be asked even of a soldier, a young man of thirty-two years, and a famous duelist. For he was both agile and powerfully upright, and yet graceful. His face, however, seemed unusually large even upon the shoulders of so big a man. The features were pronounced, particularly the long nose and the long chin. His forehead was of more than moderate height, but it sloped back, very nearly continuing the line of the nose. His brows were single lines of black, highly arched — the penciled brows gave an unexpected expression of refinement and naïveté at the same time. This expression was further emphasized by a habit of Pyndero's: he always looked about him with wide eyes, partly blank and partly innocent. But all the candor of these features was quite removed by the contrast with his mouth. For he habitually wore the faintest of smiles. Indeed, it never went out and never altered. But, with each turning or raising of his head, the meaning of that smile was new. Sometimes it seemed that he was merely compressing his lips, the unmistakable sign of stern and strong character; again, it seemed a shadowy smile of scorn and inward mockery; and, still again, it seemed that it was merely the token of a joyous heart within.

As for his dress, it was rather starched and formal than gay. His stock was high and stiff enough to have choked some men. There was not the slightest curl to the straight black hair, combed back on his head. His buttons and his waistcoat were plain in pattern and in color. His boots were also as simple as could have been wished by the most severe.

There was only one touch of brilliance and gaiety in all his attire, and that was a ruby set in a ring on his hand. But, after one had glanced twice at that ring, one began to feel that the sober costume of the new governor was made purposely drab, so it might serve as a better background for that jewel. For it was huge enough to have been a pendant. Moreover, it was of the finest sort. It was the true Burmese of pigeon-blood red. And it gave a wonderful distinction to the few gestures of Pyndero.

Such was the man who advanced upon the townsmen of Monterey, thanked them for their courtesies, and begged them to enter his house and have a few glasses of the wine with which they had themselves so generously stocked his cellar. They accepted eagerly, but, though the new governor was the very type and pattern of cordial courtesy, they found that they were presently falling into little silences. They rose to depart and tell the rest of the curious town that José Pyndero was a man of parts, which fitted well with his reputation as a soldier and as a swordsman. They also reported that pride and dignity surrounded him with a barrier, which for the time being was impenetrable.

So they left the dwelling, and they were hardly gone when visitors of another type began to approach the house of the governor. These consisted of some dozen skulking figures wrapped in blankets of different colors. They did not come straight to the entrance gate of the patio. Instead, they chose to drift around the house and, coming by a detour, to gain access by climbing the high wall. This was managed with the greatest skill and silence. One man stood against the wall. His fellows jumped to his shoulders and so drew themselves up to the top of the wall and dropped down into the patio itself behind the screen of shrubs. And this they managed without attracting the attention of a soldier who paced back and forth through the court with a musket upon his shoulder, for, when his back was turned, they fell swiftly, one after the other, with no more sound than dropping shadows. Presently, as the sentinel came to the end of his round toward the shrubs and turned to retrace his course, one of those crouched shadows detached itself from the bushes, slipped out, a knife flashing in the starlight. The soldier slumped forward without a cry and would have fallen with a crash on the hard ground had not the arms of his murderer supported him. He was lowered softly, then dragged among the shrubs, and the dozen shapes ran for the house itself.

The door was not locked, and they approached it with as much certainty as though they had seen the different people enter their respective chambers. They opened it softly. Two of them glided in. Others would have followed, but now sounded the furious snarl of a dog. José Pyndero rose with a shout from his bed, and his sword glimmered in his hand. The dog leaped at the throat of one assailant. The second shadow sprang at

Pyndero and received a foot of needle-sharp steel through his throat.

Instantly the house wakened in confusion. Voices were calling in answer to the stentorian tones of the governor. Presently a group of frightened domestics and soldiers had gathered. They found that the blanketed forms, save one, had vanished. Near the dog that had received a knife thrust between the ribs lay a tall Indian, with blood about the hollow of his throat. The governor snatched a light and held it near the dead eyes of the man. What he saw was a handsome warrior, a full six feet or more in height, his complexion a red-brown, his long hair held away from his face by a bright-colored band of cloth, the upper part of his body clad in a tunic of white cotton, his legs covered with long trousers of the same material, held close to the leg, below the knee, by a garter of cloth, and on his feet were moccasins. His upturned hands were those of a strong man. And, as the light glinted in his sightless eyes, even in his death he seemed formidable. The governor caught up the blanket that had fallen from the shoulders of the man and threw it across his face.

"Take this dead rat out!" he commanded. "Saddle horses . . . raise the town! The devils have trailed me a thousand miles, and, unless I run these desert tigers to the ground, they'll make me a present of half a foot of cold steel between the ribs. A hundred *pesos* . . . do you hear? . . . a hundred *pesos* for every man of them that's caught!"

Chapter Four

ORTIZA

When the dawn came, it found two Indians squatted about a smoky fire on the top of a high hill behind the town of Monterey. They were by no means like that splendid warrior who had died on the floor of the governor's room the night before. These, with wide mouths and high cheekbones and small brute eyes, half naked, with coarse hair tumbled across their foreheads, had only enough intelligence to keep one pair of eyes constantly watching the town below them, as though for a signal. They had near their fire two great heaps, one of dry fuel and one of green stuff. With the one they could pass on the signal by night, and with the other they could raise a tall pillar of white to be seen far off by day.

Far behind them on another hill a similar pair of Indians squatted by just such a fire, and behind these, again, was still a third on a hilltop that overlooked a pleasant valley. And those three fires had been kept burning for three full weeks of anticipation and waiting. Not that the least germ of excitement entered the breasts of the Indians, but they had been ordered to do a certain duty, and, knowing the lash, there was never a time for all those weeks, day or night, when eyes were not watching from hilltop to hilltop, and so bridging the gap between the house in the valley and the Bay of Monterey.

From the house itself, in a bell tower whose chimes sent the Indians to work and called them home again at night, an identical pair crouched night and day and day and night, one man sleeping or eating, one man with his eyes fixed upon the

34

hilltop and his hand clasping the bell rope. Such had been the orders given to them three weeks before, and they did not deviate from their instructions.

So eight men were kept in idleness and waiting, but, for that matter, Joaquín Tarabal could have sent forty for the same purpose. He was not one of those who number their servants upon the fingers of two hands, adding patiently one by one. He had not more than an idea of the number of human beings who lived by him and for him.

Indeed, *Señor* Tarabal had only vague ideas about most of his affairs and the affairs of the world. All that he was sure of was the primary importance and greatness of Tarabal. He could not have told one the price of the hides for the sake of which he reared the numberless cattle that grazed in the rich valley or roamed far across the hills and out onto the huge plain beyond. His servants oversaw that distant work. They were his eyes and his ears, but he did not really care enough about facts and figures to consult them for information. He knew, also, that they stole shamelessly from him. But he did not care. A mountain is careless of the squirrel that makes a hole in its side. Tarabal felt in just that manner. Sometimes, if he were out of humor or bored, he had one of the thieves caught and whipped to death, saying that he would discourage the knavery. But all of his people understood that the thieves were not whipped to death because they had stolen cattle and hides, but because the great master must be amused on that day. So the stealing went on as busily as ever, and Tarabal shrugged his shoulders and yawned in the faces of the honest men who came bearing him tales of plunder and knavery.

Today he chose to walk back and forth on the wall that enclosed two sides of the patio. The huge house, two stories in height and built in an ell, fenced one half of the patio; a wall, as thick as the battlement wall of a fortress of old days,

35

shut in the rest. He loved to walk in this place. It was entirely safe as a promenade, for so bulky was the mass of adobe that there was room for two men to walk arm in arm on its top. As he strolled back and forth, his eyes were constantly delighted by the sight of the valley, the plowed ground of the rich bottom lands, the sweeping pastures on either side, the sea of hills rolling on and on to the blue curve of the sky. All was his, and each little clot of color, sometimes single and sometimes in groups, meant so many *pesos*, or so much goods in trade.

Or, if he turned in the opposite direction, there was his great house, rising with fortress walls and its great wealth. Yet, if it were destroyed tomorrow and all within it, he could wave his hand and reconstruct it on a more magnificent scale than before. It would be almost worth destroying to have the pleasure of planning it all anew, for there was nothing that could not be replaced, nothing save his greatest jewel of all, and this was his daughter, Ortiza, who sat in the little balcony before that window of her room that was unbarred and looked down upon the patio. With her was her old governess, Rosa.

He contemplated the picture with an infinite satisfaction. To be sure, he did not look upon her as most fathers look upon their children. There was too little of himself in her for that. He himself was built very much like a frog, with bowed legs and with short arms and a squat, heavy body. His large head was set upon his shoulders without the support of any visible neck. His complexion was very dark — almost as dark as some of his Indians — and it had a greasy luster. His body was corpulent, but his face was not. The bony framework was too big and massive for that — so massive that it was immobile, except for a great bush of eyebrows that rose and fell with every alteration of his temper. But Ortiza was all her mother's child. She had the same great, unreadable, black eyes. She had the same waving mass of silky, golden hair. She had the same eternal quiet. She had even the same trick of canting her head a little to one side.

Therefore, if he did not love her as his daughter, he loved her the more as the most priceless possession. He could not duplicate her, not if he had tenfold as much money as was his. Sometimes it irritated him, this thought. Sometimes he shrugged his fat shoulders and thrust out his jaw, as he looked at her. He did this now, taking note that she was not busy with her needle on the film of silk that lay in her lap. So he walked on to the end of the promenade, opened the heavy, narrow door that admitted him into the main building, and went through the rooms until he came out onto the balcony where the two women were sitting. The governess rose. He took her chair without a word. He began to speak with his eyes fastened upon Ortiza, but the *ayah* did the answering.

"And now, Ortiza?" he asked.

"We have finished with nearly everything, *señor*," answered Rosa.

"Your hand and your needle have gone to sleep," growled the Spaniard.

"Poor child!" murmured Rosa. "She is weary."

"Listen to me," said Tarabal, leaning forward with his fat hands planted upon his knees, as though to compel the gaze of his daughter to turn from the distant hills and meet his glance. "Listen to me . . . you are happier now?"

"She still says that she is too young to be married, *señor*."

"*Bah!*" grunted Tarabal. "Her mother was married when she was sixteen . . . Ortiza is a year older. Young? You are old . . . too old, almost."

There was a sigh from Rosa. "Some bloom early, and some bloom late, *señor*."

"Is Rosa stuffing your head with such fool's talk, Ortiza?"

"I talk to her only of the great happiness that is coming to her, *señor*," said Rosa.

"You lie! You let her live in a dream. You've always let her do that. Wake her up, Rosa. Wake her up! The brig, *Fortune*, is overdue. We'll have young Valdez down here with us, like a man on fire. Are we going to show him a pillar of ice and call it his wife to be? He'd take ship back to Spain."

"Ah, think of that disgrace, Ortiza!" cried Rosa.

"I'd cut his throat before he left, however," muttered Tarabal. "But I say, wake her up."

He reached out his thick hand, as though to shake Ortiza by the shoulder, but, as his fingertips grazed her shawl, they stopped, hovered, and his hand was withdrawn. He remained another moment or two on the balcony, drawing his brows down until his eyes were quite lost in the shadow. Then, having been unable to find more words, he stood up and stepped back into the room. He beckoned to the governess, and she came to him at once.

"What has she been doing?" he asked.

"Sitting, as you see her."

"And what does she talk of?"

"Of her childhood and of . . . of her mother, *señor*."

Tarabal gritted his teeth. "Born a fool and still a fool! If Valdez knew her mind, he'd never marry her, not if I had twice as many leagues of land. Have you shown her the picture of Valdez?"

"I keep it before her every day."

"He's handsome. Can she find a fault in his face?"

"She says it wearies her to look at it."

"Was there ever such a girl, Rosa? No blood . . . no heart . . . no warmth."

"But when she sees him, if he is the right man, you will see her, *señor*, made into a pillar of fire. Oh, there is blood and heart in her. But the sun has never shone on her . . . she is still like a bud closed up tight and waiting for the morning."

"Now you talk like a fool again. No sun has shone on her? Have I not given her everything?"

"Oh, yes! Oh, yes! But girls are strange. Sometimes a word and a touch . . . little things . . . are more than diamonds to them, *señor*. I only pray that *Señor* Valdez is the man."

"He's her husband," answered Tarabal. "That's ended. I'll do the thinking for my women! And I'll do the picking and choosing for them. These young fools . . . they sit and dream about a lover dropping out of the moon. I've heard of it. All women are fools. All young women are greater fools."

He delivered these dicta in a voice that was perfectly audible on the balcony where Ortiza sat. And he was raising his bull voice again when his words were drowned by the heavy beat of metal against metal, and then the booming voice of the bell rolled across the patio and flooded through the room. They looked at one another agape. There was something almost like fear in their faces.

Then: "The *Fortune*'s in the harbor, with Valdez aboard her!" cried Tarabal. "I'm leaving for the town. Hang the house with flowers. Wash the Indians and give them new clothes. Wake up Ortiza. Tell her the great day has come. If she's still asleep when I come back, I'll have an accounting with you, old chatterer!"

So he stormed through the door. Even the solid stairs shook under his heavy tread as he descended, and the great bell rang faster and louder.

"Oh, Ortiza, my lamb, my darling!" cried Rosa, pressing her hands across her eyes. "Do you hear?"

There was no answer. She ran out onto the balcony, but Ortiza had vanished. So the governess first looked up in the blankest amazement, then a bustle in the patio made her step to the rail, and she saw the white form of Ortiza, lying crushed against the hard ground.

Wings were in the feet of the old woman. She sped down and rushed out to the place with glaring eyes and hands turned into stiffened claws, like some old hag of a fairy tale. From the arms of the servants she tore the body of Ortiza. She pressed her face against the soft young bosom, and then she fell upon her knees, with the girl drawn close. She threw her hand up to the pale blue sky, and tears of joy streamed down her face.

"Oh, kind God! Oh, God of mercy!" breathed Rosa.

Above them the bell still rang. It seemed that all the music was gone from its notes to those who were near. There was only the lessening crash of metal against metal, but far away rolled wave on wave of melody that made the workers in the fields lift their heads.

Chapter Five

EL ROJO COMES TO CALIFORNIA

During the night the wind came up. Instantly there was a patter of feet over the decks of the *Fortune,* the loud calling of the mate, as he gave orders for putting on sail, and the singing of the sailors at the ropes. A little later the brig was leaning before a mild southeaster and bowling merrily along for the harbor. In mid-morning they reached it and came in view of the town of Monterey, so pleasant to the eye that it looked like a painted picture rather than a real town. For the houses, with white sides and red-tiled roofs, were spotted hither and yonder over a great green lawn. To the south was the dark of a pine wood. To the north the sun flashed on a stream, and from the *presidio* came faintly and clearly the rattling on a drum, as though the soldiers were being drawn up to do them honor.

The ship came to and dropped anchor in the midst of great bustle on deck, a furling of sails aloft and a clamor and screeching of chains below. There was another stirring scene between decks, where two sailors were attempting to lead the stallion, Sanduval, to the upper deck. They took to their task gingerly, for courage that would have winced not an inch from a howling gale and a whipping mast, while they sat aloft on a yard, failed them when they confronted this novel peril in the form of the wicked eyes and the ready teeth and the lashing hoofs of the horse. They were the less ready to venture themselves, moreover, since it was known that the slave, El Rojo, had only to put his hand on the halter in order to lead the great horse on, as mild as a lamb. But El Rojo was kept in the background

41

by Valdez, who declared that it was the duty of the sailors to unload their own cargo. But the sailors knew well enough that he took that position merely in order to enjoy their terror, as they attempted the task.

Eventually they managed to slip the halter over his head, but, when they laid hold on the rope, he jerked back suddenly, with a violence that threatened to pull them within the reach of his hoofs. At that, with a yell, they relinquished their hold and tumbled backward. Valdez was convulsed with laughter and drew near to mock them, as they gained their feet once more. The head of the stallion darted forth, and the strong teeth caught at his shoulder, and with a wrench Sanduval ripped the sleeves of his master's jacket to tatters and flung Valdez prostrate on the deck. In another instant those crushing hoofs would have smashed his body, but here El Rojo leaped in between, caught the head of the horse, as a man would catch a pet dog, and actually forced the great animal back, though still with flattened ears and wild eyes it threatened death to the others above the shoulder of the slave.

Valdez came to his feet in a passion. It was the second time in twenty-four hours that his pride had been reduced, once by the foil of Mortier, and now by a dumb brute. Moreover, the jacket was the finest he owned, and he had set his heart on going ashore in his best apparel to astonish the natives. He caught up a rope, and he struck El Rojo heavily across the back with it.

"This is your doing!" he cried. "You've trained him for this. You've made a devil out of him. You've taught him to try his teeth on every man but yourself. Ah, I'll make you bleed for this, you cunning dog."

El Rojo drew back and listened in a characteristic attitude of submission, with his arms crossed and his head inclined humbly. Yet there was no fear in his expression. He saw the

42

rope, dangling in the air ready for another stroke, but he manifested no more apparent emotion than when he had met the assault of Mortier and whipped the foil from the hand of that worthy. Perhaps it was the quiet manner of El Rojo; perhaps it was a sense of the injustice in his words that recalled Valdez somewhat. He stepped back from the slave and rolled his eyes wildly around, seeking for some object on which he could pour out his wrath. That glance flicked over the sailors, but the faces of the Yankees were set and scowling, and he knew at once that to touch them with the rope end would be to have a dirk come tingling home between his ribs. So he rushed at Sanduval instead, and, whirling the rope above his head, he began to lay it on the stallion.

On head and neck and shoulders and body he rained blows that turned the horse into a raging devil. Sanduval rushed at the bars, that kept him from the man who was torturing him, and dashed his weight against them until they groaned under the shock. He even reared to a great height behind them and battered at them with his forehoofs, looking far more like a black, giant panther, tearing at its cage, than like a horse.

But the sailors were looking not at this brutal exhibition, but at El Rojo, for one of them had pointed out the slave to his companion, just as El Rojo dropped his hand to the hilt of a knife in his sash. He did not draw it, however, but folded his arms as before, though now his hands were seen to clutch his flesh with a power that made his arms tremble. He bowed his head still lower, so that he might not see what was taking place, but every time the rope whistled in the air, a shudder passed violently through the body of the slave.

"If I was him," said one tar to the other, "I'd never sleep out a watch while that long-armed devil was loose."

The other agreed with a nod. Indeed, the change in El Rojo had been so sudden, and the restraint with which he held

43

himself made his passion seem so much more sinister, that the two brawny sailors drew a little closer together and fumbled in their clothes, as if to make sure of their knives.

Presently Valdez spent some of his passion and finally stepped back and called to El Rojo to take the horse on deck. The latter instantly obeyed, and, while the great stallion was still rearing and plunging, to the amazement of the sailors, the slave slipped into the stall and took the halter rope. Sanduval came back upon all four feet and dropped his muzzle on the shoulder of his friend, who now removed the bars and led the stallion to the upper deck.

Here, as the horse raised his head and arched his tail, scenting the land odors that were blowing out from the shore, it was possible to see him for the first time in all his glory, and glorious he was! He was entirely black, with the exception of a white-stockinged off foreleg. He stood a full sixteen hands, with the muscle and bone of a lion, and a lion's manner also. Yet, so exquisitely was he made, so perfectly did the great shoulders and haunches taper down to lower legs, looking as fine and as strong as hammered iron, that, even as he stood, he suggested the speed of the wind.

"A frigate, built like a clipper," said the mate, and that expressed the unanimous opinion of the crew.

A hoist had been rigged for lifting the stallion over the side of the ship and lowering him into a barge that had been brought alongside the brig. But, when Sanduval was brought close to the tangled mass of ropes and blocks, a mass that was given a snaky life by the wind, terror sprang up in his eyes. He jumped back, taking El Rojo unawares and jerking the rope from his hand. Then he wheeled and plunged straight across the deck. There was no attempt to stop him. Three or four sailors dived for safety, as though the hard boards of the deck were water, and Sanduval, reaching the rail, rose to his hind legs, cleared the obstacle, and sailed into the air.

His body flashed in a long arc. He struck the sea with a crash and disappeared in a smother of foam, but in a moment he had his head above water and was swimming with pricked ears straight for the shore.

Valdez was in an agony of grief and apprehension. He ran to the captain and, clinging to him like a child, begged him to save the horse before it drowned, offering in his first breath a thousand *pesos* as a reward. But the captain brushed him away. He needed no bribes to make him do his duty. Sanduval was part of his cargo, and he delivered his cargo safely on shore. His loud, clear voice in an instant had a boat swinging toward the water.

There was one man on board who was even more struck to the heart than Valdez by the loss of the stallion overboard, and this was El Rojo, who ran to the rail and leaned there, with his bronzed cheeks turned pale. But, when he saw that the horse was swimming bravely and strongly, and that every wash of the waves seemed to thrust the gallant animal nearer and nearer to the shore, he raised his own head, hesitated for perhaps half a breath, and then sprang into action.

He ran first into the cabin of Valdez. There he tore off his tunic and jacket. Then he wrenched the turban from his head and exposed the origin of his name, for his hair was the color of flame — a golden red. Next, from a rack on the wall, he snatched down a scabbarded sword and raced out from the cabin again barefoot. Over the rail he went, his body straightening out like a javelin that flies quivering from the hand. Into a rolling wave he slipped, hardly breaking its surface. He came up again, several lengths of his body closer to the swimming horse. He had slipped the belt of the sword over his shoulder, so that the weapon trailed behind him, making a heavy handicap. Yet, in spite of this, he was swimming with such strong

45

strokes that it seemed to the sailors who watched that he must be inspired by the voice of his master, screaming from the prow of the *Fortune*: "Freedom for you, El Rojo! Freedom, if you catch Sanduval for me! Freedom . . . liberty, El Rojo!"

"Do you mean that?" asked the mate who was standing near him, watching the flight and the pursuit.

"*Bah!*" laughed Valdez. "What is a promise to a slave?"

But quickly all apprehension vanished. In the first place, it was seen that Sanduval had strength to spare to reach the shore. It was also seen that El Rojo, encumbered, as he swam, by something he held like a dog in his teeth — no doubt, the halter for the stallion — could not possibly overtake the great horse. But they did not need to depend upon the exertions of El Rojo.

The captain's boat was slipping over the waves, like a swallow, swinging along with the easy strokes of four oars held by hands of iron. They tumbled out onto the beach as soon as the sharp prow of their boat clove the sand. Then they ranged in an excited semi-circle in front of the place toward which the swimming horse was making. Yet, even those staunch tars would perhaps have held back the great stallion no more than a sieve holds back water. Other and more efficient allies, however, were close at hand. About the beach a number of horsemen sat in their saddles, wrapped in great cloaks that had an astonishing resemblance to Indian blankets, so essential and natural a part of the costume did they seem to be. They were watching the ships in the harbor and the plying of the boats back and forth, but, now, they began to show some interest in the progress of the stallion toward the shore. They touched their horses with their spurs, the rowels of which were armed with rusty prongs an inch or more in length. One scratch of these sent the ponies flying at full speed. So they darted up toward the point for which Sanduval was heading, brought

46

their horses to a stop as sudden as their start, and, wrapping themselves in their cloaks, waited as impassively as ever.

They were smoky-eyed, dark-skinned fellows, most of them, but if an Indian had one dash of Spanish blood in him in early California, he took upon himself the manner and the frozen dignity of the greatest *hidalgo*. Not one offered his services, but it was plain that all were eager to have a chance to show their skill with their lassos.

Old South Wind, however, had not the slightest objection to making an appeal to them. He saw that his tars were moving about uneasily on the beach, as though they had not the slightest idea of how they should lay hands on the great brute that was now working its way through the waves toward them. He called to them in bad Spanish, and he was immediately answered with a flash of eyes and teeth and a cheery: *"¡Sí, señor!"* They instantly took the coils of their lassos from the pommels of their saddles and prepared them for the cast. These ropes of rawhide were not weapons to be sneered at. Braided of thin strips of green hide, made into a thick and stiff rope, they were drawn and tightened and worked with oil until they had shrunk to a strand no thicker than a woman's slender finger, but strong as steel, and supple as a living snake's body.

There were from fifty to sixty feet in every coil, but these experts, who were raised to the use of it from their childhood, handled the whole length with the most exquisite skill. They did not open the noose and prepare for the cast by swinging the lasso above their heads. Instead, the throwing motion was a quick dart of the arm and flexion of the wrist, underhanded or overhanded, that sped the noose through the air with a cutting whistle. A man, watching for the cast and balanced on his toes to leap to either side, could not escape the noose any more than he could dodge the striking head of a snake. Moreover, the flying weight in that noose struck with enough force

47

to stagger a man. In short, the lasso was a weapon of extreme effectiveness. A sword or a knife might be useless, if the deadly noose settled over a man's arms. And after the noose had once struck and drawn taut, the rest of the lasso filled the air with writhing curves and entangled hands, legs, feet one after the other. Moreover, as the noose drew tight, the running hide cut through the skin like a knife.

Such were the tools the riders unslung from the pommels of their saddles. They fell back, their attitudes entirely careless. Some of them actually turned their backs on the approaching horse, but one could guess, beneath their languor, at a hair-trigger readiness to whirl and shoot the lasso, like a stone from a sling.

Sanduval, in the meantime, had checked the speed of his approach to the beach, but it wasn't because he saw such formidable odds gathered against him. From his rear he had heard the call of El Rojo. Now he pricked his ears and stopped swimming. A wave caught him sideways, swung him around, and ducked him into a smother of foam from a breaking crest. When he came up again, shaking his head and snorting out the salt water that had filled his nostrils, El Rojo was beside him. His golden-red hair had been turned to black bronze by the water. It was sleeked back from his lofty forehead, and he came gliding through the water with powerful and easy strokes, like a sea mammal.

The stallion checked his speed. The two came together toward the shore. A big wave caught them, tossed them up, and swung them far in. When it receded, the stallion and the man were wading through the sand toward firmer going. And now it was seen that the thing El Rojo had been carrying in his teeth, and that they had been so sure was a halter, was, indeed, a sheathed sword. More than this, the metal collar that was fitted around his neck was now shining in the sun, and altogether, with the light running and slipping on the long muscles of his arms and shoulders, he made a spectacle more wild than the stallion.

Sanduval rose from the water, with his head high, his ears flattened, and his eyes on fire with hatred of so many enemies.

"Put a halter on him!" cried South Wind, coming up hastily on shore where he had landed. "Here's one!"

He tossed a rope that El Rojo caught deftly out of the air.

"Keep far back, my friends," he called. "Keep all far back! When you come nearer, Sanduval goes mad!"

In fact, when the rope whirled past him, the stallion had reared with a snort. But the hand and the voice of El Rojo quieted him at once. He was as docile as a child to the touch of the Moslem. The riders drew back their horses with a disgruntled look. There would be no call upon their skill, after all.

"Steady, gentlemen," implored El Rojo, now leading the black stallion up where the sand was as firm underfoot as a race track, and where the great, black horse fairly glided along. "Let me first master him with a rope, and then. . . ."

The sailors obediently held back. They had seen and heard only too much about the teeth and the terrible hoofs of Sanduval during the long voyage. Only South Wind began to press in.

"And so," said El Rojo, "the thing is done."

With that he leaped onto the back of the stallion. He had neither saddle nor bridle, but the lack of these was no hindrance. Had he not, many and many a happy day on the fields of Spain where Sanduval had been raised and pastured, played with the beautiful black and taught him to run by the sound of his voice and the touch of his hand?

He gave voice and hand to the stallion now — a wild yell, such as never could have burst from a Christian throat, for

49

there was a devil of joy and of malice in the sound. It tore his own throat, and it tore the ears of those who heard. Up and down the whole beach the cry rang, and all eyes centered at once on the picture of the black stallion breaking through the circle of the riders.

But the riders on those quick-footed ponies, with those long lassos that were like arms of fire, understood at last. If they had not, the huge deep-sea roar of Captain South Wind would have told them.

"He's trying to break away . . . a Moslem slave with that horse. Stop him! Stop him!"

His words died away in a shrill clamor of bad Spanish, as those cavaliers of the beach took up the chase. They closed around El Rojo, as a flock of busy crows flap around an insolent and intruding hawk. In a trice they had condensed into a thick semi-circle. The cord was the line of the sea along the shore. Who could dodge now? But El Rojo did not attempt to dodge the ropes. Instead of fleeing, he whipped away the scabbard that clad the rapier he carried. The naked blade was out, with a long ray of sunlight quivering and running up and down the steel. His scream of joy had thrust Sanduval into a gallop at full speed. The sailors scattered back, yelling. And now El Rojo drove straight into the face of the cavaliers.

The rapier rose, a ray of the light balanced on its point. It was very strange, but each of the half dozen men who were directly facing El Rojo and who had their ropes poised for the cast felt certain that the sword was intended for his breast alone. Therefore, only three or four of the ropes were thrown, and these were thrown poorly. They struck the sides and shoulders of El Rojo, but nothing settled over his head. Before him a gap opened. Through it he sped. The rapier touched no human flesh. It had not stirred from the level at which El Rojo held it, but from before its point men scattered away like sheep.

Now they were through the line of the riders. Half a dozen ropes were thrown at them from behind, but Sanduval was running, as the shadow runs under an arrow in flight. The ropes whistled close behind, but El Rojo was free. He threw up his arms, one hand open, one holding the sword. His slick wet hair was like a copper helmet. The collar around his neck was like a gleam of dull fire. His arms and his throat and his face were Indian dark. His body to the waist was shining silver. And his yell trailed tingling behind him.

Such was the strange picture on that first day. Such was the manner of El Rojo's coming. Those who saw him sweep up into the hills said that he would never be captured, and that great things were about to happen. But even they guessed less than the truth.

Chapter Six

A FLOWER IN THE BUD

One might have thought that Louis Auguste Mortier, having come so far from France to see a friend, would have been in the greatest haste to reach the man. But, instead, he went up into Monterey and spent the rest of the day smiling behind his war-like mustaches, while Francisco Valdez raved and raged because of the loss of his slave. The entire value of the cargo, he swore, was not worth one hand of El Rojo. He would have justice and a value paid. The point of law, he said, was that South Wind had guaranteed to place him and his chattels upon the shore at the town of Monterey. El Rojo was the chief part of his belongings, and El Rojo had not been safely landed.

When Louis Auguste Mortier tired of this discussion, he went elsewhere, and, wherever he went, he found Monterey better than a captured city. He had only to stop to inquire his way in order to be asked in to have a glass of wine. And when it was learned that he was one of Napoleon's soldiers, there was no limit to their hospitality. He discovered that, although nearly three years had passed since Waterloo, no eyewitness of the great battle had yet arrived in Alta California.

The field was open to him. It was a conversational gold mine in which he was at liberty to dig as deep as he pleased, for his listeners would never weary of the treasures he described. Indeed, the whole career of Napoleon was known by hardly more than dull newspaper accounts and a few third-hand narratives. Moreover, he found that the warm-hearted Spaniards of Monterey, so far removed from the theater of the war, were

52

willing to look upon the "Little Corporal" not as a national enemy, but simply as a great man who had astonished and endangered the world. So the tales of Mortier were composed of charmed words for the townsmen, and, when they discovered that he had actually been a colonel in the Grand Army, that he had been in person at the Pyramids and Borodino, at Leipzig and Montenotte, they were enchanted. He felt that he had opened the doors of their houses and their hearts and untied the strings of their pocketbooks.

It was no wonder then, in asking the way to the house of Jean Darnay, that he found enough to delay him until it was nearly dark. Then, his head ringing with the strong, old wine that he had drunk, his heart light with the thought of all the tales he should have to tell in this virgin field, he started on the road toward the house of Darnay.

Everyone knew of the eccentric Frenchman. Everyone could tell him the road. All insisted that the place could not be missed. For that very reason, therefore, at the first forking of the road, Mortier took the wrong branch and wandered on through the dark hills until he realized, with a start, that he had gone twice the distance necessary to reach the house of Darnay. He then turned and retraced his way as fast as the horse he had hired could gallop. But presently he found, to his dismay, that he was completely lost, and that the best he could do was to wander blindly ahead.

In the meantime, since he was not guessed to be within six thousand miles of Monterey, no anxiety for the arrival of their guest to be was felt at the house of Darnay. That house stood near the main road, not far from the very crossing where Mortier had gone astray. The road dipped here into a shallow valley, or dell, that was nevertheless large enough to contain elements of a sufficient variety. There was a small hill, on the side of which Darnay's house was built; there was a trickle of water though the midst of the valley; and here and there were clusterings of big pines, lifting like blue-green clouds during the day and inky black by night. Some acres of the valley were fenced off to make a pasture for the few horses Darnay kept.

The house itself, as has been said, was withdrawn somewhat from the main highway. This was in spite of the fact that Darnay was a blacksmith. No sign announced that his shop was near, but, cutting a narrow bridle path in a detour from the road, he waited for fortune to bring him what luck it would. That detour brought travelers within sight of an adobe shed, containing a forge and the mass of iron bars and old rusted rubbish that packs the corners of all mechanical shops. Behind the shop was the house. This was built of rough logs, very solid and large and perhaps cut from the clearing near the house that now provided space for both flower and vegetable garden.

Jean Darnay and his daughter, Julie, were in the shop, and, at this moment, as he took from the forge fire a large bar of white-hot iron with his pincers and began to hammer at it with a heavy sledge, vast showers of sparks darted in low arcs to the farthest corners of the room, or struck against the long leather apron of Jean Darnay, before they turned black and dropped to the ground. These spark showers gave an excellent light by which to examine the faces of the two.

That of Julie, when she threw back her head — not to escape the showers of the sparks, but to stretch the tired muscles of her neck — was divinely beautiful for the moment. But now she looked down again to her work of holding the tongs with her gloved hands, and, when she looked down, it could be seen that, in proper perspective, her face was not beautiful at all, but simply merry and pretty. Mother Nature, having drawn in all the background and the basis of true loveliness, such as a broad, low forehead and finely drawn eyebrows and great brown eyes and a dazzling skin and a body as graceful as some dancing figure charmed into life out of a Grecian frieze — having given the girl all this, Mother Nature spoiled all by two things, the very last touches she gave to her work. For one thing, in a very reckless spirit of jest, she tilted the point of Julie's nose upward. For another thing, in the eyes, that from their color and size should have been as solemn and mysteriously delightful as the brown shadows of an old forest, nature had planted a light as mischievous and restless as the light in the eyes of any faun. Even that snowy complexion was not left unmarred. For across the very bridge of that nose there were scattered little spots of reddish brown, dim enough, and yet distinguishable. In short, Julie had a freckled face.

So that, if at the first glance she was startlingly lovely, at second glance it was discovered that Julie was only a very human, very charming girl. Of course, she might have appeared to much greater advantage if a little powder had been sprinkled across her nose, and if a cloud of silks had made her slender body seem floating in a foam. But Julie was dressed in a rude, drab homespun that was as durable and harsh as sailcloth. Her very shoes were as square-toed and heavy as the shoes of a man, though their bulk and weight only made her feet look ridiculously slender. She wore only one article of adornment, and that was a white kerchief, drawn over her shoulders with the knot in front of her throat. Such shapeless garments and such dull and comfortless materials would have been perfectly in place on a young Puritan maiden, who had not yet dared to lift her eyes from the nasal sermons of her father to the fair facts of life. But such a shroud could not kill the light in Julie. She persisted in shining through.

Her father, Jean Darnay, who stood opposite her, swinging the sledge, had the head of a prophet on the body of a Hercules. He was made powerfully from head to feet — every measure was large, so that one could guess that the fine molding of

Julie's body was not inherited from her father. But his face was quite different. Instead of blunt features to match his body, one might have said it was the face of an ascetic. His long hair flowed down almost to his shoulders. No razor had touched his face for many years at least, but, though his beard grew thick and wild, it could not mask the line of his bold jaw. With the high-arched nose, it was an eager, a commanding, a fiery countenance, but the great brow and the large, mild eyes denied all the rest.

He wielded the big sledge with the greatest ease, showering his blows as Julie turned the bar of iron. When he had drawn out the iron to a certain length, he took the tongs from her, and with a flip of the wrist that made the muscles of his forearm leap out and tremble he tossed the darkening bar into a tub of water, from which it sent up a small cloud of steam.

"It's nearly dark, Julie," he said. "Night isn't meant for labor. And, besides, you are very tired, my dear."

"I'm not steel," she answered. "You forget that I'm not steel, father."

"No," he answered, instantly darkening, "I never forget that you are weak, Julie. I never forget that all women are weak."

She made no reply to this, and they went together to the house and ate their supper. It was a simple repast of coarse bread, brown beans, and milk. It was as simple, indeed, as the house itself, which consisted of only two rooms. The larger of these was kitchen, dining room, living room, and bedroom for Jean Darnay. It contained, except for the kitchenware, little except homemade articles of furniture. Darnay himself had constructed the rough chair, the table whose top plainly showed the marks of the axe, and the shelves, on one of which were arranged some dozen books — chiefly a Bible and the works of Jean Jacques Rousseau. The other room was that of the girl. It was hardly gayer than the larger apartment.

When the supper was finished, the dishes were cleared away. Julie was not left to do this work by herself, but her father assisted, for it was the rule in his household that there should be no distinction in tasks. She worked with him in the shop, so far as her strength permitted, and he worked with her in the house. He could take his turn at the spinning wheel, or milking their cows, or cooking, and he even used the needle, though this was a thing to which he had to force himself. The dishes laid away, he took up the Bible and read to her from the Book of Jeremiah, while Julie worked at a job of mending, until the monotony of his heavy and solemn voice made her head drop lower and lower, and at last she slept.

He was so filled with the fire of the words he was reading, however, that he continued for a full half hour before he saw what had happened. He then started to reprimand her, changed his mind, and with a shrug of his heavy shoulders went on reading silently to himself. Julie slumped heavily over in her chair. One arm dropped toward the floor. Her head bent at an aching angle. Yet her weariness was so profound that the pain of her position did not waken her. Her father, looking up again, rose as though to go to her and send her to bed, but a second thought made him sink back with a frown and continue with his book. For it was a conviction of Jean Darnay that pity is a sentimental weakness to which men should not yield. He worshipped two great peoples. They were the Spartans and the Romans, and the more nearly he could imitate such heroic virtues the more highly he esteemed himself.

He had been a revolutionist, a worshipper of Danton. And when that great and terrible man was killed, half of the heart of Jean Darnay was lost to him. He remained in France for another few years, but with a constantly diminishing interest in affairs, until the domination of the young Napoleon heralded the end of the Republic. This was the final blow. He left France with his wife and his young child. The wife died on the long voyage, but he and Julie arrived at what he considered as the farthest limits of the world. In California he had settled in this lonely little valley, that was near enough to men to enable him to live by a trade, and that was lonely and silent enough to let him use his best hours for his best thoughts.

He was a man, in short, who lived almost entirely according to the dictates of reason, and who kept emotion, so far as he could, in the background of his mind. Being detected in the simplest act of gentle kindness, he felt as much shame as though he had been seen in villainy. So he let Julie continue to sleep in that torturing position and went on with his book. Yet, in spite of himself, thoughts of Julie came between him and the print. *She was growing rapidly into mature womanhood. She was twenty years old.* And every day he noted some new proof that the bud was beginning to flower. A sort of fragrance surrounded her. He felt that the next young man who saw her would stop to stare with great wide eyes. *And then what would happen?*

He had reached this point in his reflections when there was a loud thunder of hoofs up the road, sweeping from Monterey into the hills. It passed rapidly and disappeared. Then came a heavy knock at the door that caused Julie to sit up with a start and then with a gasp of pain, as the ache of her muscles passed into her conscious mind. But, before either she or her father could rise to open the door, or inquire who was at it, it was cast open, and before them stood a martial figure.

Chapter Seven

EL ROJO MAKES A BEGINNING

He wore at his side a long saber, carried very low. His boots furled loosely about his ankles. His soft, wide-brimmed hat was adorned with a crimson feather, sweeping about the band. In his belt were stuck two pistols of ordinary size and a long knife. The scarf itself was crimson, and altogether his effect was most dashing and piratical. Moreover, he was a very big man, which made his brilliancy tenfold impressive.

"Business of the governor!" he roared at them. "Business of the governor! I must have a horse! I must have a horse! Jump up, old whiskers, and get me the best nag in your pasture! Hurry!"

He reinforced his emphasis by stamping upon the floor. And Jean Darnay hesitated. He turned pale, and the soldier took this for fear — as a matter of fact, it was consuming inward fury. Nevertheless, his philosophy taught him that it was foolish and wrong for the unarmed to oppose the armed, and he knew that in California the word of the governor was hardly second in strength to the will of the Lord. So he rose and went through the door, with Julie hurrying to follow and help in the work. But Lieutenant Juan Rindo caught her by the shoulder and threw her back into the room.

"You'll stay and find me a bottle of wine," he commanded.

She cried out at his violence and his tone, so that her father returned to the door and looked in, with a face so black that the ruffian lieutenant drew back and laid his hand on the hilt of his long saber. However, the old Republican comforted

59

himself by recalling a maxim.

"Only evil women," he said, "fear the evil in men," and, so saying, he resumed the mission on which he had been sent, his heart tormented with fears for his daughter, but his soul as stern and strong as iron to put that maxim into practice.

Juan Rindo, left alone with Julie, gazed upon her with an eye of fire.

"This pig of a Frenchman," he said, "has locked up a diamond in his cupboard. But now that I've seen it, let him look to his locks!"

He laughed and rubbed his hands, and again he demanded wine. Julie started to deny that they kept any, but a second thought made her say she would run into the cellar and return at once with a bottle. She threw up the trap door that led into the dark cellar and ran down into the shadows. Juan Rindo walked back and forth, well pleased. It was the very devil's work that he had not been able to ride on in the chase. For the men who helped in the capture of the scoundrelly Indians who had made that night attack on the governor's life would be highly esteemed and richly rewarded by the faith of José Bernardo Pyndero. And who needed to be told that the esteem of the governor of California meant many *pesos* and an easy life? However, since his horse had cast a shoe and gone lame, there was no fault to be found with this station by the way. It now occurred to him that the girl had been gone long enough. He went to the open trap door and called down: "One bottle, my dear, not a barrel."

When he heard no reply, he was seized with a sudden fear that she might have escaped him, and he ran down the steps in pursuit, taking with him a lantern that had stood lighted on the table. He found the cellar well piled with stores. For, though Jean Darnay did not believe in other than a simple life, he also believed in security against hard times. Behind a stack of boxes the lieutenant found Julie. He went to her with a laugh and an outstretched hand. But the blood of Julie was up. She struck him suddenly in the face with all her might and raced for the stairs. Her quickness had taken the noble Rindo completely by surprise, and she was far ahead as she reached the stairs. But those steps were as steep as a ladder, and, though she leaped like a young deer for the top, Juan Rindo caught her, just as she had gained the level of the floor above.

He had her instantly in his arms, her own pinned against her sides. For an instant he wondered, because her face was so white and because she did not cry out. He decided that it was excess of joy at being pressed to the bosom of so brilliant a warrior as Juan Rindo. And, leaning to kiss her lips, he felt a slight prick in the middle of his back, just between the shoulder blades, exactly as though a pin were sticking into him.

He shrugged his shoulders, but the pin only stuck deeper. Then Juan Rindo, with a gasp, turned his head, and he beheld behind him a spectacle that might have frozen the blood of any man. For a blue-eyed madman with flame-colored hair, with a bronze collar about his neck, naked to the waist, barefooted, stood just behind, and the apparition held in his hand a naked rapier still touching his back.

Lieutenant Rindo blinked, looked again, and turned with a groan of fear and anger. Julie was gone in an instant and whipped behind the table, for she half expected to see the rapier pressed through the body of Juan Rindo. Instead, the strange apparition stepped back and lowered his weapon.

"You have a sword, brave lieutenant," he said.

Juan Rindo remembered the same thing and with a howl of rage tore out his saber. It seemed to Julie that that first sweeping cut was passing straight through the body of El Rojo, but, when she opened her eyes again, he was still on his feet. There had been a little shivering sound of steel on steel. Once more the lieutenant struck, and the little rapier, no more in substance than a ray of light, met the stroke and turned it softly. Then the rapier darted in. Juan Rindo, with an oath, dropped his saber and clutched his right arm. There was no blood. It was only as though a bee had stung him.

"Turn your face to the wall!" commanded the madman.

Juan Rindo obeyed. "I am Juan Rindo, the governor's lieutenant," he declared. "If I am missed, José Bernardo Pyndero will burn California and you along with it. He'll burn you by inches."

"Ah," said the other, "but that is an old story. I have already been burned by inches. *Señorita*, will you leave the room? And you, Juan Rindo, take off your clothes."

Julie fled. She found her father, leading up their best horse just as Rindo had commanded, with the saddle of the lieutenant on its back. To him she told the story, but Jean Darnay seemed in no hurry to reach the scene.

"The man of the sword shall fall by the sword," he quoted. And it seemed to Julie that she heard a faint chuckle, though it had been six months since he had actually laughed. But at length he returned to his house, and, when he reached it, he found the man of the flame-colored hair attired in the clothes of Juan Rindo, and Juan lay in a corner, with his feet and his hands bound and clad in the single garment of El Rojo.

"You . . . Jean Darnay!" cried Juan Rindo. "I command you in the name of the governor to attack this man . . . this robber . . . this . . . !"

His fury choked him.

"I am very sorry, *Señor* Lieutenant," murmured Darnay, "but you can see that I am an unarmed man. I am helpless. I cannot even run for help . . . a bullet from his pistol could run faster than I."

"You have plotted this between you," cried Rindo. "And

when the governor hears that you have sheltered a runaway slave, you'll sweat for it."

El Rojo interrupted by asking if Darnay had a file and, when the blacksmith confessed that he had, he begged him to file through and remove the bronze collar that circled his throat. It was done at once. Darnay took out a sharp file of the finest steel that bit into the metal collar as though it were wood.

In the meantime he excused himself to Rindo. "You see, *Señor* Lieutenant, I am helpless. This man compels me with his pistol. You will remember to tell that to the governor?"

"I'll remember to have you hung!" said Rindo through his teeth.

"These Spaniards," murmured El Rojo in perfect French, "are kind hearts, *monsieur,* are they not? A dog of a Moslem put this collar around my throat. But he knew no better . . . his religion teaches him that Christians are swine. Well, *monsieur,* I fell into the hands of Spaniards, and they left the collar on my neck. This simple Rindo tells me that he will have me burned in a slow fire. The fool does not know that I have burned for years. But tonight I shall give my first Spaniard a taste of the flame."

He laughed, and there was something in that laughter that made the beard of Darnay bristle. He went on until the collar was removed.

"Now," said El Rojo, "it must be welded together again. It is to be my brand, you understand? It is the print with which I write my record." He gave the pieces to Darnay, picked up Rindo under one muscular arm, as though the lieutenant were only a heavy sack, and strode toward the blacksmith shop until they reached the forge. And Julie came in the rear door. She had a feeling that something terrible was about to happen. She had not seen many men, but, of those she had seen, men who cursed and made a great noise when they were angry were the

63

least dangerous; while quiet men like her father had emotions that worked deep.

This man of the flame-red hair, however, was entirely new. He laughed when he was in a passion. She had seen his arm shake with excess of desire to plunge his rapier into the body of the man he had disarmed, and he had laughed. He was laughing again, as they reached the blacksmith shop, and Darnay, under the threat of the pistol that El Rojo held, obediently started the fire on the forge, laid in it the collar, and, after a little use of the bellows, brought forth the two glowing pieces of metal. He used a small hammer for the welding, and his strokes fell in a light and tinkling rain. But when he was through, there was only a small ridge to show where the collar had been filed apart.

"Once more back in the fire," commanded El Rojo.

"The business is finished. The welding is done," said Darnay.

"Quick!" cried El Rojo.

His imperious gesture made Julie shrink. Indeed, he was oddly changed by the clothes of Rindo that he had donned. On the lieutenant all that martial finery had appeared out of place, but El Rojo filled every detail of the picture. He had discarded the heavy saber of Juan Rindo, and in its place was that slender, feathery weapon, *La Cantante*. And the change of swords was like the change of men. How her father could dare to disobey the direct command of this hero she could not imagine, but that, it appeared, was the determination of Darnay.

"The devil fly off with you!" he growled. "Do I not know my trade? I have worked at your bidding . . . and welcome. But if it comes to changing my craft, I laugh at you, *monsieur*, for a young fool."

So saying, he heaved up a short-handled sledge, the weight

of whose head might be ten or twelve pounds. This he poised as lightly as though it had been a ball in the hand of a child. It was no slight threat. He could hurl his weapon before El Rojo could draw either sword or weapon, and even a grazing blow would bring the slave to the ground. The latter, however, had no intention of accepting such a combat.

"Very well," he said. "Do your own forging, but give me the collar."

And picking it up from the anvil with the pair of tongs, he plunged it among the blackening coals of the forge and fanned up the white fire by working at the bellows. Darnay submitted, not as one who dares not interfere, but rather as not knowing whether or not this were really an insult offered to his craftsmanship. Even so, he might have acted, but El Rojo, holding the tongs in place with one hand and working the bellows with the other, chatted with perfect ease and good nature, and his smiles kept Darnay in doubt.

"And so," said El Rojo, drawing out the bronze collar again and waving it, to give point to his words, "I return to my friends a little part of what they have given me. Only a little part, *monsieur*. For consider . . . I was born to a free name and in a free country, and yet they have treated me like a slave. A whip on the back of a freeman is a whip on his soul, also. I have been flogged, *monsieur*, by these dogs . . . by dogs like this."

As he spoke, he approached Juan Rindo, and, dropping his foot on the shoulder of the frightened lieutenant, he thrust the soldier over on his face.

"In the name of the law, I demand your assistance and protection, Darnay!" shouted Rindo.

His voice thrilled into a scream. For upon his bare back between the shoulders El Rojo had dropped the hot circle of the collar and jammed the bronze in with his heel. Juan Rindo came to his feet with a bound. He had worked the bonds from his ankles before. Now the fact that his hands were tied behind his back could not hinder him. He was through the door in a flash, with a great red circle showing on the white of his flesh. Still screaming, he faded into the night, and his voice trailed away down the road.

"That," said El Rojo, "is the beginning," and he tossed the bronze collar into a tub of water to cool.

Chapter Eight

A GOOD HEART BEHIND A WHITE FACE

Even the stern heart of Darnay was shocked. He supported his trembling daughter and stared at El Rojo, as though the latter were a ghost or a madman.

"They'll hunt you down and burn you at the stake for that," he declared.

"Have they ever hunted down the wind?" asked El Rojo, and at his whistle there came a light tapping of hoofs, and Sanduval, now saddled and bridled, thrust his fine head into the door of the blacksmith shop. Darnay drew a great breath.

"It is true," he said at length. "You have the wind at your command. But they will come for us."

"You have done nothing."

"I have seen one of the governor's soldiers disgraced. They will come for me."

"And if they do," said El Rojo, "they shall catch a nest of hornets. *Mademoiselle, monsieur, adieu!* I shall be near you when you need me most."

He stepped back through the door. They saw him, in the outer dark, swing into the saddle on the black stallion, and instantly they were gone together, with a swift rushing of the hoofs.

"Ah," said Julie, "how terrible and wonderful he is."

"*Bah!*" answered her father. "He is a boy and a fool, with his head stuffed full of books. And if. . . ."

Here his words trailed away, and they both lifted their heads to listen. Far off down the road they could hear the wail of the fleeing lieutenant, floating away into thinness and finally dying to a whisper.

El Rojo cut straight across the hills, and the black horse went, as he had gone all day, with a long and easy gallop that consumed the miles. He camped for the night in a place where there was wood and shelter for himself and good pasture for the stallion in a little meadow nearby. From the blacksmith's stock he had filled his saddlebags with grain for Sanduval; for himself he had taken a strip of dried beef — that, with water, was a delicious meal — for he had no need for delicacies. And when he had thrown off his clothes, twisted himself in his blankets, and lain down to sleep, the stars were gleaming above him through the tops of the trees, the wind was stirring among the branches, with a sound far lighter and sweeter than the faintest hum of cordage at sea, and close by Sanduval was crunching his portion of oats. Here was freedom and the surety of freedom. He felt as if he owned the world. And when he fell asleep, the same faint smile was on his lips that had made Julie Darnay tremble and wonder, for he was seeing again the lieutenant, as the tortured man leaped through the door, and he was hearing the scream of Rindo. It was a beautiful picture and lovely music to El Rojo.

He wakened early. For he was followed always with a profound conviction that he could not long continue free from the power of the law, and every hour lost in sleep was an unreclaimable hour of freedom thrown away from consciousness. So it was still the very earliest gray of the dawn when he wakened. The trees through which he began to travel, after saddling Sanduval, were ghostly dim, and only by degrees the hills began to loom and take shape. But the dawn did not change to day, for over the hills a fog had moved in from the sea, and, when the sun was high, the trees were simply turned to black, with moisture dripping everywhere from them like a slow rain. A grisly country for a traveler, one might have thought, but El Rojo could have sung like a lark.

How much ground he had covered he did not know. But presently he was stopped by the sound of trampling hoofs, and many of them were directly ahead. He made a detour to the left and presently discovered a road down which the sounds were approaching, so he drew back Sanduval to such a distance that the fog was sure to give him a sufficient screen. The sounds of horses grew clearer and clearer, with the jingling of swords in scabbards and voices here and there. They passed, like faint shadows in the distance, some half dozen horsemen riding first, then what seemed to be four couples of men on foot, and behind these, another dozen of mounted men.

"More of the whip! More of the whip!" he heard a voice call suddenly. "Are these murdering devils out for a pleasure walk?"

Instantly El Rojo heard the sound of a lash falling on human flesh. He knew that sound. It could not be a deception. He had himself felt the blows and heard the falling of the whip, and once more, for the thousandth time, he grew sick with shame and horror.

After that, he could not help following. He was drawn, as the fabled snake's eye is said to draw the victim. Presently, in a shallow hollow, the procession halted, and the commanding voice he had first heard gave orders to build a fire and prepare for an hour's rest. He took Sanduval into the shelter of a thicket, and then went forward to explore. It was not difficult. By this time a fire had been kindled that made it easier to see the forms nearest to the blaze, while those around the flames were blinded by the light to what lay at any distance in the fog. He crawled into a clump of bushes nearby, and from this vantage point he could see and hear everything.

There was a score of cavalry still busy, heaping fuel beside the fire or taking positions of ease near it, and from their talk he gathered that the party had been riding most of the night under the command of a tall man who was addressed as Excellency. The fruit of their expedition consisted of eight stately Indians, dressed in white cotton garments, their hands bound behind, their feet hobbled. They were further secured from scattering by a single long rope that passed from man to man, with a slipknot drawn around each neck. An outbreak of one would strangle himself and the other seven. They were now driven from the comfortable warmth of the fire.

"Why should these dogs lie here at their ease?" demanded His Excellency. "Drive them yonder, Sergeant, and put a guard over them. Get them up with the whip and away with them. Be quick about it."

It was done at once. A long whip, swung in the hands of the sergeant, brought the Indians to their feet, and yet there was not a murmur or a motion from them against the lash. Silently they marched ahead of the sergeant until they were half lost in the milk-white fog. There a guard stood over them with drawn sword and a command from the sergeant to sink a foot of steel into the throat of the first rascal who dared to stir. After this, the sergeant returned to the fire, and El Rojo, listening eagerly, understood presently that the captives were the remnant of a band of a dozen Navajo Indians who had trailed the new governor of Alta California some thousand miles to the seat of his government and then attacked him early that same night in his house at Monterey. The soldiers had ridden them down after a wild journey through the night. And now they were being taken back to entertain the good citizens of Monterey with the spectacle of their hanging.

There was only one chapter in the story El Rojo failed to understand or infer from the chance phrases he overheard from the lips of the soldiers or from the governor himself, and that was the reason that had made the Navajos take up that long trail. But reason there must have been, and what he guessed at was enough to make El Rojo undertake a new and perilous adventure.

He slipped back from his sheltered place and began a round-about detour that brought him up behind the stolid group of the prisoners who sat on the wet grass, shivering in a semicircle, while the guard stood over them and chatted cheerfully in fluent Spanish.

"Be of good cheer, my friends," he was saying. "I am now forced to stand here in the dark and the cold to watch you, but later I shall warm my heart, watching you kick your heels in the air."

In fact, they were so withdrawn from the heat of the fire that they almost lost the sight of it, and the men around it were only the vaguest shadows.

"And," went on the sentinel, "there is the whip."

There was a murmur from the Indians. Their heads were high, their bodies straight. They had the grave dignity of senators.

"The whip," went on the sentinel, "will keep you warm whenever. . . ."

His voice choked away, as a sash was thrown over his head from behind, and he was jerked to the ground. Dexterous hands gagged and bound him. El Rojo looked up from his work and found that not a head of the eight Indians had been turned toward him. What manner of men were these? He touched the cords that bound their hands with his saber. Their hands fell apart, but still they did not stir. The keen edge divided the ropes that hobbled their legs, and now they rose, but there was no effort to bolt suddenly. Peering through the fog he saw they were drawn and worn with the terrible labor of that night, during which they had matched their speed of foot against the

71

speed of horses and had almost won. And these were noble faces he saw. Had their skin been white, they would have been handsome enough even among the proudest Caucasians.

"Follow me!" whispered El Rojo in Spanish, and he turned away.

They stepped after him, but some swift-moving shadow behind made him whirl in time to see the last of the eight stoop toward the bound soldier. He leaped back and struck away the hands of the Navajo, just as they were closing on the sentinel's throat. Then he went on, and the eight followed him in a wide-swinging detour until they came at last to the thicket where he had left Sanduval. He mounted and struck away for the higher hills at a jog, and behind him the eight glided smoothly. He looked back, and it seemed to him that he had never seen such matchless runners, so frictionless was their stride. He increased the gait to an easy canter, and still they held their place behind him. Then, from the direction of the campfire, now blanketed out of sight behind the sea mist, they heard a sharp clamor, dominated by one thundering voice.

That was His Excellency, José Bernardo Pyndero, calling his men to horse, as they discovered the escape of the captives. El Rojo turned in the saddle and laughed silently. At that moment, however, the foremost of the Indians crumpled suddenly to his knees. His companion on either side stooped, caught him up with an arm under each shoulder, and staggered on. No civilized men, surely, could have been truer comrades in the hour of need.

El Rojo checked the stallion and flung himself to the ground. It needed only the slightest examination to see what had struck down the Navajo. The left sleeve of his tunic was soaked in blood that had been trickling from a slight wound in the upper part of the arm, ever since the men of Pyndero had surrounded them. El Rojo made his bandage quickly. From the saddlebag he took the brandy flask, with which the luxurious Juan Rindo had equipped himself for the night ride, and poured a stiff dram down the throat of the Indian. It straightened him quickly enough, but still he was far too weak for running, so El Rojo raised him in his strong arms and swung him into place in the saddle on Sanduval. He tore off his boots, tied them together, and flung them across the withers of the good horse. Behind them they heard the beating of hoofs and the shouting of the soldiers, as they scattered to get on the track of the escaped prisoners.

"Now," called El Rojo, "the time has come to run as you have never run before." And he started forward up the slope, with Sanduval cantering behind him. In the saddle swayed the injured man, his head low, his hands gripping the pommel. And on either side of Sanduval ran the rest of the Navajos. For half an hour they pushed on until they had climbed out of the mist to the top of a hill. Above them now the sky was blue, and the sun was brilliant; below the fog washed to their feet in waves like a white sea, and all the noise of the pursuit was dead.

When they finally stopped, the Indians dropped to the ground, for after the long labors of their night, that race up the hills had brought them to an exquisite agony of exhaustion. The care of El Rojo was not needed by them, however. When the breath had been gasped back into their lungs, they would be well enough. He caught the sinking body of the Indian from the back of Sanduval, stretched him on the grass, and gave him another drink from the flask.

The dark eyes opened and stared fixedly up to him. "I am ready to die," said the Navajo in excellent Spanish, "for I have seen a good heart behind a white face."

Chapter Nine

RINDO BRINGS THE GOVERNOR

The first glimpse of day, even through a storm, is wonderfully clearing for the mind. And, though the fog was gathered thick and a muffling white about him, Louis Auguste Mortier recovered his self-possession. It was hardly easier to see than when the night and the fog had been combined to blind him. But, as soon as the dim radiance of the morning penetrated the upper layers of the mist, and Mortier was sure that the sun had risen, the solemnity of the occasion — for a cold and oppressive fear had been growing in him — departed at once. He simply shrugged his shoulders and told himself that he had come to the end of a disagreeable adventure so obscure that it would not be worth the telling, even over evening wine. He was also correct in feeling that his adventure was concluded. In five minutes he had found the crossing of the ways, and in five minutes more, as the fog was lifting, he arrived at the dwelling of Jean Darnay.

He did not, however, go straight up to the house. He first retreated to a runlet of water that crossed the road not far below. There he washed his hands and his face, rewrapped his neck cloth, produced a comb and small mirror, with which he arranged his long hair, brushed the mud from his clothes as well as possible, and then, like a singer before he goes on the stage, tried his voice in a muted phrase from a song. In every respect he was like an actor about to step upon the boards. He now mounted again. His very horse felt the gathered strength of its master and, throwing up its head, galloped on with much spirit, until it was halted at the door of the house. Here Mortier threw himself to the ground, ran up the steps, and knocked at the door.

It was opened by Julie, rather pale of face and with her lips compressed, for, since the fright of the preceding evening, only the sharp command of her father had driven her to open the door. Mortier peered intently into her face.

"By heavens!" he cried. "It is the child . . . it is the baby . . . it is Julie! Ha?"

He asked this question ecstatically of the wide sky above him. Then he clasped Julie in his arms and kissed her on either cheek. She fell back, gasping, from this enthusiastic embrace, and she saw the stranger rush across the room and take her father in his arms. To Julie it was more wonderful to see her parent greeted with affection than if the skies had fallen.

Jean Darnay, enduring that embrace, had presently by his quietness compelled the visitor to give back.

"Name of names, Jean," cried Mortier, "you have forgotten me! Time has changed you also, dear friend, but your eye remains the same eye I knew in the other days. Look again, Jean! Look again, and try to remember. . . ."

"I know you very well," said Jean Darnay. "You are Louis Auguste Mortier."

The lack of emotion with which he spoke was far more damning than a complete failure to remember. Julie blushed to her eyes in shame and in sympathy for the stranger. But the latter carried it off with amazing sang-froid.

"And here is Julie, grown into a lovely woman. And you, my dear Jean, have become what you promised to be when I knew you before . . . a man with the face of a prophet. But, ah, what a day is this. I have come from France to embrace you, Jean."

"You are kind," said Darnay, a little more warmly. "Sit

down. So. Give me your hat. That is better. Now, Julie, the morning is damp. Build up the fire . . . build it high."

As Darnay spoke, Mortier darted a few swift and secret glances about the room that told him almost everything he wanted to know about the condition of his friend.

"One taste of wine, Jean, and a fragment of that excellent brown loaf that I see on your table."

"To the bread, friend," said Darnay, "you are very welcome, but there is no wine to be found under my roof."

"Very right! Very right!" he answered at once. "I use it very little myself and then only as a medicine when I am chilled or weary."

Darnay, however, was paying no attention to the explanation. He took a chair opposite Mortier and gazed upon him with eyes in which no personal kindliness or animosity appeared. It was inescapable regard. It bore down Mortier like a weight upon the conscience, and this he already had. He fortified himself, however, with a bowl of milk and a portion of brown bread. His ravenous hunger supplied the wine at that repast, and, when it was ended, he found that Darnay had not spoken a word during the interval, but Julie was lingering in the background, making a pretense of beginning her household work, but keeping her glance steadily upon the stranger. It was at once plain that hers was not the stern spirit of the old revolutionary. The joyousness was simply kept back deep in her eyes, waiting for an opportunity to shine forth. And if Mortier talked to Jean Darnay, half of his meaning and half of his spirit was for Julie.

"But, ah, dear friend," said Mortier at last, "I shall have things to tell you of all that has come about in the last twenty years. France has lived a century in that time. I shall have things to tell you . . . and of the glory of the emperor."

Jean Darnay rose from his chair. "Citizen Mortier," he said

coldly, "to whatever you have to say, I shall listen so long as it concerns only yourself and myself. But as for Citizen Bonaparte, who loved himself in everything and the Republic in nothing, I shall not listen to stories of him."

Louis Mortier was agape, and in his astonishment was mingled enough anger to turn his cheeks crimson. "What I hear cannot be the words and the voice of a Frenchman," he cried at last. "Jean, I saw Moscow, and I saw Madrid, and I saw victory at each place. Twenty nations trembled when the emperor nodded. And every Frenchman from this day to the end of time shall stand straighter because Napoleon was a Frenchman also!"

"It is not true," said the calm Darnay. "It is not true, my friend. Citizen Bonaparte is a Corsican."

"A part of France. A part of France."

"An Italian part. Why, Louis, have you forgot that this very Bonaparte began his life plotting to make Corsica free? A Genoese, Mortier, not a Frenchman. A Genoese, I say . . . an Italian. His French was abominable. He could not even speak our language, Mortier. And yet you make him a glory of France. No, no, Louis . . . a glory of Corsica, of Italy, of Genoa. But never of France. I thank God for it. His crimes are not upon the heads of our people."

The smiles were banished from the face of Mortier. He rose, as Darnay had risen.

"Is this my hand?" he demanded. "If it were torn from me and placed upon the arm of another, would it have strength to seize and to hold? No, Darnay. And if the very heart of the emperor had not been French, he could not have been the sword, the thunder of the French people. Look at me, Jean Darnay. I am not yet old. There are years of strong life and happiness before me. But I would go to die, with laughter in my throat, if the day of Waterloo could come again, with a true man in place of the traitor, Grouchy. Thirty thousand true-hearted Frenchmen, and a dog to lead them."

He wrung his hands, and the tears stood in his eyes in the bitterness of his grief.

"Ah, well," said Darnay, and his faint smile was not altogether one of scorn, "who can turn back the hands of the clock? But it was always so, Louis. You loved the revolution not for its own sake, but because it made a need for swordsmen. And now what has brought you here, to the end of the world?"

Mortier rubbed a hand across his eyes, as though in so doing he obliterated the thoughts that had just been tormenting him. When he looked at Darnay again, he was smiling.

"I have come with great news for you, Jean," he answered. "You may build a new house and hire a smith to take your place in the shop. The black days are ended for you, Jean. Your uncle, Jacques Picard, has died, and you are his sole heir, dear friend."

"And you have come for this, Louis? You have come halfway around the world to bring me what a messenger could have brought as well?"

The smile of Mortier grew somewhat stiff, but he explained at once. His own property bordered that of Jacques Picard, and the dream of his heart was to buy the Picard estate. He had been on the very verge of closing the negotiation with Picard himself, so he declared, when the old man died. And such was his eagerness that he had made the long journey to finish the transaction with the heir.

"I ask only this," said Darnay. "Why should you wish the hundred acres of marsh and swamp, Louis?"

"Because it brings my lands to the edge of the river. It gives me the hills on one side and the river on the other. I sit down like a king . . . do you see? There are bits of pasture land in it, too . . . and there is game to be hunted. But, most of all, it gives me a boundary."

"It is your Rhine, then?" said Darnay, smiling.

"Exactly," murmured Mortier, and smiled in turn. "As for the price. . . ."

"It is poor ground," said the honest blacksmith.

"I shall pay you five thousand *francs*, dear friend."

"For that swamp! Why, Louis, you have lost one thing at least, and that is your love for money."

"Five thousand *francs*," whispered the girl. "Five thousand *francs*."

To her it was a great fortune. A sudden vision filled her eyes of such a dress as she had seen in Monterey on a festival day.

"You have everything complete for the sale?" asked Jean Darnay.

"It is here." Mortier produced his paper. He produced, likewise, a heavy wallet which he laid upon the table, with a loud jangling of the gold pieces it contained.

"Ink and pen, Julie," commanded the father.

She had hardly time to place them before him with trembling hands, when her father raised his head.

"What is that coming on the road?" he asked.

The trampling of many horses was in the distance, coming rapidly toward them.

"Whatever it is, sign now," said Mortier. "We shall see who is on the road hereafter. Sign here, Jean."

The blacksmith raised his head and favored his companion with a glance that searched the soldier to the heart. The latter had faced cannon, but he had never endured a more nerve-trying moment.

"In due time," said Darnay. "I read all the papers twice before I sign them."

So saying, he began to peruse the document again, while

Mortier bit his lip in anger. The reading was not ended, in fact, before the galloping of half a dozen horses swept up to the house, halted, and heavy footfalls came up the steps. There was no knock at the door. It was thrown open by the hand of José Bernardo Pyndero himself, and behind him was Juan Rindo, his feet still bare, the white pantaloons still on his legs, but a uniform coat was drawn around his shoulders. He was trembling with the agony that still tormented him, and he was shaken with vengeful rage also.

"Which," said the governor, "is the man, Jean Darnay?"

"Yonder . . . he with the beard," gasped Rindo.

"Be still!" commanded Pyndero. "Which is Darnay?"

"It is I," said the blacksmith.

"You stood by," said the governor, "while one of my men was attacked and tortured. You saw the uniform of my lieutenant, but you did not lift a hand to help him. Darnay, you are under arrest. And who are these?"

"My daughter and a friend."

"For the sake of greater surety, they must come, too. Rindo, see to it! And then search the place for the slave, El Rojo."

"Outrage!" shouted Mortier. "Let me be heard before. . . ."

The governor raised his hand and pointed. "Silence that man," he commanded.

Juan Rindo grinned, and his white teeth glistened.

Chapter Ten

IN THE VALLEY OF SAN TRISTE

When Joaquín Tarabal arrived in Monterey to meet Francisco Valdez and escort his future son-in-law back to the *hacienda,* he found the Spaniard in his second-best jacket, for the good reason that the first had been horribly torn and spoiled — the work of Sanduval. Valdez was in a towering passion because a servant of the greatest value had also been lost. There was a curse upon this California shore, and all had gone wrong with the fortunes of Valdez. A third blow fell on Valdez when he encountered his father-in-law. He had been told that his bride-to-be was a lovely flower. Now he encountered her father and found him a veritable grotesque — a horror! His imagination leaped to the last step of his conclusions. Not only would the girl be ugly, but she would be poor also.

He could barely command his countenance to reply to the greetings of Joaquín Tarabal when the latter arrived. But, in a moment or two, he began to melt under the influence of the delight of the rancher. For it seemed to Tarabal that the youth he now saw before him was the sum of all that could be desired among men. The quality of his fine blood showed in the very air of scorn with which he looked upon the world. If Ortiza were too beautiful for him really to feel that she was his daughter — if he looked upon her with awe and wonder — how then would he feel when he could point to Ortiza and her husband and claim them for his children? With this thought swelling his heart, Tarabal surrounded Valdez with his courtesy.

"You shall have no care about one runaway dog," said

Tarabal. "In the first place, I shall have him caught for you, and, when he is caught, we'll build a slow fire and make a roast out of him . . . as an example, eh? In the second place, you may take your pick out of my own men and have a dozen, if you wish. . . ."

The rest of his sentence was blurred in the ears and in the mind of Valdez. He only knew that he had been offered a *dozen* servants if he cared to choose them. What stupendous wealth had this Tarabal that he could dispose of a dozen lives of men with a gesture? The losses of his best jacket, of Sanduval, of *La Cantante,* and of El Rojo, became less painful. There might be a great solace for his wounds of the heart and the pocketbook. And, no matter how ugly Ortiza might be, if her wealth amounted to a certain figure, Francisco Valdez cared not a whit.

He was even more impressed when he went down to the street and discovered the sort of escort with which the rich man rode. There were no less than six horsemen mounted upon magnificent black stallions, and, although they were not very large, they were all so beautifully made that it seemed to Valdez, for an instant, that he was looking upon six small copies of Sanduval, the peerless. Each of the six horses was ridden by a copper-skinned, dark-eyed fellow, whose long hair swept down to his shoulders, whose wide-brimmed hat was set about with well-polished silver medallions, and whose body was covered with a great cloak made of good cloth. Each of them, equipped like a regular soldier, carried a carbine mounted in a leather case that ran under the right knee of the rider, a pair of long and heavy pistols was thrust into the saddle holsters, and every man wore, besides, a short and ponderous saber that was more like a cutlass than a scimitar.

These grim-faced worthies, the instant their master appeared, leaped from their saddles and advanced, leading two snowy chargers of a size superior to the blacks and of equal beauty. Their trappings, too, were of the costliest nature, from the brilliant blankets that thrust out behind the flaps of the saddles to the silver fretwork that adorned even the reins of the bridles.

The heart of Valdez leaped again. All thought of Ortiza was banished from his mind. He saw only one thing — a palace in Madrid, built with gold drained from this happy, promised land. In another instant he was mounted, and they sped down the road toward the hills, while the people ran to doors and windows, as they heard the roar of hoofs, and gaped as the man of money thundered past. All of this was rich wine to Valdez.

"This white horse," he said to Tarabal, "has almost made me forget Sanduval!"

"But, not quite?"

"Ah, my dear friend," said Valdez, "Sanduval is not a horse . . . he flies with wings, like an angel . . . or a devil!"

"Then," cried Tarabal, "we'll have him back again, if I have to arm every man on the *hacienda* and send him out. We'll rake Alta California with a fine comb."

"But Sanduval could run away from the wind, *señor*."

"He may run from the wind, but he cannot run from me!"

And he spoke with such a solid conviction that Francisco Valdez almost believed. Also he bit his lip secretly. What if he should offend this absolute tyrant? What, for instance, if he should find Ortiza so terribly ugly, so exact a copy of her father's features, that he could not endure the thought of marriage? He decided on the spot that he must endure everything rather than offend the great man.

They reached the crown of a hill. Nearby a white column of smoke twisted leisurely upward toward the sky, and two men were piling green leaves and branches to raise a loftier and denser mass. Two other white arms of smoke waved against the blue sky in the distance, and now Tarabal said simply: "The fires shall stop smoking when Francisco Valdez enters my house."

This filled Valdez with new thought. If the large escort with which the rancher had met him proved the wealth of the man, the columns of smoke proved the solemnity of the occasion. Certainly he was entering a kingdom where it was best to obey the king when he advanced toward the estate of Joaquín Tarabal. They passed the third column of smoke in due time, and Valdez found himself looking down upon a lovely valley, in the center of which was a great house, with shining white walls and a roof of warm red against the green hills beyond. There were clustering trees near the walls. And over all the valley, saving in the black plowed lands, and over the hills, also, there were thick dottings of dim color. But had each one meant only a single *peso*, it seemed to Valdez that there was a prodigious host of coins in sight before him.

"What is this valley?" he asked eagerly.

"The valley of San Triste," answered the other.

"And whose is the house yonder that looks like a castle? . . . and there is a bell ringing from it, I think. Did you hear it?"

"I hear it," smiled Tarabal. "That bell shall not cease ringing until you have seen Ortiza Tarabal. That is my valley . . . that valley of San Triste. That is my house, which is called San Triste, also. And all that you see is mine, *señor*. No, no . . . it is now *ours!* For the moment your hand is joined to the hand of Ortiza, all that I have is yours. Look, look. So far as your eye goes, all is yours. And beyond that, still more and more is yours. There are other valleys almost as large as this. There are great forests with timber to build a city, if you will. There are wide, rich pastures. There is wealth that pours up out of the dirt at our feet and turns to gold without labor on our part. It is my kingdom. It is my empire, Valdez. Welcome to it. Welcome to it and to my jewel of jewels, Ortiza."

Valdez was lifted out of himself. He could not answer the owner, but the smile on his face said more than words could have said to Tarabal. Valdez rode down the slope toward the house of San Triste, with a foolish feeling that the sun was actually showering gold upon the earth.

When they reached the entrance gate, the panels of it were dragged open by three men on either side. The loud beating of the bell knocked at their ears with heavy waves of sound. And, as the wings of the gate unfolded, Valdez saw before him a pleasant picture. For all the patio was alive with people, all in gala costume. He had never seen so many flaring reds and blacks, purples and yellows, flung together in a noisy riot. They formed a hollow wedge. The hollow was the path by which Valdez and Tarabal were to advance. The apex of the wedge lay at the entrance to the house itself where now stood the good Rosa.

Tarabal stopped short, exclaiming: "What devil's nonsense is this? Where is Ortiza?"

And, dropping the pompous gait at which he was advancing, he rushed forward upon the governess, with Valdez straggling behind him. A song had been struck up by the Indians and half-breeds. But half of them stopped singing, and the other half sang out of time, when the anger of the master was seen. Tarabal had seized Rosa by the shoulders.

"Where is Ortiza? Where is Ortiza?" he yelled at her, and he shook her as though she had been a child.

"In her room . . . ," began Rosa.

"She should be whipped!" snarled Tarabal. "But come, Valdez, you shall see her in her very room. By heaven, you shall see her at once."

Valdez drew back a little.

"I cannot offend her, *señor*," he pleaded. "If our first meeting is on my part a rude intrusion. . . ."

Tarabal was beyond taking hints. He seized upon the wrist of Valdez with such force that the bones of the young man's arm threatened to spring asunder. He found himself dragged up the stairs. They came to a tall door that, like most of the others in the big house, was rimmed with stout iron bars to give it strength.

Upon this door Tarabal did not even knock, but thrust it open and swept into the chamber, pulling Valdez with him. And Valdez found himself in a girl's room. So distinct was the delicate fragrance, and such was the atmosphere, that it was as though he had heard her voice as he entered. Then he saw her lying in her bed on the farther side of the room. The sunlight, that was curtained out of the chamber, managed to slip through in one narrow torrent of gold that touched the chin of the girl and fell across her throat and splashed the hands that were folded quietly upon her breast. Within them lay a crucifix. Her eyes were closed, and about her pale and lovely face her hair flowed like a golden shadow. Beside her bed kneeled a gray-robed Franciscan, his tonsured head bowed in prayer.

Valdez himself felt that he must drop to his knees on the floor, for wonder and shock were working together in him. As for Tarabal, the change in his manner was marvelously sudden. He shrank back against the wall and dropped sidelong upon his knees, as though he had been struck down by a club. His teeth chattered. After a moment he groaned: "Father Andrea, in the name of God, she is not stolen from me? Not dead, Father Andrea? In the name of mercy, not dead."

The friar had turned toward him at the first sound of his voice, and, as he spoke, Tarabal wriggled across the floor on hands and knees, very much like the great bunched body of a toad. As he concluded his appeal, he clasped the robe of the holy man with one hand and cast up the other appealingly.

"Not dead," he moaned. "I shall build for your blessed order. . . ."

"Foolish man," said the contemptuous friar, "be gone, and let us meditate on sin and on forgiveness uninterrupted. For not all your gold is worth one thought that passes in the mind of this poor young girl you have tormented. She is not dead, but, at the sound of your voice and your step coming, she has fainted."

Tarabal shrank from the room, backing out, with his face toward the man of God. Valdez, with a thousand wonders in his mind, followed. As soon as they were in the hall, and the door closed, however, Tarabal rose to his full height and drew a breath.

"It is nothing . . . nothing, my friend. In three days she shall stand before you at the altar. But for a moment when I first saw her, it seemed that I saw the dead face of my wife . . . I am talking like a fool. Let us go down together and stop the cursed ringing of that bell."

Chapter Eleven

CANDLE FLAME

All that the gallant Francisco Valdez heard was that on the very morning before, when the ship, *Fortune*, put into Monterey harbor, and the tidings were announced by the signal smoke, and when the great bell began to toll the happy news that the husband for Ortiza had arrived in Alta California, Ortiza herself had naturally been carried away by excitement and in some manner had slipped from the balcony in front of her room and fallen to the ground of the patio beneath. There were no broken bones, but the shock had sent her to bed.

All of this seemed natural enough, yet it did not quite explain the strange words and the stranger manner of the Franciscan when he had addressed Tarabal. And when Valdez was escorted through the patio, after the midday meal, and looked up to the balcony, he noted that a tall and strong railing surrounded that balcony. It was odd that anyone could have fallen over such a defense against carelessness, no matter how excited. But Francisco Valdez was by no means in the mood to analyze carefully. His pride and his ambition were fed fat by the prospect of inheriting the great estate of Tarabal, and his eyes were still swimming with the beauty of Ortiza.

That afternoon he was conducted by Joaquín Tarabal over a section of the leagues he owned. They could not dream of covering the whole place on one excursion, but Valdez was taken to commanding points of land, from which he could survey a great sweep of country — smiling miles of hill and valley that should one day be his own. And, by the time they returned to the house of San Triste, Tarabal himself had changed in the sight of Don Francisco. Wealth had gilded him, and amiability had positively made his smile enchanting.

It was not until they had returned to San Triste that Tarabal had an opportunity to question Rosa. Then he sat alone with the governess and from her heard the story of how the girl had been seen lying on the floor of the patio, just as Tarabal left for Monterey, and how she had been lifted by Rosa and carried back to her room and put in the bed, and how, when her senses returned, she had clung to Rosa and begged like a child that she be not forced to marry this Valdez. When at length she had been soothed somewhat, she had asked that Father Andrea be brought to her. The good friar had come and had spent the rest of the day and the night in the house, never leaving the bedside of Ortiza, praying with her, pouring her full of greater peace, greater strength. When the tale was ended, there was only one thing which, to Tarabal, seemed worthy of comment.

"But to think of her daring to raise herself against me and oppose my wishes, that chit of a girl . . . against *me*, Rosa! However, that is her mother in her . . . that is her mother. And like her mother she has the strength of the weak, eh? Dear heaven, think of it, Rosa. If she had destroyed herself, she would have robbed me of all the time and the thought and the money I have poured out like water upon her. She would have robbed me of all that without a thought. *Tush!* Is that virtue? Then the prisons are full of the virtuous. It angers me. My blood boils. But do not let her know. Let all go softly, softly until the time comes, and then, if she refuses to marry him, I'll drag her to the altar with my own hands. Is she not mine? Is she not worth more than this house and all that is in it and half of my cattle, straying on the hills? Then I say that, if she keeps me from the disposal of her, she robs me . . . she robs me vilely, Rosa. Is it not so?"

"Ah, yes," murmured Rosa. "That would be too terrible."

For Rosa would as soon have challenged the power of the archfiend in horns and hoofs as to raise her voice against her terrible master. Besides, by all her lights, he was right. It was the proper power of the father to bestow the hand of his child where he would, and it was doubly his right since he had chosen for her so handsome and so high-born a cavalier as this Don Francisco, the sight of whose fine features had filled the house of San Triste with smiles and whispers, from the kitchen to the stables.

"And it will only take one glance at *Señor* Don Francisco Valdez to open her eyes," she assured Tarabal.

"As if I would not bring her a proper man for her husband!" exclaimed Tarabal. "However, this thing is at an end. And if a whisper . . . a breath . . . a dream of the truth about her fall from the balcony gets abroad, it shall be the worse for you, Rosa . . . it shall be much the worse for you."

So saying, he favored her with a glare that made her soul shrivel, like a leaf before the fire, and she stole back into the room of Ortiza, hardly daring to draw her breath. What would he do to her if the rumor should get abroad? There was a dark cellar dug three stories beneath the foundations of San Triste. And there were weird and awful tales of disobedient Indians and careless servants who had been carried out of sight into the nether regions of the mansion, and who had never appeared again. She offered up a silent prayer that God should teach her how better to serve her grim master and win his confidence.

It was now the black of night, and Ortiza was propped in her bed in the midst of a pile of pillows. A book was in her hands, but, as soon as the governess had entered, she had lowered the volume and followed Rosa around the room with her dreaming eyes. As for Rosa, she was seeing many things in Ortiza for the first time. She had looked upon her charge as the gentlest of children and, perhaps, one who was not very intelligent. The attempt of Ortiza to end her life had been one stroke to open the eyes of the governess. And the remarks of Tarabal had done the rest. Now she found that she was actually a little afraid of those quiet eyes. She was beginning to compare Ortiza with other girls of the same age and the same situation. Surely they would have been weeping and wailing. But Ortiza was as quiet as though she were half asleep. And yet how far was sleep and quiet from her.

"And now, dear," said Rosa, when she had composed her nerves as much as she could by arranging affairs in the room, "tell me everything. When there is something in the heart, it must be all talked out. Otherwise, there is sickness. Trust me, my angel. Rosa knows. She is old and knows."

"There is nothing in my heart that I wish to talk of," said Ortiza. "There is only sadness."

"A child's foolish sadness," said Rosa. "But when you see *Señor* Valdez . . . ah, then it will all be different." And she laughed wisely. "I shall tell you about him," she began. "I shall. . . ."

"I don't wish to hear," said Ortiza. "I don't wish to think of him."

"*Tush!*" laughed Rosa. "The new governor, the great *Señor* Pyndero, is to give a ball such as never was seen before in Monterey. And when you come into the room with your husband . . . he is so tall and handsome, and you, my love, in that dress of. . . ."

She discovered that Ortiza had closed her eyes, and she stopped talking. Tarabal had been right beyond a question. There was a strength of weakness in this girl, and Rosa set her mouth in a stern, straight line. She had been closed out of the mind and the life of Ortiza, and she knew that she could never

91

enter it again. In her anger, she turned part of her spite toward the somber friar, and part of it she saved for Ortiza herself. Rosa had given seventeen years of her life to the care of this girl, and now she was dismissed like a common servant. She vowed to herself that, hereafter in this house, she should be only the true servant of Tarabal. But the moment she had made that resolution, she knew in her heart of hearts that she could never entirely hold to it. So she bade Ortiza good night and left her.

To Ortiza, her going meant only a blessed time of quiet. She raised her book. It was a life of St. Francis written by an early member of that great order. But she found that she could not lose herself in the simple and beautiful story, as she had done before. Something had passed from her that could not be instantly recaptured. And presently, between her eyes and the print on the page, she found that pictures were forming of the governor's ball and all the brave cavaliers and all the lovely ladies. How would she herself stand among them? The flattery of Rosa meant nothing. She had proved on this day that her old governess feared her master more than she loved her mistress, and, therefore, nothing that she had ever said could be truly believed. It might be all a tissue of policies. It was a very lonely hour to Ortiza. The house had fallen asleep early. For Tarabal himself did not approve of late hours, and in all things he forced his own habits upon those who were near him. Sleep in the house of San Triste was a time of utter silence, indeed, for there was little to squeak or groan in that solid structure of stone and adobe, even when a storm stooped over the hills and struck across the valley. Tonight there was very little breeze — no more than enough to set up, from time to time, a distant hushing among the fig trees that grew to the westward of the house.

She hesitated, half expecting to be lulled to sleep at any

instant. But sleep did not come. She was filled with a melancholy peace and a sad happiness, such as that which is often born in the dark of the night and dies before the dawn. All of this was very new to her, and yet all the change must be traced to the mention her governess had made of the governor's ball. Even the dreadful ringing of the bell, that told of the coming of her husband-to-be, had not meant so much. It had made her seek refuge in death, but the thought of the dance made her think of seeking refuge in life.

Dimly she felt that she had powers. She had riches of resource that could be deeply mined; she herself only guessed at them, and no other human being could even dream of them. But suppose that she should choose to smile on a man — a little more than was necessary. And suppose that she looked at him a little sidewise, so that it brought a gleam of mysterious knowledge and mirth into her eyes — and suppose that she danced with even half of the grace for which the dancing master had praised her — what would come about?

She tried that smile and that side glance in the mirror that stood on the farther side of the room just opposite her bed. It showed the door open on her balcony to admit the air, and it showed the starry blue of the night sky, and with these, as she sat up, it gave her back her own reflection. She had never tried such a game before, and it seemed to her that it was as though she had slipped a lovely mask over her face when she smiled in that way. She lay back on the pillows again, shivering with excitement. What she wanted was to win a husband out of the world, not have one brought to her by the nose, like a bull to the slaughter.

Realizing what a hollow little farce all this acting had been, she tried to force her thoughts to new things. She regarded the ceiling and the shadows upon it. She regarded the noble, five-branched candlestick worked in red copper that stood beside her bed. Then, growing a little chilly, she drew around her shoulders a blue scarf of soft silk, snuffed four of the candles, and lay back to watch the flame of the fifth. It was like a little, yellow dagger blade, wide in the belly and sharpened to the keenest point, that kept stabbing into the darkness, and where the flame joined the wick, there was an oval of rich blue. Was it not strange that she had never known the loveliness of candle flame before?

Now the flame shook and shrank, until it was all blue, with only a ragged outline of yellow fire around the outer edge. Someone had told her that when evil spirits were near, a candle would burn small and blue. She sat up on the bed. Then she heard something like a whisper, but whispers could never come out of the solid floor. Yet how could she turn her head to see?

She caught her hand to her breast and forced her face around. There she saw within the door a man wearing a black cloak, a little black skullcap, and a black mask. In his hand was a naked sword blade, down to the needle point of which the yellow light of the candle ran and seemed to drip away. Her lips parted, but the cry strangled in her throat, as he raised his hand. There was such a calm air of authority that she made up her mind on the instant — it must be the wild Francisco Valdez who, having failed to see the lady of his heart during the day, had come to see her by night.

Chapter Twelve

NEITHER CHRISTIAN NOR MOSLEM

Yet that could not be. Valdez might have come masked, but certainly not with a bared sword in his hand. Indeed, even if Valdez were the wildest of blades, she doubted if he would have dared to offend her terrible father in this manner, or have entered her room, knowing that one cry from her would spread an alarm through the house and bring a score of armed servants at the beck of Tarabal.

"You are frightened, *mademoiselle*," said the stranger in excellent French. "It is the mask, then, that I take off."

He removed the black mask, and she saw a bold and keen-featured face. He took off the cap, and his hair was the color of flame — a yellow red. At the same instant the rapier was restored to its sheath, with so deft a hand that there was not even a whisper as it went home. And her wild fancy had time to tell her, in the midst of her terror, that even so it would slide home into the body of an enemy and find his life.

"If I call out, you are a dead man, *señor*."

"No. From your balcony railing I jump to the top of the wall. From the wall I drop to the back of a horse so fleet that not even the fastest of your horses could ever overtake me. I am as safe, *señorita*, as though I had a hundred armed men around me instead of these two only. So have no fear for me."

He waved his hand, as he spoke, and two figures stole into the room from the balcony. They were Indians, taller than any she had ever seen, noble figures clothed in thin white cotton garments, their long hair held away from their faces with narrow

95

bands of cloth that ran around the head. Their moccasined feet made no more sound than shadows falling on the floor. They did not look at her, but kept their eyes fixed steadily upon the face of the man with the red hair. It was a nightmare scene; it was a very vision of dread come into flesh and blood. She could not have cried out now. She could not have moved.

He of the flame-colored hair stepped to the foot of her bed. "These two will harm no one in the house," he assured her. "We have come for food and for other necessaries."

Easily into her Spanish he had slipped. Now, at a gesture of dismissal from him, the Indians stole out of the room. There was one partially rusted hinge on the door of her chamber, but under their hands not a whisper sounded to warn the house. Neither did the stairs give a sound to tell that they were descending. Then she looked at El Rojo, telling herself that certainly she must be cold with terror. But she was not afraid. He stood at the foot of the bed, but, instead of staring at her, his glance was for the single-candle flame beside the head of her bed, or else his look wandered out through the doors of her balcony to the blue-black sky of the night beyond. Ortiza understood that he was taking care not to embarrass her by a steady regard. It was something like an apology, after a knife thrust, and a faint smile came upon the lips of the girl.

"Will you leave me, *señor?*"

"If I leave, you will grow frightened . . . if you grow frightened, you will cry out . . . if you cry out, there will be bloodshed in the house before morning, *señorita.*"

Nothing could be more to the point. Now, his head being turned a little from her, she began to study his face, as she would never have dared to study the features of another man. He was not handsome, she decided. Certainly the sun had blackened him too much for that, and his features were much too pronounced, too harsh. Yet, it was pleasant to watch him.

If only he would turn a little more toward her, she could so draw his face into her memory that it would never escape her.

"¿Señor?"

"It is best that I do not hear your voice, señorita."

"Why is that?"

"I have come only once from necessity to this house. Allah forbid that I should come again."

"Allah?"

He made no answer.

"You are not a Christian?"

"Would you fear me more if I were not?"

He looked her squarely in the face now, but, instead of considering the question he had asked, she contented herself with making a number of small, but important, discoveries. In the first place, his eyes were unmistakably blue. In the second place, his forehead did not slant back, as she had thought before. In the third place, his cheeks were more drawn, and his cheekbones higher than she had guessed. And, the instant his eyes were steadied upon her, she felt aware of a cold and sharp-edged cruelty. She drew the bedclothes to her chin. It seemed wonderful that she had had the courage to speak a single word to him.

"But I'm neither Christian nor Moslem," he said. "Which of them is the worse? A Moslem made me a slave . . . a Christian kept me as one." He smiled down at her, and she felt that her breath was going out of her body, as though she had been immersed in cold water. "I have been beaten by Tunis pirates and whipped by Spanish Christians. Which shall I love the most, señorita?"

His voice had not raised beyond the faintest murmur, but his emotion had altered his color to a sickly yellow.

"You," she cried softly at last, "are the man who escaped from my . . . from Francisco Valdez."

"What is he to you, *señorita?*"

"And he was cruel to you, *señor?*"

"Why do you ask that?"

"Because it means very much to me."

He left the foot of the bed and came to stand beside her. "Then you are Ortiza Tarabal whom he has come to marry? In the name of heaven, is it true?"

"Yes."

He smiled, but she saw that his teeth were set behind the smile.

"Let me be a prophet, *señorita,* and tell you that wedding can never take place."

"What can prevent it?"

"Bad luck," he said, grinning in the same mirthless fashion. "I am afraid that there will be bad luck for *Señor* Don Francisco Valdez. Listen to me," — and here he raised a finger, and his smile went out — "such beauty was never meant for him. And such gentleness was never meant for him. You are not too proud to talk to a slave, and, therefore, you are not proud enough to take the name of Valdez."

He raised his head, as though he heard a sound that was mute to her.

"They are coming back, and I must go with them. But I shall see you again. The governor gives a ball. Look for me on that night, *señorita.*"

"You would not dare to show yourself."

"But if I took my life in my hands and came . . . tell me, would you dance with me?"

"*¡Señor!*"

"Answer."

"Yes, yes, but you must not come."

At that moment the door to the chamber opened again, and the Indians entered, each loaded with a great bundle, securely

98

tied and slung across his back. They passed out onto the balcony, and El Rojo went with them. She heard his whispered directions. One was to take his stand on the wall; the other and El Rojo would swing out the bundles from the balcony. Then they were to be dropped outside the wall, where the horses were waiting. She heard the muffled drop of one upon the top of the wall. The other was swung, and then the door to her chamber was pushed softly open, and, against the blackness of the hall beyond, she saw the bulky form of her father, half dressed, with Francisco Valdez behind him, and the heads of other men beyond.

In vain they signaled her for silence. A half-choked cry came from her throat. The answer was from the balcony: "Now, Bulé, quick! Save yourself and make off. I'll keep these back!"

The bull-voice of Tarabal, seeing that his approach had been discovered, boomed through the room. "Close on them! A hundred *pesos* for every dead man!"

They rushed across the room, yelling, but the heavy doors onto the balcony crashed to in their faces, and a bullet, fired from the outside, whistled over their heads and lodged in the ceiling. They recoiled instantly.

"Guns! Guns!" shouted Tarabal, setting the example by jerking out a long pistol. Instantly a volley beat against the balcony doors, and by the very weight of the lead thrust them open.

Tarabal ran out, and Valdez was beside him.

"The thief has the legs of a rabbit. He's jumped to the wall. Fire!"

Two or three guns spoke.

"He's done for!" shouted Valdez eagerly.

"No, he jumped in time," answered Tarabal. "Down to the stables, every man! We'll ride the dog down!"

They poured back through the room. Only Valdez paused

99

before Ortiza. Excitement had fired him. His eyes were shining, and he laughed out the words he spoke.

"No fear, *señorita!* You shall see him dragged back before dawn!"

And so he was gone on the heels of the rest. No sooner was the door to her chamber closed than Ortiza hardly paused to toss a mantle around her shoulders. Then she passed between the battered doors of the balcony and looked out. Three horsemen were fleeing across the starlit valley, and now behind them streamed a dozen hard riders.

"They are lost," groaned Ortiza. "There are no horses in the hills that can distance those of my father's. God be merciful to the poor slave . . . and save him."

The pursued and the pursuers melted into the darkness, but the sounds of shouting and the beating of hoofs came clearly back to her. Here she heard the door to her room open. She turned and faced Rosa.

"Is this your sickness?" asked the governess angrily. "Is this the sickness that keeps you from meeting Don Francisco? Your father shall learn of it, Ortiza!"

Chapter Thirteen

"EL SABIO"

It was by no means a full stable from which Joaquín Tarabal mounted his men this night. The very cream had been taken before his arrival. Eight of the finest of his black horses had been pilfered from the stables at the same time that El Rojo and his two confederates entered the house and plundered it of what they needed most. And now the eight blacks grazed contentedly among the hills. The remnants of one of the fattest of Tarabal's calves lay in the near distance. The fire, over which the choicest cuts had been held on wooden spits and roasted, was now dying down and sending up only feeble wisps of smoke. On a sharp crest to the west lay the Navajo who had been wounded two days before. Two days was a short time for a recovery, but, though he was still weak, food and sleep had done much for him. He was capable of sitting in a saddle for a short distance at best, and he was more than capable of keeping a keen lookout that swept every point of the compass. Beneath him on a level shoulder of the hill, only a little removed from the fire, seven Navajos sat in a circle, playing their game, while El Rojo stood near, looking on.

They were children, he was deciding for the hundredth time. They were simply magnificent, lion-hearted, panther-footed children. It amused him now to watch their stony faces of gravity, as they played the game. And, for all their solemnity, now and again there was a flash of an eye that told more than would violent laughter and boasting. The game was a simple one. A pole about six feet in height — the trunk of a young sapling — had been fixed in the earth, and a few inches from its base was a short stick that projected from the earth only the width of a hand. The game was to throw up a heavy hunting knife, at least as high as the top of the pole, and make it descend so that the point of the blade should strike in the shorter stick. And, for all the simplicity of the game, it was profoundly difficult. One after another, the long knives flashed upward, wheeled in a shining circle at the top of the rise, and then plunged down. But, though sometimes a splinter was shaved from the bark of the trunk, no knife was fixed in the wood itself.

And the chief, Bulé, grew more and more angry. "Is my hand old, while my heart is still young?" he asked suddenly, then flung his knife to twice the required height. So careless was the gesture that there was a great probability that the knife in falling might strike one of the circle. Yet not a man deigned to watch the flight of the missile, but each fixed his eyes steadily on the ground.

El Rojo, watching, smiled again. Down flew the knife, and luck made the point strike squarely on the center of the peg, but the blade was so slanting that the point merely chiseled a nick out of the wood, as the knife fell to the earth. Bulé uttered a slight exclamation, and then, as though ashamed of exhibiting so much emotion, he flashed a glance at his circle of companions, but not one of these had paid the least attention to him or to his words.

One of them, however, began to speak in a harsh, faint guttural to his companions, and El Rojo turned to walk away and let them have the privacy they seemed to wish. He had not taken a dozen steps, however, when he was hailed, and he turned to find that all the Navajos had risen to their feet. They had tried their best at their game, but luck had been against them. It was now time for the white chief to demonstrate his skill.

El Rojo paused only a moment. They had accepted him as a savior, in the first place, because he had brought them out of the hands of the Spaniards. They had accepted him as a worthy chief and natural leader, since he had taken them to the plundering of the house of San Triste and guarded their rear, while they fled. That was a species of moral stamina of which they had no conception. So far, therefore, he had constantly demonstrated his superiority. The moment he failed, half of their blind confidence would be gone. Yet, he could not possibly succeed at this new game that had baffled such experts as the Indians. Instead, he drew the hunting knife from its sheath and balanced it on his hand, with the hilt resting on his wrist and several inches of the blade lying within his fingertips. When he threw, it was with a flip of the wrist, turning his hand over at the same time. The heavy knife hissed out of his fingers and shot at the sapling — a long streak of light that went out as the knife point struck fairly in the center of the sapling trunk, split the narrow wand, and stuck in the crevice, vibrating rapidly back and forth.

It brought a cry from the Indians. It had been beneath their dignity to stir, no matter how close they stood in the path of the flying knife, but when they saw what had been accomplished, there was a brief outbreak of exclamations. They gathered close. They examined the wood and the edge of the knife. Then they stepped back to permit him to approach and take back his weapon. "El Sabio," they muttered to one another, "has no need of guns . . . he carries the lightning flash in his bare hands."

It had been a very lucky throw, indeed, but El Rojo approached and drew forth the knife with magnificent carelessness. He had hardly done so when the lookout cried from the top of the hill — a horseman was coming from the south. In an instant the horses were gathered, and the fire embers extinguished. In a few seconds, all were out of observation, on the farther side of the hill and lying flat in the tall grass. They saw the cause of the alarm come over the opposite crest. It was a horseman who drove before him two big mules, loaded down with immense packs. He was heading for the hollow that was just to the east of the hill where they lay in covert, and, as he came, his merry voice ran before him, singing a ballad of the road. It needed only a glance to make sure that he was a peddler.

"Bring him here," said El Rojo to his companions.

Bulé pointed. A single man rose to his feet, with lips compressed, eyes shining with joy, his fingers clasped around the butt of his knife.

"Alive," continued El Rojo.

Half of the joy left the face of the Navajo. Indeed, El Rojo could understand his emotion, for they had learned in a harsh school to hate all white faces. He had heard from Bulé himself how the expedition of Pyndero had reached the Navajo village, had been feasted and entertained royally, and in return the governor had behaved like a scoundrel. It was for this that Bulé and his companions had taken the long trail behind the governor. Obedience, however, to the white chief who had taken them out of the very hands of torture and death, and who could carry the "lightning" in his fingers, as they had just witnessed, was even stronger than their desire for revenge. The Navajo ventured one glance at Bulé, saw nothing to countermand the order of El Rojo, and sped down the slope.

El Rojo watched the runner with wonder and envy. He himself was fleet of foot, but he could not match this racer for an instant. The Navajo boy on his native desert runs down the cottontail — partly by leathery endurance which keeps him going swiftly from dawn to dark, partly by snake-like skill in still hunting, and partly by sheer dash and brilliance of sprinting. And here was no boy, but a seasoned warrior, hardened by many a long league of recent marching. He had the eyes of his six young companions upon him; he was in the sight of his chief; and, above all, the wise white man was watching. So he went down the declivity, like a thrown stone, and reached the bottom long before the mule driver came into view.

El Rojo noted the contrast. The peddler's brown cheeks shone with the fat of good living, even at that distance. The Indian was coiled cat-like behind a large stone, not peering about a corner, but trusting wholly to his sense of hearing to tell him what was happening. The peddler, coming nearer, had struck into a new song, when the Navajo rose from his place of concealment. The singing of the peddler stopped, and he clasped his hands above his heart. They saw his mouth gape open with horror and astonishment. Then his wild yell of terror rang up the slope to the concealed men.

El Rojo looked askance. Every one of those coppery faces near him was smiling, and every eye was flashing under the influence of that shriek of fear, as though each had heard the sweetest music. And he himself could not help admiring the consummate knowledge of human character that had enabled the Indian to choose his manner of capturing his victim. How had he been able to tell that the jolly singer was, in fact, a craven at heart?

The work was done, however, by this time. Up the slope rode the fat man, wringing his hands and calling upon his favorite saints, but never dreaming of trying to escape. He was escorted to the very top of the hill and to the shoulder of it where, when he saw the seven Indians waiting for him and the smoking fire and the bones of the slaughtered calf, his last bit of self-control left him. He buried his face in his hands and swayed back and forth in the saddle, moved by an agony of self-pity.

El Rojo now dropped a hand on the poor man's shoulder, and, when the latter saw a white face, he tumbled to the ground, caught El Rojo about the knees, and besought him to be his savior.

"You will not be touched," he was assured. "But something from those packs. . . ."

"In the name of heaven," cried the unhappy man, "take it all!"

His word had not been waited for. As wolves scent meat, the Navajos had guessed at pleasant possibilities in the bulky packs. In an instant their hands had torn the packs from the saddles and spread them open. So many treasures of tinsel, of gilt, of shining metal, and of cloth of brilliant colors were before them, that they could not tell what to seize first, and their chatter of comment rose shriller and higher. In fact, the peddler carried everything that small vanities, at the end of the world, could covet. In a moment Bulé was robed in a long mantle of crimson velvet, another was stuffing rings upon his brown fingers, and a third, having found a hairdresser's department in the bags, had clapped a woman's wig upon his head and danced in a swift circle, with his locks flying.

The care of the peddler had been all for his life, but, since that seemed to be for the moment secure, his heart was breaking at the sight of this plunder.

"Oh," murmured the poor man, "I am a beggar from this day forward. There is all my wealth and borrowed money on the backs of the two mules. And now it is gone in a breath. See that rare Italian lace, so yellow with age, so delicate it would befit the wrists of a duchess, now tied on the head of a. . . ."

For Bulé, to complete his attire, had caught up a length of splendid lace and knotted it about his head. Here El Rojo interfered again and suggested that it would be better to leave the packs of the peddler untouched, saving for what necessities they should find in them. His speech was met with a gloomy silence. Even Bulé was frowning.

"What wrong," said El Rojo, "has this man done you?"

"He has a white face that means a wolf's heart behind it," declared Bulé. Then, recalling that he was addressing those words to another white man, he fell silent and looked steadily at the horizon, far away. After this, he tore off the mantle and the lace, tossed them onto the pile, and gave a few gruff commands to his followers.

One by one, slowly and reluctantly, they obeyed, and what they had pilfered was restored. The peddler, in the meantime, was filled with rapture of wonder and joy.

"Whatever you may intend to do with me and my goods," he murmured to El Rojo, "I thank heaven that silks and laces will not be wasted among savages."

The Navajos drew sullenly apart, and watched the two white men with sullen looks.

"Be quiet," said El Rojo to the peddler. "For all I know, I have put a knife to both our throats." He went straight to the grim-faced Navajos. "Why," he said, "are you staying among these hills? Is it to find your chance to slip into the town, and to give Pyndero the payment you owe him of a knife thrust between the ribs? But if you rob and plunder while you wait here, you will have these hills swarming with men, like the air with wasps. For the white man fears the loss of his goods more than he fears death. If a man is killed, it is a small thing . . . but if his pocket is picked, a whole tribe must die for that theft. Is this truth, my friend?" he added, turning to Bulé.

The chief had fought back his passion with difficulty. But he knew enough of the ways of the whites to understand that there was a great deal of truth in what he had heard. Moreover, a few seconds had elapsed, and he had had a chance to let his first passion diminish. He faced his companions in turn.

"El Sabio," he said, "has spoken words as true as a ringing bell. He has given us our lives and our horses. He has put food in our mouths and knives and guns in our hands. His words must be our words."

The reply was entirely sincere. They retreated to a little distance. Pipes were drawn out. They began to smoke in utter silence, and it seemed to El Rojo that he was witnessing a religious ceremony in the appeasing of their wrath. If so small a thing could have worked them into a dangerous temper, *it was small wonder*, he thought, *that they had followed the governor so far to the north.*

Chapter Fourteen

TWO OLD SOLDIERS

The humor of José Bernardo Pyndero was as black as the pit, and for very good reason. At the very moment of his arrival in the seat of his new government his house had been the scene of an attack upon his life. And on the same night, during the pursuit, one of his best men, his most trusted lieutenant, Juan Rindo, had been caught, stripped, and branded like beef. Nor was this all. When he had apprehended the miscreants, who had attacked him, and killed some two or three in making the capture, the rest had been stolen away by that same daring villain, that very prince of iniquity, late the slave of Valdez, the noble Spaniard. Even on that very subject of Valdez his misgivings were sore. For when the Spaniard landed, he had lost slave, horse, sword, and dignity at a single stroke, and naturally he would put the blame in letters home upon the shoulders of the governor. How many of the common people he offended was not of the slightest concern to the governor. But Valdez was a different song and had to be sung in another key.

Consideration of all these things made the worthy governor yearn for matter on which to vent his wrath, and so he ordered the prisoners from the house of Darnay to be brought before him. First of all, Julie was brought. The very first glimpse of her shocked half of the governor's bad temper away. He had not seen her clearly on the night of the arrest, and he fully expected now to see a sad-eyed, bedraggled girl. Instead, he found Julie, blooming and smiling in such a way upon the guard who led her in that the latter was very apparently walking in a trance. Her dress was fresh, her hair was carefully arranged, and, instead of trembling and turning pale, she merely clasped her hands together and looked down upon the floor more demurely than in fear.

The devil take me, said the governor to the hollow of his hand. *She's a beauty. Holy patron, what a pair of eyes.* He said aloud: "You do not seem sad, *señorita!*"

"Oh, no," she answered.

The governor started. "On my honor, you seem actually happy."

"Of course," said Julie. "I am."

The governor stared. "Did I understand you?" he said.

"Because," said Julie, "I never expected to meet so great a man as the governor."

By heavens, said the governor, again to the hollow of his hand, *the little minx is making a mock of me.* To her he said: "*Señorita,* you look only on the floor."

"Because," said Julie, "I dare not look elsewhere until I have permission."

And, so saying, she looked up for the first time, full at the governor.

The latter frowned because it was the only way he could save face and appear stern. "Have you forgotten your position, Julie Darnay?"

"I don't understand, Excellency," said the girl.

"You are lodged here in prison, accused of treason against the State."

"Of course," said Julie, "that's silly. I beg your pardon, Excellency."

The governor bit his lip. "Are you about to smile, Julie?" he asked in a new tone.

"I am trying my best not to," she said.

"You may stop trying," said the governor.

He was royally rewarded with a smile that shone like the new sun.

"Now unriddle that riddle," said the governor. "You are in prison, but you are happy. Your father is incarcerated also, and by an unfortunate accident your house has burned to the ground."

"Unfortunate fiddlesticks!" cried Julie in anger. "It was that rascal, Juan Rindo. He put a match to the place. Oh, I know!"

"Silence!" said the governor.

"Yes, Excellency," and she curtsied deeply.

"Who," said the governor, suddenly interested, "taught you to make that curtsy?"

"My mirror," said Julie, and then she caught her breath and clapped her fingers over her lips.

But the governor was laughing heartily. "Julie," he said, "you are delightful."

"I am sure, Excellency," said Julie, "that you are also . . . oh, what was I about to say?"

The governor merely grinned. He was leaning forward, as though to watch her more closely.

"In one word," he said, "that old fantastic, your father, has been boring you to distraction. He has locked you up in shadows and given you books instead of young suitors to talk to. Is that it?"

"It is," said Julie, and, then blushing, she added hastily: "What I mean is. . . ."

"Exactly what you say," said the governor.

"Yes," said Julie, tossing her head. "Exactly that."

"But," said the governor, "the moment your father is free, your slavery will begin again."

Julie sighed. "I have been thinking of that," she declared.

The governor laughed again. "You shall have lodgings outside the prison," he said. "To connect you with treason is, of

111

course, nonsense. Guard, take Julie Darnay back to her cell and then come back to me for instructions." He added, as Julie was turning away: "One moment! Come closer, Julie."

She stepped to the table. She leaned a little, with very bright, very wide eyes, to listen to him.

"I am going to give you a present, Julie," said the governor.

"Thank you, Excellency."

"It is only advice, my dear."

"I shall never forget it."

"In the first place, never look at another man the way you are now looking at me."

"Why, Excellency?"

"You will be kissed, Julie."

"Oh!" she cried.

"And lock your smiles behind your teeth. Do you understand?"

"I think," said Julie, "that I do."

And, with her face so close to his, she looked him in the eye and smiled straight at his Excellency, José Bernardo Pyndero.

When she was gone, the governor rose and walked back and forth across the room two or three times, with his hands clasped behind his back under the tail of his coat, which he flipped up repeatedly as he strolled about. It was a favorite habit of his. It was an excellent idea, he decided, this decision of his to examine prisoners privately and informally before their regular trials were given. It took a little time, but it would bring him so intimately in touch with the life of the province, so very intimately. He paused at the window, and, holding the big ruby of his ring in the sunlight, he admired its rich fire and its richer shadow for a time. He was still so employed when the door was opened and Mortier was brought in. His hands were chained behind his back. But the governor, having given his man a single glance, ordered that the shackles be unlocked.

112

He was one who prided himself on his ability to read deep into the human mind at a glance. He was reading in that fashion now, and what he saw made him decide that he must have been blind, indeed, to have flung this man so hastily in prison. For he had distinction in his bearing. His head was high, his eye was bright, and there was a sort of resistless good nature about him that made the governor exclaim: "*Señor* Mortier, you are an uncle of this Julie Darnay. Is it not so?"

"It is not," said Mortier, and he added with a faint smile: "I am sorry for it, Excellency!"

The smile made the governor bite his lip. He gathered his official manner about him.

"Your name," he went on, sitting down at the table and taking up a piece of paper, "is Louis Auguste Mortier?"

"It is."

"Your occupation?"

"Farmer."

"Farmer?" echoed the governor, and, putting down the paper, he leaned back in his chair and looked Mortier steadily in the face. The half smile, half sneer, that habitually lingered about the compressed lips of Pyndero was never more baffling.

"You wear a sword, *señor*."

"When I am not in prison, yes. I have been in the army, Excellency."

"The army?"

"Of the emperor."

The governor straightened in his chair.

"Your rank?"

"Colonel."

The governor stood up.

"Is it possible?"

"I thank heaven that it is, Excellency."

"Where have you seen service?"

113

"My first battle was Montenotte . . . my last was Waterloo."

"So? And in Spain?"

"I have seen Madrid, Excellency."

The governor flushed to the eyes. "That was changed before the end. Spain wakened!"

"Most nobly, Excellency."

"*Monsieur le colonel,* I see that you are both a gentleman and soldier. I have been very hasty with you."

"It is nothing," answered Mortier, bowing. "I have known the fortunes of war. I was in Russia also, Excellency."

"Sit down! Sit down!" urged the governor. "Why, my friend, we are comrades of battle, even if we have stood on opposite sides of the fence. And if Grouchy had been a true man or a wise one, who knows?"

"Who knows?" echoed Mortier sadly. "But that is ended."

"And what has brought you to Alta California?" asked the governor. "What has brought you so far from your dear Paris, *monsieur le colonel?*"

Briefly he was told the same story Mortier had related to Darnay.

When he had concluded, the governor said: "But he has been in the same cell with you, and by this time you have his signature."

"He is as stubborn as rock," sighed Mortier. "I could do nothing with him in prison."

"I wish from the bottom of my heart," said the governor, "that I could be of service to you."

They were both seated now. Mortier's chair faced the light, so that he had to narrow his eyes in order to peer closely into the face of Pyndero. And he read enough to give him a new hope.

"Perhaps," he said, "that is not impossible."

"And yet," went on the governor, "it is a long, long trip

. . . it is many months at sea, this journey from France to California."

"Many months, Excellency."

"And for the sake of a marsh, *monsieur!*"

Mortier hesitated. Once more he examined the governor, as though the latter were a mysterious document. He seemed to decide, at length, that he must take a great chance.

"Suppose," he said, "that the marsh is no longer what it was, as Darnay remembers it?"

"True," murmured the governor. "I had an idea that it must have changed."

And the two smiled upon one another, the governor in great good humor, the Frenchman still full of hesitation.

"As a matter of fact," said Mortier, taking the plunge at once, "a large village has grown up on the marsh, which has been drained and turned into excellent farming land, and the village, the fine land, and all is in the possession of this old fanatic, Darnay, who cares nothing for money and everything for his ideas. A political madman, Excellency."

"But he has a daughter who might not be indifferent to money, *monsieur*."

"To be sure . . . to be sure." He waited in an agony of suspense.

"Yet," said the governor slowly, "we might be able to accomplish something in this affair."

The colonel drew a great breath. There was one word in that sentence that told him everything he wanted to know. "Yes," he said, "and it would be greatly worthwhile for us both. You would be my partner, Governor."

"You are kind."

The barriers were down.

"In a word, Excellency, that property is now worth a quarter of a million *francs*."

The governor moistened his lips.

"More than a hundred thousand for each of us."

"You are an excellent mathematician, *monsieur*."

"And, if I were to write out a paper in legal form, Excellency, giving you title to half of that property . . . if I were even to give you my note for something more than a hundred thousand *francs* . . . ?"

"You are too kind, *monsieur*."

"And place it in your hands the moment I received from you the signature of *Monsieur* Darnay . . . is it not possible that you might be able to *persuade* my old friend to write his name?"

"I have long been a lover of persuasion," said the governor. "Say no more. Say no more, *monsieur*. It is done."

And with a sudden overflow of happy spirits and affection, the two soldiers fell into each other's arms and embraced.

Chapter Fifteen

LORD WYNCHAM

It was a great time for Monterey. There had been excitement enough in the past few days to have lasted the town, by dint of repeated gossip, for a whole year. But new wonders continued to rain down on the little city. On the evening of the same day on which the governor had interrogated Julie Darnay and arranged it so that she could live outside the walls of the prison, there came into Monterey a peddler, driving before him two sturdy mules, upon whose backs were heaped mountains of rarities. He had come up from Santa Barbara, making the whole long journey in small stages, and so he had come, at last, to Monterey itself. He had been unwilling to wait in Santa Barbara, he explained, for the sailing of a ship to the north. That might have cost him months, and, in the meantime, how much happiness was being lost to the good wives of Monterey?

The ladies, indeed, needed only one peep into his treasures to agree with him. Before he had been in town an hour, he had already trebled his prices and saw himself on the way to becoming an independently prosperous man. For money meant nothing to the gentry who drew their incomes from huge cattle ranches strung up and down the coast. They were loaded down with *pesos,* and there was nothing on which they could spend them, unless a trading ship made port now and then with a cargo of fine clothes and trinkets and, perhaps, rare old wine to fill their cellars.

The peddler was not the only sensation in Monterey. One that far eclipsed him was announced at the same moment. Into the pleasant streets of Monterey came a tall young man, brown-faced from long exposure, blue-eyed, and black of hair and eyebrow, a combination of colors that surely spoke of Irish blood. But he was a young English nobleman, named Anthony, Lord Wyncham — a devil-may-care youth who had crossed the American continent on horseback, until his horse died, and he had then gone on, traveling on foot. Yet he arrived at the end of his prodigious journey with a rapier and a pistol. How truly like a heedless prodigal to have carried such a weapon as a rapier through the midst of Indian tribes.

But here he was, dressed in rags, cheerful, laughing at his trials and sufferings in making the crossing. He had taken lodgings at once in an unpretentious place. He had taken shelter in his chamber and refused to see anyone but a tailor, who departed in mad haste with a rush order for an outfit of clothes. Only one person managed to see him on the evening of his first arrival, and that was a wealthy neighbor who had managed to reach the room of Wyncham by strategy. Once arrived, he found the young nobleman a pleasant host. They had talked and diced for half an hour, during which the visitor had filled his ears with exciting stories and emptied his pockets of gold. But, though the sum he lost was great, the stories he heard he swore were worth twice as much.

He departed, to carry his news around the town, and, before morning, all of Monterey knew how young Wyncham, in his adventures among the Indians, had twice been tied to the stake for torture and death, only to be released at the critical moment by strangest good fortune; how he had been captured and escaped by night, racing an Indian pony across the plains; how he had taken part in a great battle between two tribes, and, having distinguished himself in fighting for his allies, had been adopted into the tribe by force and had to use a ruse to escape from them; and how, after a thousand trials, he had at length crossed the mountains and dropped into a broad valley; later he had reached the coast and then this blooming city of Monterey.

Had there been only one tithe of truth in the contents of this tale, it would have been enough to fascinate the townspeople. They were impressed, moreover, by a pride that kept him from showing his face until his rags were replaced with the tailor's suit. But the worthy tailor, calling in his apprentices and his women friends, had cut and sewed and labored all night, and in the morning the work was done.

Behold young Lord Wyncham, stepping from his room the next morning, clad as a gentleman should be clad, with a small sword at his side, a stick in his hand, a three-cornered hat perched on his head, and a smile on his face. Yet, for all his good nature, the people who saw him pass along the street, and who pointed him out to one another, were by no means willing to venture to accost him without an introduction. For his pride was stamped in his face. The very carriage of his head and the straightness of his glances told enough. But, besides that, his features were cut after a strong and imperious pattern. And his whole manner and appearance were like the description of an aristocrat taken out of a book.

His destination was noted, and people nodded when he was seen to disappear into the house of the governor. Of course, for a man of his station, it was only natural that he should go to see Pyndero. He was admitted to the presence of the governor at once, for, thick though the walls of José Pyndero's house were, they were not strong enough to shut out rumor. And rumor had already told him a hundred intriguing things about the young Englishman.

"You come as the seventh wonder, my lord," said Pyndero, when their names had been exchanged. "We have had a slave run off from a ship and steal his master's horse and sword . . .

I have been trailed a thousand miles by Indian cutthroats . . . and, when I captured them, I have had them turned free by this same devil of a slave . . . and we have had a fat simpleton of a peddler, who actually made the trip overland from Santa Barbara without losing his way, starving, or having his throat slit by the Indians. In a word, *señor*, our ears have been buzzing with news, and now you come to give us a climax."

"I see," said Lord Wyncham, "that you are too gentle in your rule, Your Excellency. A liberal use of the hangman's rope would quiet all these troubles. A few well-stretched ropes would give you quieter nights. But, as for myself, I have simply taken a pleasant ride and a somewhat less pleasant walk, and here I am at your service."

"There is one service," said the governor, "that I shall certainly demand from you, and that is an account of your travels. If you will dine with me tonight . . . ?"

"Excellency," smiled Lord Wyncham, "I have made a vow that I shall not think of those travels or open my lips about them again for seven days. You see," he explained, "I have to bring order into the narrative, and decide where I must place the shadows and the highlights. I must season the truth with lies and the lies with the truth."

"That," laughed the governor, "is ever the way with our best raconteurs."

"But, above all," said Wyncham, "one must have a good memory to recall a tale once told and always keep it in the same form. Also, one must know just where to be free with one's invention."

"You will have small need of that," said the governor, "from what we learn of your adventures."

Wyncham smiled. "One of your good townsmen forced his way in on me last night. He was hunting for excitement, Excellency, and I must be forgiven if I gave it to him."

"Then what you told him was not true?"

"Not a syllable."

"You really were in little danger?"

"None at all . . . that is, none to speak of. I found the terrible redskins so many naïve children."

"I congratulate you, my lord, but nevertheless this is bad news for Monterey."

"Not at all. By the end of a week I shall have invented enough to content them. I have read fairy stories, you see."

The faint smile of the governor deepened. "But, after all," he said, "it is really a marvel that you should have crossed without danger. You must carry a charm with you."

"For that matter, I do."

"You astonish me, señor."

"A simple charm for a simple people. A mere trick, Excellency."

"I am devoured with interest."

"I see your charming garden through the window. Step out with me, and I shall show you the mystery."

"Willingly!"

They entered the patio, and Wyncham took into his hand a heavy hunting knife with a long, keen blade that he had so disposed in his clothes it was not previously visible. This he now held, with the hilt resting on his wrist and the blade across the tips of his fingers.

"Here is my magic . . . here is my charm, Excellency."

The knife flashed from his hand, flickered across the sunlit space, and sank half the depth of the blade in the slender trunk of a sapling. There it stuck with a deep-voiced humming. And the governor exclaimed: "You need no gun, my lord, with such skill as this!"

Wyncham crossed the space, tugged out the knife, and put it away.

"The Indians," he said, "were enchanted. They could not see it done often enough. I left every tribe practicing. And in their next wars they will be throwing volleys of knives instead of bullets and arrows. But you see, Excellency, that it takes only a small thing to amuse children."

They returned to the house, and the governor was filled with curiosity to learn why the nobleman had been tempted to undertake the venture.

"When a man's income is at a certain pitch," said Wyncham, "his ambition is stultified. Then he must find other ways of amusing himself than work. And that is the only explanation."

In another moment he was gone, and the governor sat for some time in his chair, drumming his fingers against his chin, lost in thought. At length he called Juan Rindo. The lieutenant came in, walking stiffly, for his scorched back did not admit any bending. Indeed, it was a torture to him to do anything save lie on his face quietly. But he endured the torture to stay at his post with the governor, for fear another might usurp his place the moment he was gone. He faced the governor with the same half-anguished and half-defiant eye with which he had regarded all of his companions.

"Juan Rindo," said the governor, "I have just received a visit from a man who calls himself Lord Wyncham. I have received him today, and I intend that I shall receive him again. But, in the meantime, I want him watched. Have him followed night and day. Bring me a report each morning of everything he has done the day before."

Juan Rindo attempted to bow, bit his lips to hold in a cry of agony, and then left the room to execute the order.

Chapter Sixteen

ORTIZA CONFERS WITH HER FATHER

Ortiza sat half in sun and half in shadow in the orchard westward from the house of San Triste. She had walked thither, leaning heavily on the shoulder of Rosa. And it had been a wretched progress. In the first place, she understood that Rosa knew perfectly that she was entirely able to walk by herself. In the second place, her father, Joaquín Tarabal, was waddling on before her, while behind them three Indians carried as many chairs. Tarabal carefully directed the placing of the chairs. They had been all in the shade at first, but the shade had partially shrunk away. Still Ortiza did not think of changing the position of her chair. She was too intent on listening to what her father was saying. Tarabal, in fact, was waxing eloquent.

"I have been like a fool," he confessed. "I have thought that you were like a clear pool of water . . . that I could look straight through you whenever I chose. But I should have known better. It was this way with your mother. She seemed like a child, and one learned later that the child had made him a fool. She made such a fool of me many times."

"She married you, sir," said Ortiza.

"Be silent!" roared Tarabal. "Is my own child taught to answer me back?"

Ortiza lay quietly in the chair and watched.

"I know everything," went on Tarabal.

Ortiza changed color, and it was noted at once.

"What? What?" he said. "Did you think my good Rosa would serve you better than she has served me? She told me

123

all . . . how you whipped out of bed and ran to watch the slave escape . . . *ran* to watch him, though you had told me that you could hardly walk."

Here Ortiza turned her head a little, so that her eyes could fall on the face of the governess. And, though Rosa had dropped her head a little and was intent on her sewing, she felt the weight of that glance and shrank under it. Yet, she could not be sure just what was going on in the mind of Ortiza. Indeed, the more she pondered on the girl, the more she was at a loss. For Ortiza had lived a life so utterly sheltered previously, that there had been no occasion to express her emotions. At length Rosa forced her head up. She found there was a new expression in the eyes of Ortiza. It was neither sorrow nor fear, but a sort of passive enmity. She was regarding her governess with a cold curiosity, as though she were really seeing her for the first time, and Rosa was frightened. She hardly thought the anger of the terrible rancher himself could have moved her so much as that pale and patient regard of the girl.

Ortiza was answering her father: "I was at fault, sir."

"Is that all you have to say?"

"What shall I say, sir?"

"I know some fathers who are feared by their children . . . so feared that the daughters would as soon cut off a hand as disobey. But you are different. Because I have been too gentle all this time, you think that I cannot be anything else. You do not know me, child. You do not know me, Ortiza."

She could well believe that she did not. His head was turned to the head of a beast. His face was swollen with purple blood. The lids of his eyes puffed until they buried all but two gleams of light.

"What shall I do, sir?"

"What I order you. Make Valdez happy. He has been breaking his heart trying to talk to you."

"He has no heart, sir," said Ortiza.

"What the devil do you mean by that? No heart? Hasn't he come from Spain to Alta California, for your sake?"

"You are very rich, Father. One day the man who marries me will inherit it all."

"If I am pleased with him and with you. Otherwise, what would keep me from leaving all that I have to Holy Mother Church? You never have thought of that, minx. But what would keep me from it?"

"Your pride in your name," said the girl, "and in the work you have done."

If she had made fire leap from between her lips, her words could not have amazed him more. Actually to hear reasons placed against his own was miraculous, in the eyes of Tarabal. And this was the soft girl, the infant, too young to marry.

"The church would swallow your estate and think nothing of it," she was continuing. "No, you will leave it through me, I think."

"You are so sure of it?" asked Tarabal, trembling with rage. For nothing infuriates a man so much as to feel that his future action is foreknown and counted on. He likes to be a small god, his thoughts wrapped in clouds, his actions sudden, wonderful, and unheralded.

"And yet," she answered, "I care nothing about wealth."

"That is a black lie," roared Tarabal. "Everyone who lives loves money."

She was silent. They continued to look gravely at one another for a time. And Rosa, sitting by, forgot her sewing. She still clutched her needle in trembling fingers, but all of her attention was given to her master and her mistress. Her expression was that of one who sees a titanic contest. And perspiration stood out on her forehead.

No doubt those two saw many new things in one another.

At least, Tarabal drew back a little from the level and fearless gaze of his daughter.

"You know me, Ortiza," he said at last.

"I hope so, sir."

"I have ordered you to marry Valdez."

"Yes, sir."

"And you will obey me."

"I am helpless, sir."

"And you will smile on him when he comes to see you . . . you will do that, Ortiza? You will make him happy?"

"I am helpless, sir," she repeated.

He ground his teeth, hesitated a moment, and then with a shake of the head turned and retreated. Before he left the orchard, Valdez was entering it. Rosa seized on this small interval to pour forth her heart.

"Oh, my dear, my dear," she sobbed. "You know that, if I spoke against you, I have repented it since then. You know that, Ortiza? But you had cut me to the heart with your manner of talk that day. You had showed me how little I meant in your life . . . tell me that you forgive me now, dear."

"Brother Andrea," said the girl, "tells me that a good Christian must always forgive. However, Rosa, I shall not forget. You have made my father hate me."

"No, no!"

"Hush," said the girl. "However, it makes no difference. I have known that there was a danger of this for a long time."

Her calm amazed Rosa.

"Go back a little with your chair, Rosa. You must not listen too closely to my . . . lover . . . when he talks."

And she said it without changing a muscle in her face, looking steadily at Valdez, who was rapidly approaching. Yet into her words she poured an utter scorn that amazed the governess. Rosa obediently took her chair to a distance. In

126

another moment the young Spaniard was before her mistress. He greeted her with his usual careful courtesy. He took the chair that her father had abandoned and presently he was making talk about "shoes and ships and sealing wax" while Ortiza, lying back in her chair, looked up at the sunlight, cascading from leaf to leaf and pouring down through the fig trees until it collected in little yellow pools upon the ground.

"Rosa has gone soundly asleep," he murmured suddenly.

"She is only pretending," said Ortiza, without even a glance at her.

"But her head has fallen on one side. She cannot see us, Ortiza."

"I should not trust her."

"But what do I care if she sees me take your hand, Ortiza, and lean closer to you, tell you how deeply I love you, dear?"

"You are brave, *Señor* Valdez."

Still her glance was upward among the leaves.

He leaned closer still. He pressed her hand against his breast.

"Do you feel how my heart is rioting, Ortiza?"

And while he asked, he studied her face closely. There was not the slightest change of color, and the hand that he held did not tremble. He was amazed.

"It is beating very fast, *señor*," she said.

"Am I always to be *señor*?"

"Shall I call you Francisco?"

"Ah, yes."

"So be it."

"But you have not told me, Ortiza, that you are happy?"

"You have not asked me, *señor*."

"Ah, my beautiful!" he breathed. "Look at me, Ortiza."

She turned her head, and instantly their lips were together. But Valdez suddenly stiffened in his chair.

"You have let me touch your lips, Ortiza, but only as if you were a chained thing that could not escape."

"My father's will has chained me, señor. He has told me that I must make you happy."

"God in heaven!" cried Valdez. "Is it that?"

He left her as though she were fire and fled to find Tarabal. He found him seated against the outer wall of the house, facing the sun that beat fiercely against his face, and that was reflected from the white walls of the building until the place was like a furnace. But Tarabal, furling around his eyes deep wrinkles that shut out some of the blinding light, and defying the fury of the direct rays with his blackened skin, puffed contentedly at his pipe and stirred neither foot nor hand. Yet so furious was the heat that one might have expected his over-stuffed body to be rendered to lard and grow thin.

To him Valdez, approaching on the wings of his shame and his indignation, poured out his story.

"I shall not have her, señor," said Valdez in conclusion. "I shall not have her. She does not love me. It is only the fear of you that drives her forward. But I, Señor Tarabal, cannot take her unwilling. And, besides all else, there is something in her that makes me know that the man who marries her against her wish will have brought trouble into his house."

"Ah, Don Francisco," murmured Tarabal. "Is this your final conclusion?"

"It is the very end."

"But think again. The lands that go with her are great . . . even the cattle that rove on my hills are enough to make a rich man, think of that, Señor Valdez."

"Listen to me. If there were ten times as many pesos as there are rocks in those hills, I could not marry her . . . I am afraid of her, señor. She has a still, cold eye that frightens me. It is impossible for her to love a man."

128

"You are a fool!" exclaimed Tarabal.

"*¡Señor!*"

"*Bah!*" cried the rancher. "You thin-faced fool, do you think that I would let you run from California and leave my girl behind you to be talked about and laughed at? And me also? Look straight before you . . . what do you see?"

"The shadow of the bell tower, of course," breathed the young Spaniard, entranced with horror at the change in the manner and in the tone of his companion.

"When that bell rings, men on all those hills take up their guns and come toward my house. And there is not one of them that would not use a knife, if I raised a hand. Valdez, I'll see you thrown to the coyotes, or married to Ortiza. There is no third choice. Do you doubt me?"

Valdez, staring fixedly at him, knew that there was, indeed, no third choice. He began to curse silently the fate that had brought him fortune-hunting to this land of misfortune. But, when he had turned away, he hardly knew which he feared the most, the passive eyes of Ortiza, or the furious ones of Tarabal.

Before the next morning he was to be shocked again. Neither was the day ended for Ortiza. For, when Rosa went toward the house in the gloom of the evening and left the girl alone for a moment, a shadow passed to her side and, looking up, she saw a white-clad figure and the handsome face of a Navajo.

"Do not be afraid," said the Indian softly. "I have come to find out if you have any need. I have come to serve you. Tell me what I may do?"

"Go away," murmured Ortiza. "And if you come again, be sure that my father's men will run you down and hang you to a branch of these very trees."

The Indian smiled. "I was sent to stay near you, *señorita*. I cannot run away."

"How long have you been near me?"

"All day."

"Where have you been?"

In place of answering, he said: "*Señor* Valdez has made you unhappy?"

"How do you guess that?"

"I saw your two faces while you talked. Do you wish him to be taken away?"

"No, no! And who sent you to me?"

"El Sabio."

"The wise? And is he the man of the red hair?"

"It is he."

"Go back to him," said the girl. "Tell him that it is ruin for me and death for him if he or you come near me again. Tell him that all is well with me. That I am happy. Go."

And the Indian departed as silently as he had come.

Yet, perhaps he had only seemed to obey. For, in the middle of that same night, Valdez wakened with a causeless start, lighted the candle beside his bed, and looked around him in a nightmare of alarm. Suddenly he cried out in horror, for in the pillow, just beside the hollow where his head had lain, was the hilt of a knife. He drew it out. The blade was as keen as a razor. The pressure of its own weight had served to drive it through the down of the pillow. And yet how daring was the hand that had done this and how cunningly secret. Had he not wakened before the operation was completed, could he doubt that the same knife would have been buried in his heart? The cold of his horror departed enough to permit him to shout. In a moment his room was filled with men, and Tarabal was waddling behind them.

To them Valdez showed the knife and the deep slit that had been cut into the body of the pillow. The explanation was not long in coming.

"It is one of the knives that was stolen from my house," exclaimed Tarabal. "The devil, El Rojo, is still playing a game with us. But what is the meaning of this one? Search the house! See what has been stolen!"

But nothing was stolen. In fact, Valdez had rather shrewdly guessed that nothing would be found amiss. This dagger, thrust beside his head in the night, was a warning. Of what? To leave all connection with the house of Tarabal behind him? But if he did that, he would have the power of the rich rancher turned against him, and that was equivalent to signing his death warrant. He sat up the rest of the night and meditated, white of face.

Chapter Seventeen

BLACK SCHEMING

The prison at Monterey was so small that the soldier in charge was only a sergeant. But, small as the prison was, there was more to it than met the eye. It was a little, compact adobe structure of six or seven rooms or cells. Yet it could hold far more than six or seven prisoners at once. The reason was that, while it had only one story above the ground, there were three stories beneath the level of the foundations. It was known that men had entered that prison and never appeared again. Therefore, justice wore a stern face for breakers of the law in California.

Sergeant Diego Perin was proud of the mysteries of his establishment. He had been in charge for fully fifteen years. He knew every inch of the place and most of its history before he had come into the command. All of which made him valuable. But, more than this, he had the character of an ideal jailer. He was one of those fat men who talk a great deal and appear to have all their affairs wagging constantly on the ends of their tongues, but, as a matter of fact, Diego Perin never talked about anything of importance. He was as full of rumors and whispers as an old grandmother, but he was as barren of facts as a desert. He constantly wore a smile. He had the reputation around the town of being a most jovial fellow, and men wondered that he should have been entrusted with so grave a charge as that of the prison. But the smiles of Diego were fed by his knowledge of the weakness of others and his own strength.

He smiled this morning over his breakfast because the eggs were fresh and the wine strong. But he continued smiling after he had received the order of the governor. It was only a few words, scribbled on a small slip of paper that he had extracted from the envelope. But it had so much meaning for Diego, that he propped it up against a cup and continued reading it over and over again as though there were as many items of interest in it as in a newspaper. He continued reading it until his breakfast had been completed.

Then he rose, took from a recess a bundle of keys of many sizes and in all states of rust, and went to execute the orders of the governor. He went to the cell of Jean Darnay, unlocked the door, and bade his guest a cheerful good morning.

"It is time," said Darnay, with equal cheerfulness. "I knew that I could not be kept in this place much longer. I presume that you have come to remove the irons and set me free, my friend?"

"I suppose," said Diego, still smiling, "that you knew all the time that you would not be kept long in the jail?"

"It was impossible for me to doubt," answered Darnay. "I have committed no crime. There is nothing for which they could make me suffer."

"No doubt that is true," said Diego. "No doubt you will presently be set free. Today, however, I have only orders to change your cell. Walk before me, *Señor* Darnay. Walk slowly, moreover. You see that I carry a pistol in my hand. My great hope is that I shall not have to use it. But I am a nervous man, and if you were to start or to make a sudden movement, who can tell? The pistol might explode of its own will. You understand?"

"I understand," said Darnay.

He stepped through the door into the corridor. He was directed from behind down a flight of steps until they reached an oak door braced and framed with thick iron plates. Here he was told to step to one side, and Perin unlocked the door and ushered him down another flight of steps. These were cut in the earth and paved with large stones that were slippery with moisture. At the bottom of the flight they reached a second door. This was likewise unlocked, and they went down and down into a region of foul air, where Darnay was surrounded by a chill that ate into his bones, and where he heard the constant dripping of water.

Presently he was directed through an open door, passed down two or three steps, and found himself in a den some eight or nine feet by six. The floor, the walls, the ceiling were all of large stones mortared together. But they were now so far below sea level that beads of water stood out on every hand. And one end of the cell being lower than the other, a little pool was collected over its surface. A set of rusted leg irons were sunk in a large stone in a corner of the cell. These were locked around the ankles of the Frenchman. In exchange, the manacles were taken from his wrists.

"How long am I to be here?" he asked.

"Only a little while, no doubt," said the good-natured sergeant. "Perhaps new prisoners are expected in today, and they have only cleared out the upper cells for a time."

"I shall bear witness," said Darnay, "that I have been imprisoned tyrannically, without examination or trial. Will you have word of that taken to the governor?"

"Certainly, *señor*. I shall carry the message myself."

"You are kind."

"I am only glad that I have been of some service, *señor*. But I am sure that you will not be here long."

"I hope not. In the meantime, I presume that I may have a bed placed in the cell?"

"A thousand pardons, *señor*. It is the cursed regulations that check my desire to serve you well. But the rules have it that the dungeon cells shall be equipped with no beds."

"Is it possible? Very well. Let me have two or three boards to keep me out of the wet."

"You wring my heart, *señor*. Even this is forbidden. The cells must remain as they are."

"But this water . . . these wet stones . . . such a place would kill a dog in a few days."

"It is an unhappy place, *señor*."

"And I am charged with no crime, or certainly none can be proved against me."

"I shall make mention of all this to the governor. Certainly he will see that your condition is bettered."

"Again, I thank you."

The sergeant took his leave, locked the door behind him, and, stepping into the passage, he gave way to a fit of silent laughter, so violent that it shook his fat body like jelly. And it kept the lantern that he carried in the crook of his arm jingling against his hip.

He wiped his eyes, however, and went on to his office. There he promptly forgot all about the Frenchman and the Frenchman's demands. But in the afternoon came another Frenchman, *Monsieur* Louis Auguste Mortier. He bore with him a note from the governor, commanding that he be admitted to the cell in which Darnay was confined, without being searched, and after he had been provided with a lantern.

The sergeant examined the note and the signature with the most scrupulous care, but there could be no doubt of it. Not only was the signature perfect, but the entire note was inscribed in the hand of the governor. So he gave Mortier a lantern, admitted him to the subterranean cell of Darnay, and departed, according to orders, leaving the key in the lock.

When he was gone, Mortier raised the lantern and saw

Darnay seated with his back leaning against the wall of the cell and his crossed legs resting upon the wet stones. He could not repress a shudder.

"Jean!" he cried. "In heaven's name, what is the meaning of this? This is too terrible."

Darnay rose to his feet. "I thought that I had left tyranny behind me when I abandoned France," he said. "But I should have gone to a desert island. Wherever there are two men together, one will try to torture the other and break his spirit. But I am touched to the heart, Louis, to see that you have not deserted me. The dog of a sergeant swore that he would carry my complaints to the governor. He has not done it, and through some mistake I am left abandoned in this hole in the ground. Go at once, Louis, and represent my condition to the government."

Mortier shook his head. "Alas, Jean," he said, "you do not know what is in the mind of this man, Pyndero. He swears that you are responsible for the disgrace of his lieutenant, and therefore for the disgrace of the military dignity and power of Spain."

"He is mad!" cried Darnay.

"He is. He was reasonable enough, however, to let me come to see you here, Jean. But I bought his favor with five hundred *francs*."

"A dog that can be bought . . . not a man. What, Louis, is he waiting to be paid before he lets me go?"

"That is why I have come to you. You have been working a long time . . . you have lived simply . . . surely you must have saved up some store of money, no matter how small, Jean."

"No, no. I scorn money, Louis. I have ever scorned it. I have worked for the food I eat, the house I live in, the clothes on my back and the back of my girl. That is all. And while I am here . . . what of Julie, dear friend? What of my girl?"

"Alas, Jean."

"Speak to me, Louis. They have not dared to place her in such a dog's kennel as this?"

Mortier nodded his head, his hand pressed across his eyes, and Darnay, having raised his hand as though he would register a curse in the heavens, lowered it again and said more calmly: "Then they have the knife at my throat. But I have no money, Louis. Go back and tell Pyndero that."

"Jean, dear friend, in that case you must die."

The blacksmith started. "So be it, then. God's will be done. I have lived long enough."

"But Julie, my friend."

"Julie . . . Julie?" groaned the old revolutionist, struck with agony. "What can I do? Oh, God, that I had power to blast Julie and myself and all this country with fire."

"Money alone will help you, Jean."

"And they have burned my house. They have beggared me before they demand gold."

"You have friends, however."

"Not one. I have shunned them all . . . no man has come into my life since I left my France."

"One, however, remains."

"And who is that?"

"It is I, Jean."

"Dear Louis, God bless you."

"I have six thousand *francs,* besides enough to buy my passage home. With a thousand *francs,* I am satisfied that the governor will rest content. With five thousand I shall pay you for the estate. We shall both be happy, old comrade."

"You are a good man, Louis. You will have my prayers from this day. Go to the governor at once."

"As swiftly as my legs will carry me. But . . . I have the

document and the acknowledgment of the sale with me. And here is a pen and ink that I have brought on purpose. Let me have your signature, Jean."

"Do you distrust me so much?" asked the blacksmith, nevertheless picking up the pen and dipping it into the ink.

"Distrust you? By no means. But I have been through many a hard campaign, and I know that one should never relinquish the assault before the objective is reached. Eh, Jean? So, if you please. . . ."

He spread the paper before the prisoner, as he spoke, and pointed out the place for the signature. And now all would have gone well — indeed, the pen of Darnay had scratched the first letter of his name — when it seemed to him that the hands that held the paper trembled a little. He was not sure. But he stopped writing, and the moment he did so, he became more certain that the hands were unsteady.

"The chill in this cursed place has made you tremble, Louis," he said gently.

"Yes," said Mortier.

But there was a certain thickness in his voice that caused Darnay to look up, and, as he did so, he saw that his companion was pale, and that his teeth were set.

"Louis!" he cried, stepping back. "What is wrong?"

"Nothing," gasped out Mortier. "Sign, Jean."

But the pen dropped from the fingers of Darnay.

"There is more to this than I see," he said slowly. "I shall not sign today, Louis."

"You fool, you wear out my patience. Do you think that I will carry my charity with me endlessly? Beware, Jean."

"Is it so?" answered the other, drawing himself up. "Then understand me, Louis . . . I doubt your honesty in this. Frankly I doubt it. If I am wrong, God forgive me. But I feel that there is something here I must know."

So close had Mortier come to the goal of success that he could not endure the sudden disappointment. He gave back with a curse and dashed the ink pot upon the floor. The glass flew, tinkling against the stone walls.

"Then you will rot here, you fool! The governor keeps you at my wish. I have offered you freedom and money. Stay here and die like a fool if you choose." He groaned, as he saw that he had spoken enough to damn him, and fury at that thought spurred him on. "But still I shall wring it from you, Darnay. I have not come this distance to be beaten. I shall have the sale completed, Darnay. And for five thousand *francs* I shall buy what is worth a quarter of a million. Do you hear me?"

But Darnay had turned his face to the wall and folded his arms.

Chapter Eighteen

THE BODY OF FELIPE

Juan Rindo was in the greatest distress. The governor had a way of rubbing his hands together when he was most angered, so that the great ruby twisted and brightened and dimmed and shadowed like the eye in a snake's head. It so fascinated poor Juan that he could not help watching the ruby rather than the face of his master.

"I told you," said the governor coldly, "to get the best man you could find and put him on the trail of Wyncham."

"Excellency," said Juan, "I combed the streets of Monterey. Everyone agreed that there was only one man who really knew the country and could do such work as I described. That was Felipe."

"What name?"

"Only that name, Felipe. He has no other. He is an Indian . . . or almost a pure Indian, sir."

"Why did you put one of those brutes on such a trail? I told you that I must have an excellent man . . . a man with brains and hands and a silent tongue."

"Felipe has all of that."

"And yet he is an Indian?"

"Excellency, he is a famous man for his own work."

"However, he is two hours late this morning. He should have reported long ago."

"He should, sir, and for being late he'll find trouble on his hands."

"I warrant he will," said Pyndero. "But mark this . . . my

140

time is gold, and a man who steals it I shall not have around me."

Juan Rindo quaked. "Consider, Excellency," he said, "that the trail of Wyncham might have taken Felipe to such a distance that he has not had sufficient time to return and to report."

"But Wyncham lives in Monterey."

"Perhaps he left the town last night."

"We'll soon find out."

He pulled a cord that jangled a bell. To the servant who appeared he spoke a few words, and presently the man came back, bringing with him a little old fellow who must have been seventy years at the least. He was withered and bent and battered by time.

"What did you see?" asked the governor.

The other turned his eyes upon Juan Rindo. In all of his body there was no spark of life, save in those black and burning eyes.

"You may speak," went on Pyndero, "before Rindo."

"I saw his shadow on his window curtain more than half the night. Then he went to bed."

"How do you know that?"

"I climbed up the wall and looked through the window. The moon was shining on his bed."

"You climbed up the wall?" exclaimed the governor, amazed, and reviewing with a glance the trembling limbs and the meager strength of the old man.

The latter held out his claw-like hands. "Patience lifts mountains," he said, chuckling. "Patience wears out stone and catches eagles."

He laughed again. He was babbling out his life's secret. But it was such a secret that, even when other men knew it, they could not profit by it.

"I believe you, father," said the governor curiously. "I be-

141

lieve that you actually climbed the wall, clinging to each little projection, in danger of falling and breaking your crooked old back if your fingers slipped. You saw his shadow on the curtain half the night and . . . ?"

"Sitting very still, as if he were writing."

"Very likely . . . very likely. Of course, he will have long letters to write home to all his friends about his adventures. Very likely, Pedro. Now you may go."

The ancient fellow hobbled out of the room, stooped over, and made little motions with his right hand that was held near his shoulder and plainly showed that he generally walked with a staff.

"You see," said José Bernardo Pyndero, "that my good old Pedro Sandiz has shattered your story entirely. Wyncham did not leave Monterey last night. I tell you, Rindo, that your man has been drunk. That is the only reason he is not here."

Juan Rindo shivered. He might as well have been drunk on duty himself as to have his own hireling accused of the crime.

"Ah, Excellency," he said when he could speak, "you do not know how carefully I made my inquiries about this man. He was spoken of to me as a wonderful bloodhound who could not be thrown off a trail. Men spoke of him with horror. He had been known to unravel great mysteries. An old woman had been dead for three years. One of her younger brothers became suspicious that there had been something strange in the manner of her dying. So, after the three years had passed, he set my man, Felipe, on the trail. And in a month of work, Felipe unearthed the whole story."

"What was it?"

"Her own daughter had murdered her to get the inheritance of her mother's money and house."

"*Phaugh!* What a story!"

"Disgusting, Excellency."

"But to the point," admitted the governor.

"And there are other things. Everyone knows about him in Monterey. You can ask anywhere."

"Such as what?"

"If a horse is lost, they send Felipe. He tracks the horse almost as if he had the power of scent. If a robbery is committed, they bring Felipe. He sits around on the place of the crime for a time. He seems to soak up impressions of the criminal, and then he disappears. A week, a month later, he brings in his man."

"He is a fighter, then, also?"

"Like a mad dog, I have been told."

"A mad dog," said the governor, "might do very well against some men, but he would be worse than useless against such a fellow as Lord Wyncham. Nevertheless, Rindo, what you have told me restores my confidence in you. If Felipe is not here now, it is because he has actually found a long trail of Wyncham's . . . perhaps the trail he traveled in coming toward the town . . . by the way, along what trail *did* he come into Monterey . . . through the hills?"

"No, Excellency. Along the shore of the bay."

Here a knock fell on the side door of the governor's room that he used as a sort of audience chamber. Rindo went to it.

"It is one of my men who has been hunting for Felipe," he said, turning toward Pyndero again.

"Bring him in, then. I'll find out what he's learned myself."

Rindo, accordingly, set the door wide, and his soldier entered, covered with dust and blinking as though at a great light, to find himself in the dreadful presence of the governor. Rindo murmured sharply to him, and he recovered himself sufficiently to straighten and salute.

"And what," said the governor, "have you been doing to find the trail of Felipe?"

143

"Riding, Excellency," stammered the man.

"Where?"

"Around the town, Excellency."

"And you found the trail?"

"Not the trail, Excellency."

"If you were not following the trail, what were you following?"

"I went where the horse wished to take me."

"Are all your men fools?" thundered José Pyndero, losing all patience.

"Pardon, Excellency," murmured the soothing voice of Juan Rindo. "My man has something to tell me. But he is afraid of such a presence as this. . . ."

"Speak to him yourself."

Rindo bowed and, smiling, approached his private.

"Blockhead . . . you dumb brute," breathed Rindo through his teeth and his smile. "What did you find?"

He received an answer that made him recoil.

"What is it?" called the governor. "After all, he *did* find something."

"Yes, Excellency. . . ."

"Well, well. Go on."

"He found Felipe dead."

"The devil! Where?"

"Where?" repeated Rindo.

"In the hills," said the soldier, gathering a little more confidence as he saw the impression his tidings had made upon the governor.

"How did you find him?" asked the governor, rising from his chair.

"My horse was wandering through the hills. I had no thought of which would be the best direction to ride in. I came past some thick shrubbery. A coyote dodged out of the brush. I thought nothing of that and rode on. But after a time I came

144

back by the same place, and again a coyote dodged out of the shrubs.

" 'There is something hidden there,' I said to myself. I went into the brush. And there I found Felipe, lying on his face. When I turned him over, his eyes were open, but he was cold and stiff."

"How had he been killed?" asked the governor.

"A knife thrust between his shoulders."

"He had been stolen on from behind, eh?"

"I do not know, Excellency."

Pyndero shrugged his shoulders. "You have done very well. You will discover that I have not forgotten you hereafter. Now go to your corporal and give him my order to take a cart for the body and bring it in."

The soldier saluted, and so departed.

"You see, Rindo," said the governor, "you were wrong, after all, and so were all the good people in Monterey. The shadow of Lord Wyncham is seen on his curtain half the night. He is then seen in person, sleeping on his bed from that time forward. And yet, your man is found dead among the hills, stabbed from behind. I tell you, Rindo, he had gone off on some private business of his own. He had gone out on some stabbing match. And the other fellow did the first stabbing. That is all there is to it."

"Excellency," said Rindo, "this man has no enemies."

"Tut, tut, Rindo. No enemies? A devil of a man like that without enemies?"

"Excellency, men do not hate dogs because they have teeth."

"Eh? That was sharp enough, Rindo." The governor rubbed his hands with pleasure at the thought. A nicely pointed remark was to him as precious as a well-delivered thrust inside the enemy's guard. "Go on, Rindo," he said. "Your mind is working this morning."

"No matter what we know about Lord Wyncham's being in town all night, it must have been something connected with Wyncham that Felipe trailed into the hills."

"But what could be connected with Wyncham?"

"I only know that Felipe was a bloodhound, Excellency."

The governor sighed. But his eye was bright. He began to foresee that his stay in California would not be as altogether dull as he had often dreaded.

"Now, Rindo," he said, "forget all about Lord Wyncham. I no longer have any suspicions about him, and, if he should ever learn that I once *did* have suspicions, I shall know that you have been talking. That is all. The fellow who found the body of Felipe . . . let him have a week off duty with double pay."

Chapter Nineteen

WINDOW CONFIDENCES

Now Julie Darnay was convinced that the man was mad. He ran through the most ridiculous motions and postures. Of course, she could not see all the absurd things he was doing, but he leaped here and there, like one of wits as light as his feet, and they were as light as thistledown. He flickered back and forth across the floor of his room, like a shadow thrown by a fire and quivering on a wall.

Certainly he was mad. It could not be a dance. Sometimes, as he stooped forward, he bent over until his body made an acute angle with the floor. Again he leaped back, half the length of the room. She stared with great eyes. Most wonderful of all, it seemed to Julie, was the silence in which he performed these maneuvers. Even supposing that he had taken off his shoes, she was close enough, to be sure, to have heard the pounding of his bare feet.

And then all was made clear. For she saw the frail gleaming of a ray of light that issued from the right hand of the man. It was a sword, and what she had seen was a dummy-foil drill. He had been going through his exercises in the privacy of his room. All that she had seen was instantly given point. Those grotesque leaps and sudden glidings to and fro now became sinister things, and they were beautiful because they were sinister. Where she had thought him a frantic clown, she now felt that he was the very paragon of a graceful gentleman, and, whereas she had been between pity and smiling, she now found that her heart was beating more quickly.

147

Presently he came to his window in order to breathe and rest, and Julie Darnay found herself looking upon the shining black hair and the bold features of Lord Wyncham. She swung the shutters of her window wide open. Oh, that he would look upon her. In an instant her wish was granted. He saw her at once, and, leaning from his window, he kissed his hand to her. Julie, as a matter of course, blew a kiss back to him, but she had not reckoned on the effect it might have.

For he was instantly out his window, hanging by his hands. He was in his shirt and knee breeches, but his feet and legs below the knee were bare. Now he worked his way along the wall of the house, clinging with the tips of his fingers to such rough projections as he found, though Julie could see nothing that seemed capable of affording a hand hold from the distance at which she looked. He was presently just above the top of an adobe wall. Down to this he dropped, staggered, in imminent risk of falling to the ground, then whirled, raced along the wall, went up the wall of her house, with the ease of a flying bird, and behold him, in ten seconds, sitting in the window of Julie's room, laughing at her, with the wind lifting and blowing his long, black hair. She had never seen him so close — only a glance now and then when he had chanced to pass her in the street — but now she saw enough to enchant her. He was as brown as a berry, and the brown, wherever the sun struck his skin, turned it bronze, with the rich red of the blood shining through it.

Julie was frightened, but only enough to brighten her eyes and put a tingle of color in her cheeks. "Your lordship," she cried, "seems as much at home in the air as a bird."

"I have seen enough to make me fly, *señorita*."

"But," said Julie, "what if people see you here?"

"They will say that we are eminently respectable. We converse at a window in the open sun."

"But you, my lord, have come to see a girl you have never known."

"I have seen you two times in the street, Julie Darnay, and I made a solemn vow that the third time I saw you, I should certainly speak to you, even if you were surrounded by a whole bevy of swordsmen and jealous lovers and brothers and what not."

The smile flashed on her lips and in her eyes. "I am sure, *señor*, that you have no fear of swords."

"So?"

"I have been watching you fence at shadows in your room."

He turned his head, observed the position of his window, and then looked back at her with a sharper glance. She felt that he was rather alarmed than embarrassed when he found out that he had been spied upon.

"One must have exercise," he said.

"After walking three thousand miles?"

"That is nothing. But now we may consider that we know one another?"

"It is very improper, your lordship?"

"Not at all."

"But where could you have found out my name?"

"The governor speaks of nothing else."

"The governor?" cried Julie.

"Why not? He is a man of taste."

"The governor," echoed Julie.

Suddenly she was remembering that Pyndero was a bachelor, that he was the king of this country, that she herself might, by lucky chance, mount to the pinnacle of success, that she might become his lady and be the greatest woman in Alta California. Then she would wear wonderful gowns and receive famous visitors in the name of her husband.

All of this swam before her eyes, but so quickly did she

make the illusion vanish that the shadow lay on her face only an instant and then was gone. She was able to smile as brightly as ever into the eyes of Lord Wyncham. For a Spanish governor was a Spanish governor, but an English lord was quite a different thing. Moreover, they were romantic fellows, these English, and one could not tell in what fashion they might be taken off their feet. Julie felt that she would be a fool, unless she played all of her cards as well as she could and as quickly. She had read a great deal of the Bible, but sundry romances she had come upon had sunk into her mind far more deeply than Holy Writ.

"He is in distress," said Lord Wyncham, "because your father is unfortunately confined to the jail for a few days, and perhaps you will not be taken to his ball."

"Oh," breathed Julie, "the governor's ball?"

"But I," said Lord Wyncham, "have vowed that I should risk a rebuff for the sake of his friendship and attempt to meet and know you, *señorita.*"

She smiled at him, and then they chuckled together over his not too ingenious story.

"Even if you came barefoot?" she asked.

"I have been at sea a great deal," he explained, "and I'm more at home in bare feet than in any shoes."

"So am I," said Julie, and then she blushed at the confession.

"But the ball?" he asked.

"What of it?"

"Consider the disappointment of the governor, if he learns that you are not coming?"

"How can I go when my poor father is in prison?"

"But, of course, it is nothing serious. He will be out at once."

"Of course," she nodded. "But is it not strange that they should keep him so long when he had done nothing at all?"

150

The black brows of Lord Wyncham lowered a little, and his blue eyes stared searchingly into her face. "Very, very strange indeed," he said.

"Ah," cried Julie, "when you look like that, I think that I have seen you before."

"Really?"

"Just a trick of imagination, of course. But about my father . . . yes, I am worried."

"Let me suggest something. Perhaps that rogue of a governor is only keeping him confined until you ask to have him set free."

"Ah, do you think that?" She clapped her hands happily together.

"Very like."

"I shall certainly ask him then."

"At the ball?"

"Where else?"

"I am glad you are going, *señorita*."

"Thank you."

"And you are going with me, I shall hope?"

"Why," laughed Julie Darnay, "of course. I thought that was all settled."

Chapter Twenty

A BOUT WITH THE FOILS

The governor found himself drawn so closely to the young Lord Wyncham that sometimes he discovered that he was on the verge of disclosing secrets that should have been left safely obscured. For instance, on this morning Wyncham was speaking of Julie Darnay.

"She is full of mischief," he said, "and, when I mentioned the name of the governor, she grew rosy. Oh, her heart was stirred, I warrant. For that matter, where is there a girl of her age who wouldn't be touched at the thought of dancing with a governor?"

"Wyncham," cried the startled governor, "you didn't tell her that I was wishing for her at the ball?"

"Why not?"

"I can't receive a nobody there."

"She's too pretty to be a nobody."

"And you let her think that I'm very interested?"

"Of course. I have saved you at least a week's time, and broken the ice completely for your acquaintance. I have so prepared her that, with only one or two lies of moderate strength, you will find her smiling up into your face."

The governor tapped with his fingers against his upper lip. It was his favorite way of covering a smile. He was delighted with Lord Wyncham. It was the very frankness of his rascality that intrigued the governor. His own misdoings were kept religiously behind the veil. Now he hardly knew which to admire the most — the careless manner with which Lord

Wyncham lied, or the equally careless manner with which he told the truth.

"Wyncham," he said at length, "you are original . . . inimitable."

"Not at all," said Wyncham. "I have copied every man I have ever met. I am at this moment intently studying some of your mannerisms."

"Nonsense!"

"It is true, nevertheless. I was raised in poverty."

"Really?"

"A truth. In the meantime I have observed many types of people. I have talked to lords and ditch diggers."

"How could that have been?"

"My father was a second son. He could do nothing worthwhile all his life but pray for the death of his older brother, without heirs. And, by dint of making that one prayer and no other, he at length was able to succeed. His brother died. He stepped into the estate with a sigh of relief. And so here I am in Alta California."

The governor nodded again. "You couldn't stand the quiet life?"

"I could not. I was not ready to marry and settle down, and, since I had the estate in prospect . . . port has ruined my father's chances of a long life . . . the lovely ladies became so attentive that I knew it was only a matter of time before I should be caught."

"Wyncham! What, fled from the beauties?"

"Which shows my wisdom. I fear nothing in the world but a smiling girl."

"*Tush!* They are nothing, when a man's mind is set."

"I'll tell you this, Governor . . . Julie Darnay is determined to beg her father's freedom from you, and I'll wager that she wins it."

"You'll lose, then," said the governor. He spoke so deliberately that in a moment he regretted what he had said. "Of course," he added, "I am simply waiting for justice to take its course."

Lord Wyncham smiled with perfect openness. "I see," he said.

José Pyndero knew that it was best to drop the subject there. But his conscience was tingling a little, and he could not help pressing on. A little imp of the perverse was leading him. "You see what?" he asked.

"I didn't guess before that you wanted something out of the old Frenchman."

"Sir?" cried the governor.

"Excuse me," said Wyncham, and laughed.

But Pyndero, having been pricked, as though with a keen sword's point, could not help keeping to the subject. "What the devil put this into your head? What could I get from an old blacksmith?"

"Nothing, of course. Besides," added Wyncham smoothly, when he saw that the governor was disturbed, "I'll wager that the girl wins. What, Pyndero? I know you. A bright smile and then a sad one . . . a sad look and then a gay one . . . and you'll capitulate."

The governor shrugged his shoulders. "I'll make a wager on that."

"Whatever you please, except money."

"A bout with the foils, then. Two touches out of three, my lord."

"I'll take no odds, Your Excellency."

Pyndero smiled. He had conquered so many times in practice with the foils, or in earnest with the unabated points, that it had become impossible for him to conceive of defeat.

"Perhaps you know best, Wyncham. We'll walk into the

patio. Two touches, my lord. The first to make two touches wins. Is that it?"

"If I lose?" asked Wyncham.

The governor considered.

"Your penalty then must be to come to play with me every day. I am out of work and practice."

"And if you lose?"

"Why, then I must listen to Julie."

"And set Darnay free?"

The governor hesitated. Then, as one who recalls that, after all, there is no real danger, he nodded. "I set free the old blacksmith. But," he added, "what makes you so earnest to get Darnay out of trouble?"

"I have seen Julie. That's answer enough."

"You think you'll get her favor by setting her father free?"

"Why not?"

"Because, unless her father's in jail, Julie is. He's a grim old warrior, you know, an old revolutionist. Danton is his god. He gives Julie very little liberty."

He jerked out these short sentences, for he was busy, as he spoke, taking down foils from the rack in which they hung. He selected half a dozen — for he had weapons of every sort — and he offered Lord Wyncham the hilts. The latter tried one, lunged with it, nodded with pleasure, tried another that he liked still better, and signified his willingness to trust to his luck with that foil.

"A very good choice, too," said the governor, looking upon his guest with greater respect. "You have my own eye for the weight and the balance of the foil."

They had reached the patio when a name was brought to the governor. He bade the servant bring his guest to the patio at once.

"Here's a man you'll be glad to have watch your play," said

the governor. "An old French soldier. Colonel Mortier has fought his way from one end of Europe to the other with Napoleon. Besides, he's a good judge of fence. He took a foil against me the other day and gave me some excellent exercise. A little too free in his style, however. He seems to try to rush in and bear everything down. And that will never do against an artist . . . never, never!"

Mortier appeared while the governor was still speaking, and just as the latter and Wyncham had removed their coats and prepared for the engagement. He was introduced to Lord Wyncham, bowed his acknowledgments, and then took a chair nearby to act as judge.

Lord Wyncham came on guard with such careless ease that one would have thought him facing a child. Mortier, who had tasted defeat at the hands of the governor on several occasions, smiled with sour expectation. They engaged at once, and the governor pressed straight in, with the confidence of a man who knows himself and his sword, having proved both on a thousand occasions. In an instant he had cornered his antagonist, and Mortier, rubbing his hands together and delighted to the bottom of his heart to see a representative of "perfidious Albion" humiliated, leaned forward to watch the touch.

Something, however, went wrong at the critical moment. Lord Wyncham was working no harder than ever, but there seemed to be something wrong with the timing of the Spanish swordsman. At any rate, between two motions of his sword, Wyncham glided to the side and was free. José Bernardo Pyndero blinked with astonishment and pressed in again. Once more he drove his antagonist the length of the patio. Still, struggle though he might, he could not slip past the point of the Englishman. There was little danger of a counterattack. Wyncham fought purely on the defensive, and even on the defensive he seemed perfectly indifferent to the outcome of the match. Luck, it seemed, was fortifying him.

At the farther end of the patio the governor feinted in low carte and then thrust full at the head, a venomous attempt that might have torn out one of the eyes of Wyncham, had the button gone home. The Englishman, however, avoided the point with a movement of his head, and, stepping in at the same time, he offered with his foil at the defenseless breast of Pyndero. It was a manifest opening, but Wyncham did not take advantage of it.

Instead, he leaped back, saluted, and set to work without his smile, as though for the first time he had been induced to take the match seriously. In three seconds the governor was giving back. Neither was it tactical maneuvering to draw out the enemy. For José Pyndero found himself struggling, as he had never struggled since boyhood against any swordsman. For ten years he had felt that he was the leading blade of all Spain. But Spanish swordsmen were not in the front rank. The stilted and involved teachings of Carranza still weighed down the aspiring fencers of the nation. But war brought new ideas to Pyndero. For five years he had labored to perfect himself in the French system. And now it was five years since he had met a man who could even distantly approach him in the perfection of his sword play.

To feel that he was matched here by an obscure and youthful noble at the end of the civilized world, so to speak, maddened the worthy governor. He fought now with a scowl of concentration. Perspiration dripped from his forehead. In truth, he was nearly exhausted, whereas Lord Wyncham was almost as fresh as ever. He was breathing heavily, but that did not disturb him. His gliding footwork was as smooth and as deft as when he began. He lunged as far, he recovered as swiftly as when he had opened the encounter. He had changed his style. Rather, he had taken upon himself all styles. Sometimes he used a rather straight arm, with a long and awkward Italian guard. Sometimes he pressed in and attacked with all the flexible neatness of the French school. And, again, he was a combination of all schools. His quick, short parries clipped away the blade of Pyndero. His point hovered like a phantom before the face and the breast of the unlucky governor. With his back to the wall, Pyndero tried a counterattack. He had hardly begun when a time-thrust nailed him fairly in the center of the breast.

He had been beaten fairly and squarely. Had they been fighting with true rapiers, he would have been a dead man, with a foot of cold steel through his heart. For his own part, he was too stunned to speak, but he heard an exclamation from Mortier, and both he and Wyncham turned toward the Frenchman. The colonel was in the exact position from which he had watched the decisive thrust. That is to say, he was half risen from the chair, bent over, his arms somewhat extended, his eyes bulging. Amazement had been carried to the verge of horror in his face. It brought home to Pyndero the full greatness of his fall.

"There are two touches needed to win!" the governor cried. "On guard, *señor!*"

"On guard," said Lord Wyncham.

He brought his sword up as carelessly as ever, and this time he paid a penalty for it. The nervous blade of the governor slipped inside his guard and touched the Englishman on the shoulder.

"Now!" cried Wyncham. "Now, in all seriousness, Your Excellency!"

They went at it in a fury. But the governor, having tasted success, seemed to be invincible. He pressed back Lord Wyncham. In thirty seconds he had scored again, and Lord Wyncham threw down his foil with a laugh.

"By the Lord, Pyndero," he cried, "a touch only serves to

158

wake you up and turn you into a fighting devil."

"Ah, my lord," returned the governor, who had dropped into a chair and now was gasping back his wind and mopping his purple face with a handkerchief, "I thought I had gone to sleep. I was completely wrong in everything, but when I waked up, you admit . . . ?"

"Masterly work," said Wyncham.

"Yes," said the governor, "I say freely, my lord, that you are the finest blade I have ever encountered. And with a little more experience . . . in fact, I was a little worried to begin with . . . though, after I had solved your style . . . after that first touch. . . ."

"After that, of course, there was nothing to be done," said Wyncham. "Exhausting exercise though, eh?"

Yet he was already breathing easily, and, while the governor lay stretched in his chair, gasping and panting, Lord Wyncham was calmly donning his coat. In a trice he was as cool and comfortable as ever. His appearance also changed as soon as the coat was donned. Without it he had seemed to be twice his real bulk. For his shoulders were extraordinarily wide, and his arms very long. In action, with those long arms shooting in and out, one extended behind him to give balance, and the other darting in and out, he had seemed fully twice the size of the governor. But, now that he had donned his coat, he was perfectly normal. The governor, if anything, was the more imposing man.

"Wine," called the governor, when he could breathe more easily.

Wine was brought, wine chilly from the deep and moist cellars of the governor's house. It was an old claret. It filled the narrow glasses with a heart of red fire and with purple shadows.

"To the sword," cried the governor, giving his toast, "and

159

to a worthy swordsman" — nodding to Mortier — "and to a brilliant one," thereby saluting Lord Wyncham.

"To the sword," responded Wyncham readily, "and may none of us ever meet with abated points."

"Amen!" cried Mortier heartily.

They drank, and Wyncham at once took his leave, pursued by the governor's reminder that he had promised to come to fence every day in case he were beaten. So he departed, and the governor lay back in his chair and smiled contentedly upon the ceiling.

"But do you realize," said Mortier, who quite understood the vanity of his new friend, "if those had been real rapiers, you would at this moment be a dead man, my dear friend?"

"*Bah!*" scoffed the governor. "I was only testing him. If the sword had been real, he would never have scratched me with the point." Yet his brow was clouded.

Chapter Twenty-One

PYNDERO DECIDES

"After the first touch," went on Mortier, "a strange thought came to me. I could have sworn. . . ."

"What?" asked the governor, angered by this dwelling upon his misfortune. For, after all, to one who has been a duelist, the first touch, if it be over a vital spot, has a significance that a hundred touches afterward cannot possess.

"But when you touched him twice in succession, I knew that it could not be."

"What could not be?" asked the governor, more and more irritated.

"Excellency," said Mortier, who recollected that he could speak as freely as he chose, because the governor was his partner in their business venture, "of all the people I have ever met in the world, and I have met a good many, you are the finest swordsman. . . ."

"A thousand thanks, my dear Mortier."

"Except," continued the Frenchman, "one man."

"Ah," said the governor, his joy departing.

"And that one man," went on Mortier, "I thought for a moment, in spite of myself, I was watching at work as Wyncham drove you before him."

"Hmm," said the governor, scowling.

"But when you touched him twice in succession, it removed all my doubts."

"This acquaintance of yours," said the governor dryly, "is so great a fencer that it would have been impossible for me to

161

get a sword's point near him?"

"Exactly," said Mortier.

"Your pardon," sneered the governor. "Such a man does not live."

"Your pardon," answered Mortier sternly. "I have myself fenced with him. Recollect, Your Excellency, that I have crossed foils with you a number of times. You are a brilliant swordsman. But the other was a genius. He had the arms and the shoulders of Wyncham, very long and snaky quick. He had the same footwork, moving about like a floating shadow over the ground. I have fenced with you and found that you far surpass me. Yet it was not impossible for me to touch you once, while you were touching me three times. And, in actual fighting, that one touch of mine might come first. If the worst came to the worst, I should not consider a duel with you as a death sentence."

"Certainly not," said the governor, but his face was stern.

"This other artist, however," went on Mortier, "was as sure as death. In his hands I was helpless. He drove me before him. He turned away my thrusts and lunges, as the roof turns away the hailstones. He could have stabbed me to the heart at any instant. I was filled with wonder. In fact, Your Excellency, when I first watched Lord Wyncham, I could have sworn that he was the man."

"And who was this great genius?"

"A slave."

"What?"

"That same El Rojo who stole your Indians from you, Pyndero, who rides Sanduval, and who has branded and made a fool of your lieutenant, Rindo. That is the man . . . the slave of *Señor* Valdez."

"A slave and a fencer? In the name of heaven, *monsieur le colonel.*"

"Very strange, eh? But this Wyncham is a strange man. So strange, as a matter of fact, that, when I saw his style of fencing, I was half convinced he was El Rojo."

"But that slave has red hair. Is that not so?"

"It is true . . . very true, my friend. But there is black dye for red hair, and there is black dye for red eyebrows. You understand? Also, there are wigs."

"But his voice, Mortier!" cried the governor.

"When he was on the ship, I never heard him speak except a very soft-voiced monosyllable or two. He kept in his place and was never obtrusive. That's why I can't place him at once by his voice."

The governor was shaking his head. "Pure nonsense. I trust that I can recognize the manners of a gentleman, and Wyncham certainly has the correct air."

"He could have picked that up."

"By watching his masters? A Spaniard and an English gentleman are as unlike as the two poles."

"Very true. But El Rojo went to an unusual school, where he could learn all manner of things. He was on a pirate ship, you know."

"I've heard something about that."

"And he had all manner of men for companions when he was rowing in the galleys. He had Englishmen, Frenchmen, Italians, Spaniards . . . men from half the world sat beside him. What he learned in that way must have gone deep. And if he could pick up fencing and become such a consummate artist, you must admit that he could pick up other things, too. When I consider with what perfection he played the part of the humble, submissive, contented slave for days and months and years, no doubt waiting for the opportunity to escape, that at last he seized so daringly . . . I say, when I saw all of these things, I was ready to attribute anything to El Rojo. He is really

163

a Yankee in blood, you know. His father was an American merchantman whose ship was captured by the Moors. He and his wife were killed by bullets during the battle. The crew and the youngster were taken prisoner and enslaved."

"The devil! A perfect romance! What is his true name?"

"He always told Valdez that he had forgotten . . . he was only five or six at the time he was made a slave. But I have no doubt that he remembers well enough. To conclude, I say that this El Rojo is such a remarkable fellow that, for some minutes, during the fencing bout, I believed he must have turned himself into young Lord Wyncham. However, I saw him twice touched at the end, and that showed me I had been mistaken."

The governor had grown very thoughtful. "At least," he said, "there is something curious about Wyncham. He lies too well, for one thing."

"You think he didn't really come across the continent?"

"I don't know. I can't make up my mind to one thing or the other. So I am having him watched. We are going to find out a bit about that gentleman, you may depend upon it." He added briskly: "And, in the meantime, I sent for you to hear the full details about Darnay. You know there was no chance to talk over everything yesterday."

"I told you about the substance. He couldn't be stirred. I lost my temper and blurted out the whole truth. I told him that what had been worth little or nothing, when he was in France, was now worth a quarter of a million *francs*."

"The devil!" exclaimed the governor.

"It *is* the devil. What can we do if he fails to sign?"

"Let him rot in the prison."

"And if he *does* sign?"

"He will rot there just the same. I cannot have old fools like Darnay running about through Alta California, telling tales, whether people believe them or not."

The careless manner in which he spoke made Mortier look down to the floor to keep the fear out of his eyes. He had sadly underestimated the strength of the governor, he saw. Yet, even as he listened, a new thought came to him that perfectly solved the problem and cut the Gordian knot for him. Having arrested Darnay and having exposed his designs to the old man, the governor dared not set him free, or the Frenchman would pull a towering scandal down around the ears of Pyndero. Therefore, Darnay was, even now, as good as dead. It only remained for Mortier to win the heart of Julie Darnay and to marry her. Then, the instant that Darnay died, Mortier's wife would become the heir to the estate, and he, through his wife, could lay his hands upon it.

All of this was so simple that tears of joy rose to the eyes of the soldier. He said good bye to the governor shortly after this and rose to leave. "As for Darnay," he added, "why should we both worry about him? Monterey has forgotten about him already. Because, in fact, the town never started to talk about him. There is only one danger. This girl, Julie, may begin to start tongues wagging. And, as I remember, it would only take a word or two from her to start a young man making a fool of himself."

"All very true," said the governor.

"But suppose that I monopolize some of her time? It is known that you receive me. Suppose I tell her that I am working for the liberation of her father?"

"A good idea, Mortier."

"I am off to find her this moment."

"Good luck, my friend, and *bon voyage!*"

Mortier laughed and departed. But, when he saw he was in the street, he made one serious mistake. He looked back at the house of José Pyndero and smiled, then shrugged his shoulders, and walked on. The mistake was so serious because the governor was watching him from a window, and Pyndero saw clearly both the smile and the shrug.

It was not a great deal, but it was enough to start his thoughts. He spent some time walking to and fro, turning the question over and over in his mind. And, having been a soldier himself, it did not take him long to begin to understand the probable tactics of the Frenchman. Julie was the point of attack. She was the point that must be secured.

Only one way occurred to him, and that was to pay her some attention himself. Unless he greatly misunderstood her, as long as she had the slightest hope of such a dignitary as the governor of the province, she would not take the addresses of the colonel seriously. And, on the spot, Pyndero decided that he must excite those hopes in her mind. It could be easily done. One flattering conversation might be enough to sink the ship of Mortier.

Having come to this resolution, he let his thoughts run on to other things. Truly his stay in Alta California was anything but dull. Yonder in the hills — how near he could not guess — were the Indians who would lurk about until they had either accomplished their quest by sticking a knife between his ribs, or until they had been run down and butchered. Yonder, too, was the miscreant, El Rojo, and last of all, the mystery of Wyncham. On that point, also, he decided that he would take the field and do his own detective work. That very night he would start on the trail that had brought Felipe a knife thrust between the shoulders.

Chapter Twenty-Two

"STOP THE CARRIAGE!"

It was known that the governor did not have a carriage. For that very reason *Señor* Don Joaquín Tarabal had decided that he, the richest man in California, must have one. Since he must have a coach, he must have it of the finest type. Therefore, it was ordered in France. No one knew at what immense expense it was built, painted, gilded, and furnished in velvets. No one could guess the huge cost of boxing the great vehicle, part by part, each part wrapped tenderly, so that no harm might come during the voyage. And, again, there was the expense of the long trip around the Horn and up the western coasts of the Americas.

At any rate, the coach at last reached Monterey, was assembled on the beach, and, having been rubbed and polished until it shone, had been rolled into town behind a team of six horses. Since that day nine years had elapsed, and the great coach had been used three times. Nevertheless, Don Joaquín did not regret the expense. It pleased him that he had under a shed such a thing as this to exhibit to visitors to the ranch. And when a stranger arrived, he never failed to lead him to the door through which he could see the magnificent carriage. Indeed, every day of its existence that carriage was polished, and the leathers oiled and rubbed, and the metal work burnished, so that, when a ray of sunshine fell upon it, it was sure to give back a blinding light.

In nine years it had been used three times. It was on the third occasion that Lord Wyncham and His Excellency, Governor Pyndero, saw the coach. It was the afternoon of the same day on which they had fenced in the patio of the governor's house. And, having gained a mutual respect for one another, when they met on the street in the afternoon, they started a stroll together that ended in a long tramp. As for the governor, he was deeply interested in learning all that he could concerning the young English nobleman. To verify that title, he would have given his year's salary to have at hand someone who could say whether or no there was such a patent of nobility, and who at the present held it. To be sure, when he was with Wyncham, his doubts almost ceased. But when he was away from him, a thousand apprehensions crowded into his mind.

He could not help remembering the manner in which Mortier had connected the young lord with the escaped slave, El Rojo. And, again, he could not help dwelling on the singular story of how Anthony, Lord Wyncham, had crossed the continent. However, he was forced to admit that such an extraordinary fellow was as apt to be telling the truth as lying. He could not be sure which was the case here. But he knew that a man who fenced as Lord Wyncham did, necessarily possessed both imagination and cool nerves. By a closer association with him, it might be possible that he would let fall a few valuable hints.

The governor, however, was wrong. The conversation of my lord was entirely about America. He did not even dip into his experiences crossing the continent, but confined himself to topics of the day in Monterey. He chatted of Mortier. He had seen pretty Julie Darnay and had something to say of her. On the whole, he seemed marvelously pleased with California and the life there. When he would move on again, he did not know. One thing tempted him to stay. His boast had been that he could live for a year on his wits. And it was so easy to win money at dice from the good citizens of California that my lord felt it would be going against manifest Providence if he turned his back too soon on such a store of gold. And here the governor could not forbear laughing. It tickled him to the core of the heart, the unprincipled recklessness of this man. He recognized the same strain in himself. He felt that they were brothers in all but blood and, for some time, as he walked down the road, he was smiling to himself and vowing in the silence that, if ever he had at hand a dangerous and difficult task in which reward and peril were equally balanced, he would call upon young Lord Wyncham as his partner in the work. For, though he believed the man capable of almost anything, yet he felt that his pledged word would hold Wyncham, as steel chains might hold another man. With his lordship as an avowed partner, all would be well between them. And with such a co-worker, what could they not do together?

He sketched a dozen bold schemes. He would supply the thews and the sinews of war. There was the possibility of getting together a gang of miscreants, setting them aboard a trim little sloop, mounting a few long-guns, and ranging her up and down the coast as a pirate to seize the shipping. What an ideal commander would the young lord be, thought the governor. And if the spoils were split into three equal parts, one for the crew, one for the man who led them, and one for the governor who kept them from being captured, they would both become rich.

This dream, however, could not be realized until he had learned more, much more about his companion. And, if he continued his inquiries, it was not at all improbable that he might be able to learn so much that he would have Wyncham at his mercy. For it was very strange, indeed, that such a man should have left England at his own pleasure. Far more likely that that skillful sword of his had penetrated the breast of some well-known man, and that he had saved his neck from the rope by fleeing across the seas. It was very likely, also, that he was only a younger son, and that he had falsely assumed the title of Wyncham in this obscure corner of the globe, hoping that no one would be capable of confronting him with the truth about his position. All of these possibilities concerning the young man must be probed, and, particularly, the governor was eager to learn how it happened that Felipe, on the trail of Wyncham, should have been knifed in the back while he was far away in the hills, and Wyncham at the time sound asleep in his room in Monterey.

That silence of the governor's had endured a moment or two, and he was about to speak again when a distant rumbling, that had been growing softly upon them during the last few minutes, turned the corner of a hill, and the thunder dissolved into the bumping of wheels and the grinding of tires and the patter of many hoofs. A few seconds more and they found themselves looking down upon a strange spectacle. It was like a small section of a triumphal procession transplanted to the California wilderness of bare, brown hills.

First of all, there appeared a solitary rider on a black horse — a black horse whose bridle, saddle, reins, and trappings were whitened with silver mountings. If the horse was magnificent, the rider was still more so. He was a half-breed chosen for the grace of his horsemanship and the splendid dignity of his bearing. He was equipped now with a long cloak that furled back over his shoulder and rippled in the wind. Along the side of his great black hat a white feather curled.

He was enough in himself to have made a city stare. But he was merely the herald of the splendor that followed him. This consisted of eight black horses, only less glorious than the stallion that was mounted by the first of the party. Like him, they were harnessed with silver-worked harness, and a postillion rode on one of each span. These postillions, to furnish a slight

170

change in the color scheme of white and black, were clad in long crimson coats, with trousers of blue velvet; their hats were white and their plumes black. Behind the stream of the eight dancing horses the driver appeared aloft on a seat blazing with gold, with a splendid functionary seated with folded arms beside him. But the driver was a strange contrast to all the joyous lavishness of the rest of the picture. He was a squat humpback, with huge, long arms and great hands.

There was no need of the postillions, even to manage the eight horses, had it been chosen to handle the team with reins. As it was, the little man did nothing but give orders that quickened or slackened the pace of the team. He had resolutely refused to dress in a fine uniform. Instead, he wore a dirty gray shirt, coarse, cowhide boots, and a ragged hat slouched down about his ears. One could imagine the fury of the rich rancher, as he strove to curse his driver into finer clothes. One could also imagine the surly scowl of the clod, as he shrugged his shoulders. But, at length, he had conquered. He was necessary to that equipage. He could pick up any horse of the eight with his voice and make it lunge into the collar, or, without a word, he could soothe the most restive.

Certainly he was the only jarring note in the entire group. The two horsemen, who trotted on either side of the coach, were hardly, if at all, inferior to that gorgeous horseman who led the troop. Behind the carriage, at just a sufficient distance to escape the clouds of dust the wheels raised, rode eight horsemen, by twos. Considering the space occupied by the horses and the intervals between each span, and the great length of the brilliant carriage itself, the procession stretched along a considerable bit of road. When the leader had come around the shoulder of the hill, it was still some moments before the roar of the cavalcade swung into view. Last of all came half a dozen enormous brindle-colored dogs, each span held on the leash by an Indian runner, more than half naked and gray with the dust. They were spectacular brutes and seemed from their color and bulk to be a cross between the English bandog and a greyhound.

"What prince is this?" exclaimed Lord Wyncham, when he saw this procession start up the slope toward the place where he and the governor were walking.

"The devil knows, not I," answered the governor. "But I see plainly that I am to be outdone by one of my subjects in my very seat of government."

He smiled at Wyncham, partly in good humor and partly in vexation.

"What use is a carriage like that in the California hills?" asked Wyncham.

"None under heaven. Yet, I think I have heard of it. It is one of the seven wonders of Alta California. It is the carriage of *Señor* Don Joaquín Tarabal."

"And who," asked Wyncham, "is he?"

"You have been this time in Monterey and have not heard his name? Come, come! A man could more easily live six years on the earth without seeing the sun."

"You forget, my dear friend, that I have spent my time, since my arrival, talking about myself and relating my inventions about my trip across the continent rather than asking questions about other people. But this looks like a cavalry charge, not a pleasure drive."

"It is the great Joaquín Tarabal in person," said the governor. "I recognize his horrible frog face even at this distance. I have never seen him, but he has been described to me. He is the richest man in the province. He has more *pesos* than he himself dreams of. He is only troubled by one thing, and that is the lack of things on which to spend his fortune. He is one of these lucky devils . . . he married a charming girl . . . killed

172

her in a year or so . . . but she left him a ravishing daughter. He could not find a husband for such a queen among the men in California, of course . . . so what does he do, but send to Spain, and there he buys a husband from the ancient and famous family of Valdez. He has imported that husband, and no doubt that young man is now riding in the carriage."

"And the beautiful daughter?" asked Wyncham.

"Of course."

"Then we shall ride the rest of the way back to Monterey in the carriage with them."

"Impossible! In the first place, all of the seats are filled, and in the second place, neither of us has any claims on *Señor* Tarabal."

"I say," said Wyncham, "that I shall ride to Monterey in that coach."

"My lord? You may now see for yourself that every seat is filled. In spite of its bulk, there are only places for four, and every place is taken."

"Your Excellency," said Wyncham, "is impossible."

"Sir!"

"You have no imagination. I shall sit in the coach and talk to the lovely Miss Tarabal."

"The *señorita*, sir?"

"Of course. I say that I shall stay in the coach and talk with her until we reach Monterey."

"Valdez will have your throat cut, even if you could manage it. But it can never be done. Do you expect to hold them up? They have enough men to riddle you full of holes, even if you were the finest swordsman in the world."

"True," chuckled the Englishman. "But there is one thing which is stronger than swords or bullets. Look . . . what a wonderful bit of a show it is. See those white plumes, shaking between the ears of the horses. Pyndero, I wouldn't give up this picture, not for a hundred pounds, and I swear that I shall be in the heart of it."

"A hundred pounds, then, that you never get there."

"A hundred pounds, Excellency. Do you mean it?"

"Upon my honor. A hundred pounds to you if you actually ride into town in that carriage."

"It is too simple. However, if you insist upon giving away money. . . ."

The leading horseman was now not more than fifty feet away from them, and he had raised a bright red staff that he held across the pommel of the saddle to warn the pedestrians out of the way. Lord Wyncham stepped hastily to the side of the road, but, in so doing, he stepped upon, or seemed to step upon, a stone that rolled under his weight and cast him with a cry to the earth. There he lay for an instant stunned, then struggled to his feet, but slumped over to his side with another exclamation.

"The ankle, Pyndero!" he cried to the governor. "I have twisted it. I shall not be able to walk for a week at the nearest."

"Then," said the governor coolly, "you have lost your chance to dance at my ball. I am sorry, Wyncham."

The latter, in the meantime, had tugged off his boot with a groan and was wrapping a handkerchief around his ankle. The carriage would by this time have rolled on, with Tarabal buried securely in his own comfort and caring not a whit for the ease of any other person in the world, but Ortiza had risen suddenly from her place, and, standing straight up, she cried: "Stop the carriage! That man is badly hurt!"

Chapter Twenty-Three

"A THOUSAND TIMES KIND"

To Francisco Valdez it had seemed a strange thing that anyone should dare to halt this impressive equipage. He had been used to splendor enough during his life, but such extravagance, here at the end of the world, seemed to him more than imposing. He was over-awed. And such a clear, strong voice of command from Ortiza was the very last thing he expected. To be sure, all through the journey toward the town his respect for her had been increasing, but it had been her passive strength he admired. She had watched him from her seat with an indifferent eye that had gradually quelled him more and more. Every foot of the way that was sounded off by the rapid hoofbeats convinced him more and more clearly that he could never be happy as the husband of this woman. He could not take her into his life and assign her a small, obscure niche to fill, as many husbands he knew did with their wives. He could by no means do that. She had a quiet strength that would make itself felt. No, he could never find happiness with her. Instead, what would betide him?

When he thought of marriage with Ortiza, he thought of the knife he had found buried in the pillow beside his head, and the instant he thought of leaving the country without marrying the girl, he thought of the wrath of Joaquín Tarabal. Which force was the more to be dreaded he could not make up his mind.

But now came this clear cry from Ortiza, and the driver from his high seat sent the command on to the eight horses and brought them to a halt. The brakes made a shrill squeal, and the big vehicle stopped with a suddenness that jarred the four people in it and threw into disorder the gallant horsemen who followed in the rear.

From farther back the six great bandogs, seeing the fallen man by the roadside, began to press forward, slaver of eagerness dripping from their jaws and plainly showing that they had been raised for the manhunt and trained to it. The three attendants hurled their whole force back on the leashes, but they were dragged along in spite of their efforts. It was only a sudden roar from Tarabal, who saw the direction the dogs had taken, that stopped them. He leaned from his seat, bellowed a stream of curses that checked the great dogs, made them touch their tails between their legs, and then rolled back into his seat.

"Drive on!" he commanded. "What do you mean by stopping here, Juan?"

"The *señorita* commanded," grumbled the driver.

"He is badly hurt, Father!" exclaimed the girl.

"Since when," demanded Tarabal, "have you begun looking out for the troubles of strange men? You are fifty years too young for that. Drive on, I say!"

The driver spoke, the eight horses, at the word, leaned together into the collar, and, just as the heavy coach began to roll ahead, the fallen man was heard to say loudly to his companion, who was kneeling beside him: "No, no, Excellency. I shall manage to get back to the town. Do not ask them for a place in their carriage."

The word "Excellency" had a wonderful effect upon the rancher. He sat up, blinking. "Stop," he called to the driver.

The team halted. Tarabal leaped from the carriage, like a youth and an athlete. He approached the place where the two were.

176

"What's wrong here?" he asked cordially.

"Nothing," said the governor hastily. "That is, nothing of the least importance. My friend has turned his ankle a little. It is something that often happens to him. And then, in five minutes, he is as well as ever."

So saying, he smiled and nodded to the rancher. The latter searched his face, and he saw enough to convince him. He had heard the newly arrived governor described. That description fitted perfectly the man he now saw before him in the road. And something like the warm sun of courtesy instantly poured into the heart of Tarabal. Yet, what could he do? He was dismissed with a polite gesture. He turned to retreat toward the coach, grinding his teeth because he had lost this chance of rendering a service.

"You are wrong this time, Excellency," said Lord Wyncham. "The ankle is badly wrenched. If I can put my weight on it in ten days, I shall be only too happy."

Tarabal turned with a sigh of relief and pleasure. "Then," he said, "you must certainly take a place in my coach. I shall be only too happy to bring you comfortably into Monterey."

"You are a thousand times kind," said Wyncham. "I have not the honor of your name. This, however, is His Excellency, the governor, *Señor* Don José Pyndero."

"And I," said Tarabal, bowing as low as his obesity would permit him, "am a thousand times happy to find His Excellency. I am Joaquín Tarabal of San Triste."

The governor bowed, but he did not seem overpleased. "And this," he muttered, having been forced to the point, "is my friend, Lord Wyncham."

To keep from gasping aloud in his joy, Joaquín Tarabal bit his lip. He felt that an immense wealth had been poured into his hands. He was so happy that he could have sung and shouted in his joy. The governor of the entire province was

177

here before him and about to come under an obligation to him. With the famous governor, that man of war, was the brilliant young English nobleman whose name had lately made such a stir through the town of Monterey. He could hardly believe that with one stone he had knocked over two such birds. First of all, he wanted to pour out a blessing upon the head of his daughter, who had first stopped the coach; next of all, he could have taken up and kept as a treasure the stone that had caused the downfall of Wyncham.

He himself picked up the head and shoulders of the fallen man. On the stern faces of his attendants something akin to smiles appeared at the sight of their terrible master deep in the rôle of the good Samaritan. Half a dozen of them left off their smiling to rush to the assistance of the rancher, to take the burden from him. But he stuck to his post. Under the rolling fat of his arms and shoulders were muscles of such an immense strength that the burden of Wyncham was nothing. The governor carried the minor portion of the nobleman's weight.

So they reached the carriage, where Valdez rose to give his place to the unfortunate Wyncham. But he had no sooner seen the face of the latter than he cried out: "By the eternal heavens . . . the rascal, El Rojo!"

It caused a commotion. Tarabal dropped his share of the burden hastily, and the head of Wyncham would have struck the dust had not the governor dexterously caught the falling body. He broke into loud laughter at the same time.

"The Frenchman, Colonel Mortier," he declared, "made the same mistake. By the Lord, Wyncham, they are taking you for a slave."

"Upon my word," breathed Wyncham, and he looked fairly into the eyes of Valdez. For an instant they stared at one another.

"I could have sworn," said Valdez, "and yet . . . ?"

The sight of this man in the arms of the governor convinced him.

"My eyes have failed me," he said. "But even the voice seems to me perfectly that of El Rojo."

Ortiza, at these words, sat up in her place and looked wildly upon the young nobleman, who was placed in the seat that had just been vacated by Valdez. His hat he took from his head in order to pass a handkerchief over his forehead, as though to remove a perspiration brought there by pain. And, as the hat was taken off, and the jet black hair of Wyncham was exposed, she sat back again against the seat.

The new arrangements were quickly made. Valdez and the governor were mounted on either side of the carriage, on horses taken from the attendants, and the dismounted men ran in the rear, in the dust cloud that the carriage kept raising toward the sky.

When the introductions were completed, Valdez finished his hundredth apology for having mistaken the noble for his runaway slave, and the equipage began to rumble on its way again. On the instant, Lord Wyncham stepped to the center of the stage. He forgot the pain of his injured ankle that the motion of the carriage must have turned into a perfect torture. He was even able to smile and, though his face was a little pale, that nerveless Spartan, Tarabal, frankly admired the courage of the Englishman. The latter, with the open-hearted directness of his race, was paying his admiration to Ortiza. He should have been left to roll in the ditch in pain, he declared, if she had not first brought attention to his unlucky position. And he declared, in a picturesque speech, that he would never forget her kindness.

She had contented herself with watching him in the same calm, disinterested fashion that had so repeatedly sent chills through the blood of Valdez. The latter, from his position beside the coach, noted several things with perfect contentment. The first was that the governor was staring in wonder and joy at the new beauty. The second was that the English nobleman was even more impressed, to all appearances. The third was that Ortiza seemed oblivious to both of them. One tithe of her attention went to the man who sat opposite her; the other nine-tenths was given to the road that stretched before her, or to the quiet of her own thoughts.

But some reply was demanded when the Englishman had finished his speech of acknowledgment.

She merely said: "You are too courteous, *señor.* You are as courteous as you are rash."

"Rash, *señorita?*"

"Very, *señor.*"

"I cannot understand."

"But is not that true of the very brave . . . the rash . . . that they do not know when they are in danger?"

Valdez pricked up his ears. Here was more talk than he had expected from the girl, to be sure. Tarabal himself was scowling upon her forwardness. Yet she herself was as unperturbed as ever, and with the same cold eye she held the Englishman at a distance.

"I cannot pretend," said Wyncham, "to such a distinction. But how can I be in danger?"

"It is your ankle, of course," said the girl, "to which I refer."

"Naturally, *señorita.* But how am I endangering that?"

"By letting it rest upon the floor of the carriage, *señor,* as if you had become quite unaware that it was injured."

There was an exclamation from the rancher. But Wyncham, looking down at his foot that he had allowed to drop to the floor of the coach, broke into careless laughter. He picked up his boot and dragged it slowly onto the exposed foot.

"As a matter of fact, *Señor* Tarabal," he said, "I have

180

imposed on you and should have won out, if it had not been for the keen eye of the *señorita*. I had made a bet with the governor that, in some manner, I should contrive to be carried back to Monterey in your carriage. And, as you see, I am in a very good way of making him forfeit his hundred pounds, unless, *señor*, you now deprive me of my seat."

Tarabal laughed. His manner of laughter was to throw back his head, open his mouth to an incredible width — while his eyes disappeared in a maze of wrinkles — and then launch forth a torrent of noise.

"You shall stay here, now," he bellowed, "if the Archangel Michael came down with a sword to claim your place. It was all a fraud, then, my lord?"

"It was . . . and a shameless one," murmured Lord Wyncham.

"But," said Tarabal, "it has cost the governor a hundred pounds."

"And *Señor* Valdez has gallantly given up his seat," said Wyncham. But, though he spoke of the Spaniard, he looked straight at Ortiza.

She, however, seemed unaware that she was addressed, for she was looking down to the floor of the carriage, and her hands were folded in her lap. Yet, he began to understand that her mild eyes had seen deeply in him.

181

Chapter Twenty-Four

THE GOVERNOR INVESTIGATES

The Tarabal family had come into Monterey for the governor's ball. It would not do for such a man to let his daughter come in alone; neither would it do to come in the day of the ball. He must move in state, make his presence felt, let the townsfolk gape at his splendor, and then depart a few days after the ball was over. José Pyndero, considering these things, could not but smile. Yet, he was glad from the bottom of his heart that the rich man had made such a decision. It had given the famous Pyndero a chance to see a girl who stepped farther into his heart than any woman he had ever known.

It had not been her mere beauty of face. But, in addition to that and above it, there had been the quiet insight that had enabled her to see through the pretense of Lord Wyncham. That amiable actor had drawn the wool over the eyes of all the others, but Ortiza had detected him, and it still made the governor chuckle to think of it. The adventure might have cost him a hundred pounds. Indeed, he had offered to pay it, but Lord Wyncham, when they arrived in Monterey, had insisted that, since he had won the bet by a sham, he could not collect the money. And the sum was sufficient to make the governor happy to have an opportunity to avoid the payment. He decided that Lord Wyncham, whatever else he might be, was a gentleman as well as a subtle knave. And he felt that he was drawn still closer to the Englishman. Between them, they would do great things in California.

But that night he decided that he would start out on the

trail of the nobleman and take up the work Felipe had left off so disastrously. It was a task for which he had a strong taste. Formed in the school of those half-bandit and half-patriot guerrillas, who had first made a stand in Spain against the overwhelming power of Napoleon, and who had first shown to Europe that mere battles in the field will not conquer the spirit of a nation, he had never lost either his talent or his love for single-handed excursions, for danger, and for personal daring and risk. Tonight, he decided, no one should know him when he sallied forth.

It was a chill evening. The wind had rolled a drenching fog in from the sea. It covered Monterey with a dismal white fog, wet and of a penetrating cold. Against this he prepared himself by throwing over his shoulders a heavy woolen cloak of gray. He put on his head an old hat, whose drooping brim most effectually masked the upper part of his face. On his hip he buckled his favorite rapier, having first made a dozen passes with the blade to assure himself that its balance was as familiar to him as ever; on the opposite side of the belt the sword was balanced by a long and heavy, double-barreled pistol. He had used that weapon more than once on the dueling field. He only hoped that there might come an occasion for him to use it again before morning.

Thus equipped, he viewed himself in the mirror, decided that all was well, and started forth. He let himself out of the house by a secret postern, from which no guard would watch his exit. Then he stole away by back paths until he reached the house in which Lord Wyncham was lodged. He circled behind this, hunted through the grounds for a moment, and, finally, with the point of his sword, he pricked a figure that was crouched among the brush. The man arose with a hissing, indrawn breath. A knife glimmered faintly in the fog, as he turned.

"You keep your watch like a fool, Pedro," said the governor.

"A spy should have eyes in the back of his head as well as in the front."

"Ah, Excellency," murmured the old man, rubbing the place where the sword had touched him, "I was set to watch one man, and I am watching him."

He pointed to the dimly lighted rectangle of a window in the back of the house above him. On the curtain was printed the shadow of a man, seated in a chair, with a hat on his head. Naked candle flame, it seemed, supplied the light in the room. For the silhouette wavered and quivered and seemed to have a faint restless life of its own.

"Just as it was the night before?" asked the governor.

"Exactly similar, Excellency."

"Writing, no doubt?"

"No doubt, Excellency."

"An odd thing, Pedro, but, when I looked carefully at the forefinger of Lord Wyncham's right hand today, I saw no stain of ink."

"Of course, he would wash it away."

"Nonsense! A careless fellow like him would not have the neatness to write for hours at a time without covering his hands with spots of ink, and he would wash it carelessly also. There would certainly remain, in spite of his washing, some darkening from the stain."

"You understand such things, Excellency."

The governor, however, was arguing with himself, not with his spy. "Besides, no matter how much he had to write, such a pleasure lover as Wyncham, such an inveterate dicer, how could he find the patience to sit for hours scribbling?"

"Nevertheless, Excellency, there he sits. Your eyes will tell you just what mine have told me."

"My reason," said the governor, "tells me quite another thing."

"And that, sir?"

"It is not Lord Wyncham who is sitting there."

"Not Lord Wyncham!" gasped Pedro. "That is his room, Excellency. I swear to you."

The governor was a little shocked by the suddenness with which he had himself come to his conclusion. "Not a doubt of that," he said. "You are not a complete fool, Pedro."

"Just in that way, he sat there last night, Excellency."

"I don't believe it."

"For hours!"

"Impossible!"

Pedro was spurred to speak above his natural courage. "You have said so, Excellency."

"Which does not make it true. But, I say again, that is not Wyncham who throws the shadow on the window."

"You must be right, Excellency. I am only poor Pedro Sandiz. Therefore, you must be right."

The governor was not slow to catch the irony that informed this speech of his spy. "Therefore," he said, "I shall prove that I am right. Your eyes tell you that Lord Wyncham is in that room. My reason tells me that he is not there. Let us see whether the eyes or reason is the stronger."

"How shall we find out?"

"Leave that to me."

He looked about him, stepped close to the wall, considered his plan for an instant, and then made his preparations. He drew off his boots, cast aside his heavy cloak, in spite of the wetness of the night, and unbuckled his sword. He left these things in the keeping of Sandiz.

"And if the sword is lost while I am gone, your life shall be lost when I come back," he informed his spy.

With this last warning he began to climb. It was not easy. Though the wall was rudely built and old, affording many holds for hand and foot, it was slippery with the wet of the fog, and

Pyndero drew himself cautiously up until he had reached the top of the wall. From this point his work was much easier. He drew himself across to the window on which the patient shadow fell.

He could not hold on forever in that awkward position. Therefore, he tried to open the window. It stuck and squeaked, and the governor gave over his effort, grinding his teeth with rage and mortification. What would be thought in the town if the governor of the province were found striving to enter a window of a peaceful house in the middle of the night? But, to his astonishment, the shadow on the curtain inside the window did not stir in answer to the noise. He tried the window again. This time it slid up easily enough. He passed his leg inside the sill, prepared his pistol for a quick shot, in case there should be a sudden attack against him, and then he stepped boldly — almost jauntily — into the room.

At first the flare of the two candles dazzled him a little. But the figure in the chair beside them, however, did not stir. He rubbed his eyes again, with a cry of astonishment. For what he saw in the chair was no more than two pillows piled the one above the other. Over them a cloak had been huddled, and a wide-brimmed hat had been placed upon the whole structure. He turned to the window. There lay the silhouette, as life-like as possible, but Lord Wyncham was not there.

This explained, then, how the clever Felipe had been found far from the town of Monterey. Perhaps it explained, also, how he had been found with the knife buried in his back, squarely between the shoulder blades. For the governor could remember now how Lord Wyncham had hurled his heavy hunting knife and sunk the blade half its length into the solid wood of a tree. It was only strange, perhaps, that the man should have attacked Felipe from behind. But, the more he thought of it, the more natural this all seemed to José Pyndero. Lord Wyncham was only a gallant gentleman on the surface. At heart, he was a cunning adventurer, coldly playing a dangerous and deep game. Perhaps in that game the governor himself was no more than a simple pawn.

Pyndero began to search the room, but he found nothing. There was not more than a few articles of dress, a few sheets of writing paper, without a word inscribed on it, and, hanging in their sheaths from a peg in the corner of the room, two long hunting knives. The governor felt a damp of cold perspiration on his forehead, and he was attacked by a shuddering weakness in his vitals.

He went back to the spy at once.

"And you found, Excellency, what?" exclaimed Pedro.

"I found," said the governor, with a voice of the greatest good nature, "just what you said I should find. I found Lord Wyncham . . . writing."

He gave the fellow a broad piece of silver. After all, nothing must be known, nothing must be breathed until he was sure. But of this much he could feel reasonably sure: that, if Wyncham knew the governor was watching him — and if he did not know, then why these precautions to delude a spy? — the life of José Pyndero was in the utmost danger of being snuffed out swiftly and with not more noise than a thrown knife makes, whispering in the air.

Chapter Twenty-Five

A MESSAGE FROM HIS EXCELLENCY

However, there was not the least immediate fear of the knife of Wyncham. For he sat in the room of Julie Darnay, speaking softly, for fear the voice of a man, heard from her room, might gain her a scandalous reputation. As a matter of fact, nothing could have been more innocent than his call. He was at this moment pressing into her hand a purse of gold coins, and Julie protested, but protested with only half her heart.

"Why?" she cried to him. "Why should you do it, *señor*? I am only a stranger to you, and yet you have showered me with gold."

As she spoke, she leaned back in her chair, her head tilted a little, looking at him half in sadness and half in wonder. Wyncham, indeed, sat eagerly forward, but it was to admire her as a picture and not as a woman. He was even smiling a little, as though he well understood that she must have studied angles in her mirror for a long time before she perfectly understood in what position her face was most charming.

"Why do men bet on a horse race?" he said, to counter her question.

"Because they think their horses will win."

"And I, Julie, am certain that you are going to win."

"In what way, my lord?"

"A rich marriage."

"Of course, they will never look at me," said Julie, but her color and her smile belied her words.

"Of course, they will," said Lord Wyncham. "You will be

a great lady one of these days."

"My lord," cried Julie, and she actually turned pale with excitement. "You really think so?"

"I know so. They cannot resist you, Julie. You understand how to entangle them. If it were only your beauty. . . ."

"Oh, *señor*."

"For you *are* lovely, Julie. If you were in London, people would find you a sensation."

"Now you are laughing."

"You would enjoy that, Julie . . . being a sensation?"

She watched him narrowly, for she could never quite be sure what was going on in his mind, and whether his smile meant admiration or contempt. It was impossible to tell.

"It would mean being stared at by great people wherever you went. It would mean hosts of *billets-doux* from people you have merely glimpsed and forgotten. It would mean a shower of presents. There would be old wine for your table, rare lace for your shoulders, and glorious jewels for your hands and your throat. Would you like all that, Julie? And to be pointed out and gaped at in every assembly?"

"Of course, that would be glorious."

She had closed her eyes in exultation, and, therefore, she did not see the cynical glint in his amusement.

"Very well, Julie, if ever you go to London, you will enter your heaven at once."

"Oh, but how shall I get there?"

"We'll find a rich marriage for you here in Monterey, and then you'll torment your husband until he's taken you to the great city. You understand?"

"Perfectly!"

"And in the meantime you'll be happy enough."

"But *your* happiness, my lord?"

"Is in seeing you play the game."

189

"With all my heart, then."

"Who has called today?"

"*Monsieur* Mortier."

"The excellent colonel? Ah, is he to be caught?"

"*Bah!* He is too old."

"But if he's rich?"

"That would be different. However, he's not rich, though he talks as though he might be some day."

"Very likely. He has the way of a man who is likely to carve out his fortune, even if he has to do it with his sword."

"What do you mean, my lord?"

"Nothing. Mortier is an old friend of your father's, I believe."

"They were boys in Paris together."

"Charming. And Mortier came all this distance to call on his friend."

"No, to buy a small property from my father."

"Small? Twenty thousand miles to buy a *small* property?"

"Five thousand *francs* is all."

"Well, well, well. I begin to change my mind. But what is Mortier doing to get your father from prison?"

"He sees him every day, and he brings me word that my father is well cared for."

"Then why is no one allowed to see him? Why are not you allowed to see him?"

"*Monsieur* Mortier says it is the governor's way of punishing my father."

"Nonsense. The whole world knows that your father loves nothing so well as a chance to be alone."

"That is true. I had not thought of that."

"In fact, Julie, I shall not be surprised to hear that Mortier does not see him at all. He is simply saying it to make you cheerful."

"You think that?"

"And that your father is in terrible danger in that prison."

"My lord!"

"I have made inquiries. He is not seen in the upper part of the prison."

"Then the underground cells. . . ."

"It seems possible."

She considered the thing for a time. "Then he is having plenty of time for thought," she said at last.

"You are not very fond of your father, Julie?"

"Why should I be? He made a slave of me. I was never free for an hour."

"Then you will not worry about what happens to him in prison."

"Of course, I'll worry, but not a great deal. I know that he'll be saved before anything terrible happens to him."

"What makes you so sure?"

"You know why we are in trouble?"

"Through the escaped slave, El Rojo."

"When El Rojo left us, he gave his word that he would help us if we should ever be in need of help."

"And you trust his word, Julie?"

"Of course."

"A poor slave, while the governor and all of his troops stand against him, to say nothing of the walls of a prison?"

"You have never seen that slave, my lord."

"Of course not."

"I tell you, I saw him half naked and with a slave's collar around his neck . . . but a king with a crown could not have been greater. And his red hair was like flame on his head. Oh, I shall never forget him. I worshipped him . . . I loved him."

"Julie, Julie. This is wild talk."

"He is worth it. If I could find him, I'd walk barefoot tonight to reach him."

"And give up London?"

"He could take me around the world if he chose. He could do anything."

"A wonderful man, indeed. And yet he is very poor, Julie, I take it?"

She sighed. "Yes, yes. Of course, that is true. But, thank heaven, no one will know what I have just said."

"I shall keep your secret, Julie. For, after all, only a very foolish girl would love a man without money, and I take it that you are not a fool, Julie."

She laughed, and Lord Wyncham rose to depart.

"Keep Mortier interested," he said, "but do not commit yourself. We must aim high. Everything is possible. There is the governor himself without a wife."

"But he," Julie protested, "could not go to London."

Lord Wyncham stared at her a moment, then swallowed his mirth, bowed to her, and was gone, as he had come — which was through the window. He climbed like a monkey to the ground. As he reached it, he cut away around the building, wrapping his cloak closer about him as a protection against the fog. He began to sing as he walked, a sure proof that his spirits were high. At last, standing on a corner between two houses, he whistled a tune that was interrupted, in the very midst of a bar, by the sudden looming of a figure as white as the fog before him.

To this fellow Lord Wyncham murmured only a word or two, then hurried on, and did not pause until the square façade of the prison butted its way through the mist. He now circled the building until he came to a lighted window, a rectangle of milky white. He pressed his face close to the glass and made out, inside the room, only the hearty figure of the sergeant who was luxuriously at work behind his table at a solitary repast that the brother of one of his prisoners had brought to him.

For it was known in Monterey that the way to secure good fare for a prisoner was to furnish good fare for the sergeant — and more than he could eat. For Sergeant Diego Perin had always two or three corners of his being where still another delicacy could be tucked away.

Lord Wyncham thought for an instant. Then he tapped on the window. It brought the sergeant hastily from the table.

"Who's there?" asked the keeper of the prison.

"Sergeant Perin! Sergeant Perin!" called Wyncham.

"Well?"

"Open the window at once. A message from His Excellency!"

"Why through the window and not the door?" growled the keeper. But he had not the moral courage to refuse to listen to the governor's voice by proxy through the window. He threw up the window accordingly and thrust out his bullet head.

"Now," he said, "what is all this trouble about?"

The answer came in the form of a heavy sword hilt dropped upon the back of his head. He slumped over the sill, like a loosely filled sack, and in another moment Wyncham was through the window and had deposited his man on the floor of the prison. He worked in leisurely fashion, first blindfolding the good sergeant and then binding hands and feet with rope, a quantity of which was in the room. When this was done, he sat on the stomach of Diego Perin until that worthy gasped and groaned and recovered his senses.

Then Lord Wyncham rose and tickled the flabby throat of the sergeant with the keen point of a hunting knife. A prayer to the Virgin to intercede for his wretched soul babbled forth from the lips of the sergeant.

"Softer," commanded Wyncham.

The prayer was whispered — half murmur and half sob.

"The cell of Darnay. Where is it?" asked Lord Wyncham.

"I shall lead you there at once."

"Describe the way."

It was done.

"Now the key?"

"There are five very large keys in the bundle on the table. It is the one from the head of which some of the rust has been worn lately."

"How many other guards are in the prison?"

"Not one."

"If you lie, when I hear a sound from one, I shall first come back to cut your throat."

"I swear on the cross."

"Good," said Wyncham, and straightway gagged the poor man until he could barely breathe.

That done, he took the keys from the table and, as an afterthought, bore along with him the half bottle of wine which the sergeant had not yet consumed. In the outer corridor he hesitated again, but, though he listened for some moments, he heard no sound, and he began to feel that the sergeant might have told him the truth about the guards. So he went on down that long and damp stairway that had been described to him. The taper that he carried burned blue and small, as he descended toward the lower portion of the steps. At length he reached and unlocked the door.

A foul air rolled out to him and made him curse in astonishment and horror. He called the name of Darnay, and, receiving no answer, thrust the taper into the doorway. There he saw a sight of misery and terror. The Frenchman lay on his back on the floor. His long hair flowed down into a green pool of standing water that covered the stones. His eyes were closed. His face was encrusted with filth and blackened blood that had flowed from an abrasion above his right eye. Perhaps he had received that wound in falling from exhaustion. His cheeks were sunken. He looked a dead man, and one to whom death has not come very recently, at that.

Wyncham could not go to him at once. When at length he reached him and raised his head from the sickening water of the cell, he felt his brain reel at the thought that any human being should have been compelled to exist for even an hour in this horrid dark and foul air and filth.

He felt for the beat of Darnay's heart. For a time it was imperceptible, but at length he made out a faint and slow pulsation. He pried the teeth of the senseless man open and poured a mouthful of the wine down his throat. While he waited for it to take effect, he found a key with which he could unlock the leg irons that held the prisoner. Then he dragged him to a drier part of the cell and began to work the arms of Darnay to help increase the circulation of his blood. Once or twice he paused, for the silence in the prison began to weigh on him, and it seemed that small sounds, like whispering spies, were creeping down the stairs. Eventually Darnay gasped and opened his eyes. He stared wildly into the face of Lord Wyncham.

"Courage," murmured Wyncham. "You are with a friend at last."

"A friend," whispered Darnay, and closed his eyes with a smile.

He was given another swallow of the wine that caused his eyes to open again. A third swallow seemed to clear his brain, and a faint color appeared in his cheeks.

"What is this?" he asked, making a feeble effort to sit up.

"Freedom," said Wyncham.

"God has sent me death and a happy dream," said the prisoner. Presently he said in a louder voice: "Who is here?"

"A friend."

"I have never seen you."

"A first meeting, but not the last."

He lifted Darnay to his feet. The Frenchman staggered.

"Steady," said Wyncham and, passing his left arm around the victim, he supported him strongly out of the cell and up the long, slippery stairs. The action brought new power to Darnay. Presently he was carrying some of his own weight. So they gained the top of the stairs, turned down the passage, and came to the door. Wyncham kicked it open and, instantly, from either side, stepped two white-clad forms, almost invisible in the smoke-thick fog that had drifted more and more heavily over the town.

"Take him," said Lord Wyncham, speaking in Spanish. "Give him good care. This is the man . . . this is my friend. Let him be fed and tended well. He must sleep and rest and eat. Now, go quickly!"

There was no spoken answer. Instead, the two white-clad men lifted Darnay, and in a moment they were lost in the fog. A little later the dull pounding of hoofs began. Wyncham waited to hear no more, but, having closed the door of the jail carefully behind him and hung the bunch of keys on the outer knob, he himself disappeared into the fog.

Chapter Twenty-Six

THE COLONEL RECEIVES A VISIT

The governor was himself preëminent in the pursuit of the villain who had broken the prison open, gagged and bound the jailer, and taken Darnay away to safety. Of one accord it was taken for granted that the same miscreant who had freed himself from slavery, branded with burning metal the governor's own lieutenant, freed from impending death eight murderous Navajos, plundered the house and the stables of the great Don Joaquín, and laughed to scorn the efforts of the government to catch him, must be the man who had also stolen from the arms of justice a second prisoner. In a word, it was El Rojo.

Pyndero, therefore, rode foremost in the pursuit, but hardly to be outdone by him were his two friends, Lord Wyncham and Louis Auguste Mortier. The governor was better mounted, but the Frenchman and the English nobleman rode like men possessed. Yet, for all their scouring of the hills, they could not find a trace of the fugitives. Darnay was stolen clean away. They labored until the dawn, and then they returned wearily to Monterey. It was a solemn and silent return. For the governor this was an eminently serious affair. He had been bilked of his prey, and this was not the first time. Law and order had been brought into disrepute by the villain, El Rojo. Men would begin to laugh at the efforts of José Pyndero.

In fact, he had already heard rumors of such laughter here and there. Like many another man or beast, laughter was more terrible to José Pyndero than swords. When he reached Monterey again that morning, his mind was made up. He would wait until the ball was over. Then he would initiate a reign of terror in California, and it would endure until he had wiped out the Navajo murderers, who lurked in the hills, and El Rojo as well who led them. That thought of El Rojo, indeed, was beginning to haunt the good governor. If he fenced, his skill was compared by Mortier to that of El Rojo's. If he mounted a horse, its speed and beauty were contrasted with the great stallion, Sanduval, that El Rojo had stolen. If he went for a stroll among the hills, his lieutenant begged him to take an escort, for fear the terrible El Rojo would swoop down with his band. The very air was filled with that name.

Yet, he would not destroy the festivities of the ball by immediate martial preparations. He would imitate the sleeping lion until the dance was over. The next day he would show Monterey the metal of which he was made. In the meantime, he could have eaten fire. He remembered courtesy, however, enough to thank Mortier and the Englishman from the bottom of his heart for their efforts. Then he rode on to his house. A little farther on Wyncham detained Mortier, while he finished an anecdote, and then these two separated with laughter.

It was only the beginning of an arduous day for Mortier. He spent the first half of the morning improving his appearance. Then he called on Julie, but he was encountered at her door by a maid who let him know that her mistress was not yet out of bed.

"What!" exclaimed Mortier. "Not up yet on the very day her father has run away from the law? This is a sad day for her. Wake her and tell her that Louis Mortier, her friend, has come to condole with her. I must see her, at once."

But the maid showed not the slightest inclination to take his advice. She was a bold-eyed half-breed, and now she looked him over as calmly as though he were a beggar.

"The *señorita* will sleep. She is very tired," she said, and shrugged her shoulders eloquently.

"Name of the devil!" broke out Mortier through his teeth, and then found that the girl was regarding him with more respect. If he could afford to fly into a fury, it was apparent that he must be a great gentleman. He at once took advantage of her changed demeanor. If he could not see her mistress, he would at least find out something about the maid. But, though she seemed to wish to tell him all that she could, he found that she was kept back by a great fear. Of course, her wages were not being paid by penniless Julie. Who, then, supported the maid? If Mortier could find out that, he felt that he would have Julie in his power. Someone in the town had taken a fancy to the girl and was beginning to shower her with money and attentions.

Since he could learn nothing, in spite of half a dozen coins that he dropped into the palm of the maid, he decided that her employer must be a man fully as important as he was. Instinctively his mind turned to Lord Wyncham. But all he could do for the moment was to go away and wait until Julie should be out of bed and dressed to receive him. He came back in an hour, but he found her in the midst of throes of grief for her father, declaring that he was lost, and that her good name was stained by his conduct. She cast herself into a chair, clapped her hands to her face, and swayed to and fro in the blackness of her grief.

It was all a sham, as Mortier knew. She was merely trying to get rid of him quickly. But he stopped the demonstration, as he might have stopped an attack with a time thrust.

"Julie," he said, "since you are in sorrow, and since you are now almost alone in the world, I have come to ask you to marry me."

The sobbing stopped at once. She was so amazed that she looked up and allowed him to see that her eyes were quite dry.

"In the name of heaven, what do you mean?"

"Marriage with a man who will devote his life to making you happy, Julie."

"You are not laughing at me? But you would seem more like my father than like my husband."

"I am older, Julie, and, therefore, I have had a chance to learn how to fight a way through the world. Besides, I come of a tough stock. My father was sixty-eight when he shouldered a musket and marched to Valmy. I'll be hale and hearty at seventy-five. You need have no fear of my years, Julie. I'll be able to care for you."

Julie burst into violent laughter.

"Damnation!" exploded Mortier. "Do you laugh at me?"

"I . . . hysterics," gasped Julie, and promptly she began to weep. Perhaps it was the mere excess of laughter that had brought the tears to her eyes. Mortier, however, could not imagine for two successive minutes that he was actually being mocked. He was convinced that the honor of a proposal from him for her hand had simply unnerved the girl, and he decided that she must have time to think things over. He dropped to his knees beside her.

"Take the day to think this over. In the morning I shall come to see you again, Julie. Then you may have your answer ready. *Adieu.*"

He went out, twirling his mustaches like a grenadier who had just been decorated by his emperor. Perhaps it was well that he could not look through walls and see the joyous mirth of Julie the moment he was gone. But he spent the rest of that happy day walking on air, preparing a suit for the ball, having a barber trim his mustaches and hair, and estimating a way in which he should spend the income from a quarter of a million *francs*. If he invested it very safely, at three per cent, it was still certain to bring in for him a noble sum of more than ten thousand *francs* a year, to say nothing of the produce from his own farm. He had completed hours and hours of these pleasant calculations, and was smoking his good night pipe, wrapped in a dressing gown and with slippers on his feet, when there fell a gentle rap upon his door.

He opened it at once, swinging it wide in his bluff fashion, and he was amazed when a figure, standing before that door, wrapped to the eyes in a sweeping black cloak, glided into the room before he could make a move in opposition. Mortier, however, had fought in fifty battles and a hundred skirmishes, and he was not the man to be suddenly unnerved. He did two things at once. He kicked the door shut and at the same instant reached for a belt that hung from the wall. His hand came away from it with a naked rapier, prepared for action.

"What sort of manners are these? Coming into a man's room without being asked? Slipping in like a shadow? You'll slip out again, too."

With this he whirled upon the intruder. To his amazement, he was confronting El Rojo. He could not believe it. The excess of his good fortune choked him. With such a prize as this, he would become the most famous man in Alta California and the best friend and benefactor of the governor. Nothing would be too good for him. There was, also, the handsome cash prize that rested on the head of the slave. Valdez had offered much; the governor had offered more; and Joaquín Tarabal had contributed a generous portion. Decidedly this would be a good night's work.

Now the rascal sat upon the bed, cross-legged. He had thrown off his cloak. It lay in a ragged-edged pool of black around him. His golden-red hair, like flame, stood wildly on his head. He was dressed in a cotton tunic that left his arms bare from the shoulders. His feet were bare and powdered with dust almost to the knees, to which his trousers were turned up. Altogether he looked the most athletic figure, the most agile, and the strongest man Mortier had ever seen. But the heart of the Frenchman warmed. In the belt of El Rojo did not appear that slender rapier that he so well knew how to handle. Instead, there were only two hunting knives, heavy in the hilt and long in the blade. But what were a dozen knives compared with the long rapier in the hand of Mortier? In a word, he felt himself to be the master of the situation.

"El Rojo!" he exclaimed.

"I am he," nodded El Rojo. "Allah be with you, my old shipmate."

Mortier puckered his brows and stared more closely at the other. "That voice," he said. "I could swear. . . ." But here he remembered the black, glossy hair of Lord Wyncham and shook his head. "What madcap business has brought you here, El Rojo?" he asked. "Do you not know that a price is waiting for the man who captures you, and that it will be paid whether you are taken alive or dead?"

"I know all that," answered El Rojo, "and it is nothing to me. Because, *monsieur,* I understand that so great and brave a man as Colonel Mortier would never betray a poor escaped slave for the sake of the reward."

So saying, he gave Mortier a smile that might have meant anything, and that, at the least, had little mirth in it. With this he crossed the room, opened the window, and attached to a beam above the window a long lariat of rawhide he had brought with him under his cloak.

"What is the purpose of that?" asked the colonel.

"A second stairway in case the first one is blocked," said El Rojo. "They have a way of tagging along close behind me, and I am rarely at liberty to return as I came."

"Still," said Mortier, as full of curiosity as he was of satisfaction at having this valuable prisoner in his hand, "still, El Rojo, you have managed to stay free in spite of them all. It is a marvel. How have you managed to do it?"

"It is a simple thing."

"Ah!" And the Frenchman leaned forward.

"I have made eight men trust me. When you have accomplished that, you can do just as I have done . . . or so can any man, *Monsieur* Mortier."

There was an irony in this remark that made the good colonel take notice. "You have made eight men trust you? Nonsense! I have been trusted by an entire regiment of gallant Frenchmen."

"So?" said El Rojo, and his white teeth glistened again. "But I, *monsieur,* am trusted by eight Navajos who have trailed a foeman a thousand miles, and all for what? A mere nothing, you will say. He mistreated the tribe of those men. But I say, *monsieur,* that those eight men multiply me. They make me eight, instead of one. And that is why I am a ghost upon which the governor will never be able to lay his hands, until I put my trust in the wrong man."

With this he glanced so sharply at Mortier that the Frenchman felt sweat start out on his forehead. It was almost as though the treachery in his mind had been read.

"Tell me one thing, El Rojo."

"All that I may, *monsieur.*"

"Where is *La Cantante*?"

"Safe with Sanduval."

"And Sanduval is safe in town, waiting for you?"

"Exactly, *monsieur.* You see to the very heart of my mystery."

"You seem gay, El Rojo."

"Why should I not be? I have played a game so long."

"Well, well. Tell me, was it you who saved Darnay from the prison?"

"Of course. He was in trouble on account of me. I was forced to save him. I had promised him long before that I should befriend him if I drew him into danger by branding Rindo in his house."

"Very true, El Rojo. And when you talked with Darnay, did he speak of me?"

"Only a word, *monsieur*."

"And that?"

"He is a sick man, *monsieur*, and he babbled something about an estate of a quarter of a million in France . . . robbery . . . persecution . . . fairy talk, *monsieur*."

"Ah! Well, my good friend, El Rojo, the things he babbled about were true."

"Impossible, *monsieur!*"

"Why impossible?"

"Because then you would be a villain."

"In a sense, yes, and in a sense only a reasonable man . . . a general maneuvering for a great victory."

"You are rash to tell me such things, *monsieur*."

"Not at all. You are to take the place of the excellent Darnay in the prison, El Rojo."

"You would betray me, *monsieur?*"

"The reward means something, and the fame of taking you means something more."

"It would bring a curse on you, *monsieur*."

The colonel laughed. "My sword will answer such curses," he said.

"As you please, *monsieur*. But I entreat you to reconsider. You are damning your soul."

"Do you think that I care a fig's end for damnation and souls, poor Rojo?"

"Yet, in the name of mercy, sir, I beg you not to take me like this."

"Are you losing nerve, Rojo? Are you begging?"

"On my knees, *monsieur!*"

And, in fact, he fell upon his knees and clasped his hands. But Mortier merely laughed.

"You surprise me, El Rojo," he said. "However, I suppose you are only to be pitied. Stand up. Prayers will do nothing with me. And. . . ."

Here he broke off his words, for El Rojo had leaped from his knees to his feet and toward the window, outside of which his rawhide rope stretched down to the ground. But Mortier quickly interposed his rapier's point and drove back El Rojo. Then the colonel, having first locked the door and placed his back to the window, had his man securely in a trap. Here he could keep him so long as he chose, and when he had extracted from him all the amusement and information that he cared for, then he would turn the slave over to the authorities and the grateful, vengeful Valdez.

"What will Valdez do with me?" asked El Rojo, now abandoned to despair and burying his face in his hands.

"He has a number of ideas," said Mortier, "and any one of them is probably enough to discourage flight in the future. At least, they all seem strong enough to me. He has thought of cropping your ears, or of slicing the end off your nose, or of branding you in the center of the forehead. Any or all of these things might be done, and there would be an accompanying flogging, of course, in a public place."

"It could never be done!" cried El Rojo. "You, *monsieur,* would never permit it. There is too much humanity in you."

"*Bah!*" said Mortier. "I am a soldier first of all."

"And is this all the pity I win from you?"

"All, El Rojo."

"Though I have voluntarily come to you?"

"You have voluntarily put your head in the jaws of the lion.

Therefore, you must pay the price for having proved yourself a fool."

"Very well, *monsieur*," said El Rojo, standing up, and not the slightest sign of fear remained in his features. "Very well, you have spoken as I expected you to speak. But I could not be sure. I wished to have you condemned by your own lips before I acted against you. And you see, *monsieur le colonel*, that you have done that thing for me to perfection. You certainly could not dream of asking for mercy from me."

"Are you jesting, El Rojo?"

"A sharp jest, *monsieur*."

El Rojo raised his hand. Then, too late, Mortier whirled with a groan of fear toward the window. But a form was already sliding through the window, and, before Mortier could swing around with his rapier, he was struck to the ground by a flying body that leaped at him. Another followed. He was trussed in an instant, and, staring up, he found that two tall and strong-shouldered Navajos were standing above him, with their arms folded, and their faces carefully impassive, although their chests were still heaving from the efforts of climbing the long rope to the window of Mortier's room. How like stealthy-footed cats they must have climbed. And how noiselessly, too, they had glided through the window.

He looked to El Rojo. The latter had produced and lighted a long-stemmed pipe — so very long, indeed, that the joints of the stem separated and had to be screwed together. The slave had thrown himself back on the bolster of the bed and, having lighted the pipe, sent up a cloud of smoke, puffing slowly, leisurely.

"There is only one place where men know how to enjoy tobacco, and that is south of the Mediterranean. You should go there to learn, *monsieur le colonel*."

The colonel gazed desperately toward him.

"El Rojo," he said, "I can make you rich."

"Your ransom," said El Rojo, "will be cheaper than money . . . it is merely to write a paper . . . and not a long paper at that."

Chapter Twenty-Seven

A MIDNIGHT CALL

As everyone in the governor's household knew, it was a capital offense to waken the great man earlier than the hour he had appointed the night before. It was, above all, of importance on this night that he should not be disturbed, for the next evening came the great ball, with preparations for which half of Monterey was stirring. But when Mortier came to the house of the governor in the dead of the night, there was need of one look into his face to make the sentinel at the entrance pass him on to the sentinel at the door that opened from the patio of the house itself, and thence he was brought to the door of the governor's room and bidden wait there until the official was awakened.

The last ceremony called forth an outbreak of abuse, but Mortier did not seem to hear the sounds. He had fallen into a nearby chair and lay in it with a fallen head, only writhing now and again with a convulsive shudder. At length the door of the governor's room burst open, and José Bernardo Pyndero came out in a fury.

"Where's Mortier, then?" he demanded. "Where's Mortier? Is this a joke? Has he gone away again? I'll have every man in my service whipped if. . . ."

Here he caught sight of Mortier in the chair, and, striding to him, he laid a hand upon the shoulder of the Frenchman.

"What brings you here between midnight and dawn, *monsieur?*" he asked sternly, and, as he received no immediate answer, he let his fury have a free rein. "Are you drunk?" he thundered. "Have you dared come here with a befuddled brain and. . . ."

Mortier raised his head.

The voice of the governor fell away to a mutter. "Have you seen a ghost?" he gasped then. "Have you seen a ghost, Mortier?"

Still the Frenchman did not reply, and the governor took him by both shoulders and raised him to his feet. Mortier staggered, but kept his dead eyes fixed upon the face of Pyndero.

"Name of names," breathed the governor and conducted Mortier suddenly into his own room, the door of which he locked and bolted. Then he placed Mortier in the most comfortable chair and laid a cushion behind his head.

"Now," he said at length, visibly moved with horror, "tell me what you can. What has happened?"

"El Rojo," said the dull and lifeless voice of the Frenchman.

"That fiend . . . what has he done?"

"He came to my room."

"Impossible! You could have called twenty soldiers by leaning out your window and shouting."

"Through the window came the Navajos."

"Ah!"

"Wine," panted Mortier.

It was brought in haste to him by the governor's own hands. When he had swallowed some of it, he seemed stronger.

"He wanted what?" urged the governor.

"A confession."

"Of what? Tell me, was it he who rescued old Darnay from the prison?"

"It was he."

"My score against that red-headed demon will never come to an end."

"You will never beat him . . . you will never catch him, Pyndero."

"That will be seen in time."

"Time will see him make a fool of you, my brave José."

"But with you . . . what could he want with you?"

"A confession, I say."

"Of what?"

"Of a thing that means as much to you as it does to me."

The governor sank onto the edge of the bed, as though his legs had been knocked from under him.

"Darnay?" he asked.

"He came to hear something that had to do with Darnay."

"Of course, Darnay had told him everything that you had told Darnay. What a fool you were, my friend, to have told Darnay that his ground had become as rich as a buried treasure."

"A black fool. I should have cut his throat after telling him that. Then I could have married the daughter."

"Julie! She will know now what has been done to her father . . . and by whom, and why."

"I think that there may be some doubt as to that."

"How can there be?"

"El Rojo swears in the name of Darnay that, if Darnay is restored to his good standing . . . and if he is allowed to come back to Monterey . . . and if ample restitution is made to enable him to rebuild on his land, where the blacksmith shop stood . . . he, El Rojo, undertakes that not a word of my confession shall be made public."

"The word of a slave for all these things?"

"The word of a slave. It is enough, Pyndero."

"I cannot believe it."

"You *must* believe it."

"What will come to José Pyndero if it is known that he has

been a part of this horrible affair? There is a devilish truth in that. I should be blotted out of sight of favor. I should be ruined at once. They might give me the prison and be done with it."

"The same cell in which Darnay was rotting, for instance."

"Enough!" gasped the governor.

Mortier poured out another glassful of wine with a trembling hand and drank it off. Some of it spilled across his chin and over the white front of his shirt, where it left a stain like blood.

"I must do all those things," said the governor. "I am at their mercy, and I must act as they dictate. Be sure, Mortier, I shall never forget that it was owing to you that I was mixed up with this cursed affair. But, whatever else you may be, you are brave, Mortier. How did they wring the confession from you?"

"Help me to stand up."

He was raised at once from the chair.

"Take off my cloak, Pyndero."

The governor obeyed, and found the body of the Frenchman swathed in cloths beneath the cloak. Those cloths he lifted. There was a groan from Mortier. The governor went on with the investigation, working with all possible delicacy. At length the back of Mortier was exposed. At what he saw upon it, the governor fell back with a cry of horror.

He could understand now what he had seen in the face of Mortier, the thing that had brought him so readily through the sentinels. It was the agony that he had striven against, but that had finally conquered him. It still remained in his staring eyes and in the weak and sagging lines of his mouth.

"My poor friend," said Pyndero. "My poor, poor Mortier!"

Tears came into the eyes of Mortier and then rolled one by one down his face. His whole body trembled, so that the governor could see the Frenchman shuddering, and he knew that only the ghost of a brave man was standing before him. The spirit of Mortier had been totally broken. He replaced the bandages.

"It was El Rojo who did these things to you?"

"The Indians . . . the fiends . . . working under his orders. As they worked, he told me stories of the galleys . . . and of the prison in Tunis . . . and of how he had been treated like a dog in the household of Valdez."

"And at length . . . ?"

"I . . . I gave way, Pyndero. I sat down and wrote everything as it had actually happened."

"Then we are both ruined."

"Unless El Rojo keeps his word."

"A slave's word! But I must build upon it until I have managed to plant six inches of cold steel between his ribs. In the meantime, Darnay must be pardoned. The action against him must be explained away. I shall say that Rindo gave false testimony, discharge the fool, and give Darnay money for what the fire consumed."

"So be it," murmured Mortier.

He had closed his eyes, and his lips trembled more than the light of the candle that was playing against his face. It was not hard to guess that he would never again have the courage to hold a sword and face a swordsman.

Chapter Twenty-Eight

TWO WALTZERS

The house of Governor Pyndero was large, but it was not large enough to accommodate the crowd that poured toward it on the evening of the ball. For everyone came. The whole town felt that it had a right. The only sort of entertainment the governor could give was one to which everyone was invited. And so Pyndero had thrown up before his house a great tent, where the hundreds could stand and watch the dancing and applaud it. They could even join in themselves, if they chose.

The outer shell of the ball, if it might be given that name, began in the middle of the afternoon. And from that moment Monterey enjoyed a public holiday. Before long the violins were singing in the great tent, and the fandango was under way. Lord Wyncham, who visited the tent together with the governor, announced that he was vastly disappointed. For he had expected the dance to be fast and furious. On the part of the women, on the contrary, it was entirely statuesque. They glided about with their arms hanging stiffly at their sides, and their eyes directed toward the ground. The men did better, capering gracefully around their partners.

Now and then, when a waltz was played, some couple would whirl down the tent, amidst the gasping and the cries of admiration from the crowd. But the waltz was too new. And though the Emperor Alexander had danced it in London two years before, the news of the imperial sanction had hardly reached California. The dance was considered rashly immodest. It made elderly ladies blush and elderly gentlemen frown.

213

But Lord Wyncham and the governor openly approved and applauded — which was a great forward step in the history of the progress of waltzing in California.

All the sport was not dancing, however. The ladies had come equipped with large numbers of eggshells that had been emptied of their contents and filled again with cologne and sealed up. Their game was to steal behind some man who watched the dancing and, flipping off his hat, crack the egg upon his head, so that the perfume ran in every direction down his head and face and over his clothes. This was simple enough, yet the real art of that game was to escape into the crowd before being detected by him who had been attacked. The egg breaking on the part of the ladies was matched by an equally singular custom on the part of the men. Occasionally, when one of the ladies danced near the edge of the crowd, a hat was dropped upon her head by one of the men. It was a singular method of paying a compliment. If the hat were worn throughout the ensuing dance and then taken off and held out by the lady, it meant that the gentleman who reclaimed it was her partner for the rest of the evening. But if the hat were shaken off, the repulsed gallant was forced to step out onto the floor to reclaim his fallen hat, and he received the smiles of the crowd. These were the broader when a girl kept on the hat for a considerable time before she shook it from her head.

Such was the scene that Lord Wyncham and the governor looked upon for a time. Then they retired toward the house again, as the time drew near when the governor's private party was about to commence. For, besides the entertainment in the outer tent, there was another in the house of the governor itself. To this the gentry had been bidden. Here was another orchestra. Here were opened wines of a finer quality than those that flooded the common gullet of the town in the big tent. Here came the opulent ranchers from the surrounding leagues of country, and with them came the rich Joaquín Tarabal, waddling through the door, with his daughter on his arm, and his beady little eyes darting here and there in an eager search for admiration of her. Here came, too, Julie Darnay, and around her arose the greatest murmur of all.

The famous Lord Wyncham had himself gone to fetch her. It was no wonder that he had paid her this honor. She could repay him or any man amply in cash. For this day it was known that she had inherited a handsome estate in France. Half a million *francs,* some said, while others, more mild, reduced the figure. But she had suddenly become, from a modest blacksmith's daughter, a prize worth marriage. The greatness of the change made her seem more dazzling. All the crowd knew of the story was that Mortier was a villain — that he had managed to have Darnay thrown into prison by deceiving the excellent governor, that El Rojo had saved the blacksmith in the nick of time, and that, finally, Mortier had fled from the town and disappeared, probably in a small sloop that was trading down the coast. As for the persecuted Darnay, he was back again in town, weak, sick, but on the road to recovery, after a terrible experience in the jail. He had refused to talk. But it was said by those who had talked to the doctor who attended him that the eyes of the old Republican had burned like two fires when he was asked what had happened to him in the cell.

Another man had disappeared with Mortier, and that was no other person than the fat and smiling sergeant who had charge of the prison, Diego Perin. He was gone, and people wondered what could have been on the conscience of the happy jailer. Then came obliging rumor and solved all. The wretched Diego Perin had been bribed by Mortier, who wished to wring the fortune of Darnay from him by torture. It was the money of Mortier that had brought Darnay to the very verge of death. Consequently the corrupted jailer and his briber had fled at the same time, before punishment could overtake them.

This dark background was what made Julie Darnay so exceedingly brilliant by contrast. In fact, she was very lovely when she entered the house. Not in vain now were the hours during which she had hummed to herself and danced along the shadows of her father's house. For now no less a person than young Lord Wyncham claimed her hand and waltzed with her in the presence of the governor. There was not another couple on the floor — so slowly had the new dance taken hold among the aristocracy of Alta California. But, though all eyes were fastened upon them, Lord Wyncham was maintaining a close and important conversation with Julie.

"Julie," he said, "tonight is the greatest night of your life."

"And why?" she asked.

"Because you make your first impression, and that is something that can never be lived down or up."

"I'm doing my best. Am I failing?"

"No, no."

"Because," said Julie, with the frankness of power, "there is only one other girl at the governor's house."

"And who is she?"

"Of course, you have watched her much more closely than I."

"No, on my honor."

"Then I'm afraid to point her out to you. It is the daughter of Tarabal. How could such a pig of a man have such a lovely daughter?"

"She is too pale and quiet," said Lord Wyncham. "You are quite wrong about her, Julie."

"Very well. Wait until she begins to dance. Then you will see the men lose their heads. I know. I know."

216

"How can you know so much about men, Julie?"

"Because, sir, every girl is born with as much knowledge as that."

"Very well," said Wyncham, "then I shall take your advice and pay a great deal of attention to the *Señorita* Tarabal."

"She has a beautiful name," said Julie, looking him fairly in the eye.

"What is it?"

"Oh, *monsieur*, you rode in the coach with her, and yet you say you do not know her name?"

"Of course not. I have forgotten it."

"Good," said Julie, smiling. "That is very good, indeed."

"Do you think I am not telling the truth?"

"Oh, *monsieur*, I never think."

"Julie, you are mocking me."

"A lord, and I mock you? Oh, no!"

"However, Julie, I want to point out something to you."

"What is it?"

"That fellow, Valdez, who is to marry *Señorita* Ortiza. . . ."

"I see," said Julie, "that you have remembered her name. Quite by miracle, my lord."

"It popped into my head, you know."

They smiled frankly at one another.

"I don't blame you, sir," said Julie. "She is a picture."

"I hope," said Wyncham, "that she is something more than that." He added: "But, as I was saying . . . have you looked at Valdez?"

"He's too pretty a man to be looked at twice. He would have made a lovely girl."

"You are laughing at him. The Valdez family is very old . . . very famous, very rich."

Her eyes had opened a trifle with each phrase he spoke. "In that case . . . ," she said.

217

"He is not what you thought, eh?"

"Of course not."

"Julie, if I were not in love already, I should fall in love with you."

She was so astonished by his confession, made so very frankly to her, that she almost lost her step. Now she looked up to him a little wistfully.

"Have you gone so far with Ortiza?"

"It is all on my side, Julie. You will have to help me."

"With all my might," said Julie, and, sighing, she looked down to the floor.

"What I want you to do, of course, is to call off the dog."

"You mean I'm to attract *Señor* Valdez?"

"Julie, your understanding is divine."

"But he will never look at me . . . so great a gentleman."

"The king of England would look at you, Julie, and more than once."

"If you command me," said Julie. "Of course, I am under great obligations to you, and I must try my best. But you can't hope he's such a fool that he'll give up the fortune of Tarabal?"

"It seems to me," said Wyncham, "that he's wretchedly unhappy there in the midst of the Tarabal millions. There is a crease between his eyes where he has been wearing a steady frown."

"That is true," murmured Julie.

"And when Tarabal looks at him, he shrinks, as though he felt a whip."

"I see that, too."

"Look a little closer, Julie, and I think you will see that he is even a little bit afraid of Ortiza herself."

"That gentle, beautiful girl? She is a lamb."

"Very quiet, Julie, but you have not looked closely enough at her."

"Ah, my lord, what do you mean?"

"That she is full of danger."

"How can she be? Yet, when I look again, I begin to understand what you mean . . . very quiet, but always thinking, and nothing can move her. She is like stone."

"Exactly, Julie."

"But are you not afraid?"

"Of course not."

"I understand. She is another world to conquer. Very well, then, I shall do my best with *Señor* Valdez. Besides, I have directions from my father to obey you in everything, my lord. God keep you tonight!"

They had come to the end of the dance, and, as they were walking across the room in the midst of applause, she made this remark, and it stopped Lord Wyncham.

"What do you mean by that?" he asked.

"I hardly dare to guess," she said, "except, perhaps, that you are in very great danger here, my lord."

He looked steadily at her. "I haven't the slightest idea," he said. "What do you mean?" And then, shrugging his shoulders, he went on with her.

Chapter Twenty-Nine

WYNCHAM SPEAKS

Governor Pyndero did not dance. He had to set his teeth to
keep back the desire. He felt that on the occasion of this first
social event of his giving, it would be wiser for him to restrain
his impulse and spend his time in sober conversation with the
citizens who were heaviest in pocketbook and in name. This
policy, in due time, brought him to the side of *Señor* Tarabal.
The vanity of the rancher was well known. And the governor
was instantly in the midst of praises of the carriage, the ranch,
the house, the daughter of Tarabal.

"And now," said the governor, "she looks like a princess,
as she dances with Lord Wyncham."

Tarabal rolled himself from side to side, so huge was his
satisfaction. Mere words could not express it. The governor,
for his part, looked steadily in the direction of the dancers
whom he had just pointed out. As a matter of fact, he had
spoken at random. But his own words now sharpened his
vision, and it seemed to him that Ortiza was lovely, indeed —
a discovery he had made long before — and that Lord Wyncham was actually a worthy partner for her. This, however,
was a distinctly new thing.

He said it over to himself and stared. Unquestionably they
were getting on well together. She was flushed, and her eyes
shone. She was talking gaily with my lord. Yet, what was
Tarabal saying?

"You see that she is fighting to appear happy, Your Excellency?"

"Fighting?" said the governor.

"She has been ill all evening. She was not even sure that she could come to the ball. I persuaded her, but she has sat here, pale and silent, with not a word to me or even to my son, Valdez."

"Ah!" said the governor, and looked again at Ortiza.

He had the greatest respect for the opinion of Tarabal in all matters that had to do with finance. But it occurred to him that he might be slightly off in his estimate of his daughter. At least, the recovery of Ortiza had been singularly rapid. She was dancing with a light and joyous grace that certainly counterfeited the most perfect health. And, as she tilted her face up to Lord Wyncham, she was like a flower. The blood of the governor rushed into his head, receded slowly, and left him very pale.

"Has she ever been like that with *Señor* Valdez?"

"Girls take their husbands for granted," said Tarabal complacently. "I think this Englishman will have dreams tonight."

"Very likely," said the governor. "Very likely."

He could almost read the lips of the two and catch their words. But, if he had been actually able to hear them, the governor would have turned even more livid than he was already.

"I shall not listen again, my lord," she was saying, and with that she bent her head so that he could not see her face.

"And yet," he said, "I guess that you are smiling."

"*¡Señor!*" she cried, but when she looked up and strove to frown at him, the laughter broke through. "What shall I do?" she said. "I am helpless . . . I cannot keep from laughing at you."

"And yet," he said, "I have never in my life been more serious."

"But, of course, you are not!"

"You are sure?"

"I have seen you once, my lord."

"There you are wrong."

"Have I really seen you before?"

"I can prove it."

"Well?"

"When you thought of the ball tonight, you remembered something that a strange fellow vowed to you."

"Ah?" murmured Ortiza, and actually blushed with interest.

"Shall I tell you what it was he promised you?"

"How could you know it?"

"That he should dance with you at the governor's ball."

"But will he come?"

"Do you hope so?"

"Oh, no! He would be ruined, of course. They would stab him with a hundred swords."

"If he did not come, he would be ruined in *your* estimation, *señorita*."

"Indeed, no! Could I ask a poor slave to venture his life merely for the sake of keeping a foolish promise?"

"Slave?"

"Is he not the slave of Valdez?"

"He is not! He was stolen by pirates. He was enslaved by the father of Valdez. But he is as free by his birthright as I am free."

"But how could you know of him?"

"I cannot tell you."

"At least his real name, if he is a free man."

"His first name is Anthony."

"The same as yours, my lord."

"The very same. And I'll venture to say that, if he has promised to meet you and dance with you at the governor's ball, he'll keep his word."

"Impossible!"

"I shall wager with you on it."

"As much as you please, sir."

"But I cannot place a bet when I know beforehand that I have won."

"What do you mean?"

"Ah," he said, "have you not guessed? Then look at me and guess again."

She looked obediently into his eyes, until her smile went out, and her eyes were great and staring.

"It cannot be," she whispered at length. She grew limp with sudden weakness. "Oh," she whispered, "you were made to do it."

"I had given you my promise."

"But no one dreams who you are?"

"Half a dozen people dream, but they are not sure. Mortier dreamed the truth. So does the governor. He is not sure, by any means, but he is feeling toward the truth with a cat's paw, and, when he is a little surer, he will strike. He is watching us now, as we dance together, and he tells himself that something is very wrong."

"Where have you found the courage to live among them all these days?"

"A wig, blackening for my eyebrows, make-up have done it very well. It keeps me in the shadow and lets Lord Wyncham be seen. What fools they really are."

"And how desperately clever and reckless *you* are."

"I had sworn to meet you here and to dance with you."

"But not to stay all these days in Monterey before the ball, exposed to worse than death every moment."

"It has all been a very pleasant game, and I have had helpers."

"Who?"

"Eight Indians."

She shuddered. "Can you trust them?"

"With my life."

"Swear one thing."

"I shall."

"That after this dance you will leave the ball."

"And so draw suspicion on my head?"

"You would not do that."

"I say, the governor is watching me like a hawk."

"But you must not stay. If you should be found out. . . ."

"I should risk all for the sake of the next dance we are to have together."

"What can I say to convince you?"

"Nothing."

"You would still jest."

"I am mortally serious."

"How can you be?"

"Because it is love. Do you dream that, otherwise, I should have stayed? I was armed. I had a horse fast enough to defy pursuit. I only stayed in the first instance to help the poor devils, the Navajos. But when I saw you that night, I could not leave. I have been near you ever since. I, or one of my Navajos, has never been beyond the sound of your voice. Does this help to make you see that I am serious?"

She could not answer. When the dance was ended, she told her father that she was ill and must go home at once. It was not hard for Tarabal to believe her. She was sickly white. And, though he would gladly have had her stay and complete her triumph, he was so proud of the admiration she had already attracted that he was ready to agree to anything. She insisted on one other thing — that Valdez should not be disturbed. He was too happy, it seemed, with the new heiress, Julie Darnay. And, besides, there was no need for his escort.

So Tarabal said secret farewell to his host and slipped away.

224

As they moved toward the house in which they were staying in Monterey, her head was bowed, and she did not speak.

"Ortiza," he said when they came to the house, "you are sick and unhappy?"

"I am only afraid," she answered suddenly. "I am sick because I am afraid."

"Afraid of what?"

"Nothing," she said, and passed on into her room.

There she studied her face above the candlelight in her mirror for a long time. And what she found there was enough to set her smiling at last. One would have thought that she had read to the end of a pleasant story. Finally she took the candles from the mirror and put one on each side of the window.

Chapter Thirty

A GLORIOUS IDEA

There was no question that the ball was a flaming success. It was a triumph both in the governor's house and in the great tent. Eventually all the guests from the house moved out into the rioting crowd in the tent. Of all the merrymakers, there was none who attracted such attention as Julie. People who had thought her eclipsed by Ortiza, while the latter was dancing, began to doubt what they had seen. For it is very, very hard for the eye to remember the truth. And Julie, before the ball ended, was the queen of the night. Yet, when the festivities ended, no one was surprised when Valdez was given the honor of escorting her back to the house where her father lay sick and weak.

The ball broke up in five minutes. The guests departed, and through the streets of Monterey reëchoed the waves of their laughter and song. The governor stopped Lord Wyncham and drew him aside.

"I need five minutes' talk with you," he said, "and a bottle of wine. Wait for me in the house until I've finished with the herd."

He accompanied the invitation with a kindly pressure of his hands, and Lord Wyncham obeyed. In fact, the governor's invitation was simply a politely worded command. He heard the merriment move away from the house and the great tent. As the silence began, the governor came back into the room where Lord Wyncham was seated. He struck at once into the heart of his business.

"Wyncham," he said, "I have in mind something of such importance that it cannot wait. I must talk about it tonight. Come into this room with me and we'll be sure of silence and no interruptions."

He led the way, and through a casement in the chamber they could see the lights on the brig, *Fortune*, and the skeleton of her masts, lifting up above the black water and nodding from time to time across some of the lower northern stars.

"What has put this affair into my head," said the governor hastily, "is the manner in which you crossed the continent and handled the Indians along the way."

"Have I ever told you the way?"

"Only by inference. I gathered that they were easily managed by you."

Wyncham shrugged his shoulders.

"And what I now want to do is to get a message to that rascal, El Rojo."

"A message of sword points and powder and lead, Pyndero?"

"Not at all. You must guess again to get at my meaning."

"I have no other guess, sir."

"Wyncham, what has struck you, since you arrived here and began hearing of El Rojo? What has impressed you about the man?"

"That's he's a slippery scoundrel who'll be fruit on the gallows some day."

"I doubt it. He's too uniformly successful, Wyncham. That's why I want to get a message to him. Uniform good luck is something that all of us could very well use in our affairs. Am I right?"

"Unquestionably," said Wyncham.

"In short, Wyncham, I want to bury the sword between El Rojo and me. You'll perhaps wonder what use the governor

227

of a province can make of an escaped slave. But, I tell you frankly, that the man has my admiration, and I am appealing to you to reach him. You love adventure. I think you'd be willing to attempt to get in touch with him for me. Frankly, it's a message I can't confide to anyone else, and it's a message no one but you could get any closer to El Rojo with than to the knife of an Indian hunter. You understand me?"

"Why, it's all clear enough, Pyndero. You want me to try to locate this slippery devil and give him a message of good will from you."

"With guarantees, you know."

"I'm to try to convince him that you mean what you say by my lips. And I'm to put it in such a way that this ex-pirate will believe me."

"You can do it, Wyncham."

"I thank you. That's a large trust, Pyndero."

"You are inclined to smile at me. I wonder if you do not secretly despise my scheme. Perhaps you even wonder how I could use such a fellow. But I tell you, Wyncham, that there are more angles to the life of a governor of California than you dream of. He would mean a fortune to me, and I would mean a fortune to him. Is that plain?"

"I take your word for it, but this is a devilish ticklish task. Besides, I have no liking for the knives of these Indians."

"Nonsense!" cried the governor. "They don't know even the alphabet of their craft compared with you. You could kill them at thirty paces, as if you were using bullets. Confess that you have no fear of their knives, and that it is only your infernal love of leisure, my lad."

"I cannot confess it. Yet. . . ."

"Let me see those knives. You keep a pair of them ever about you, do you not?"

Lord Wyncham delayed long enough for a man to count

two rapidly. Then he produced from his clothes two long-bladed weapons, so long, indeed, that it was wonderful where he could have concealed them. He handed them to the governor.

"Ah," said the latter, "here they are. And yet with knives like this, and your skill to use them, you insist that you will not attempt to get in touch with El Rojo for me?"

"To a stranger," said Lord Wyncham, "it would seem that you were almost threatening me."

"Why, you fool," cried the governor, "of course, I am!" As he spoke, he jerked out a double-barreled pistol and dropped it across his knee. "You have seen me shoot, Wyncham?"

"I have never had that pleasure, and I hope, Your Excellency, that I shall not see it for the first time this evening."

"Your hope is mine. All depends on you. My soul, what a cool devil you are, Wyncham. But with pistols I've practiced many a mortal long hour. I'll knock an orange out of your hand at twenty paces, my good friend."

"Very wonderful," said Wyncham.

"All of this boasting, by the way, simply to bring you to reason."

"I shall try my best to act inside of reason, Pyndero."

"Then you see that the game is up?"

"I cannot possibly follow your meaning, sir."

"I'll help you to it, then."

With this he rose and, keeping the muzzles of his weapon directed straight at the breast of Wyncham, he walked across the room and buried the fingers of his left hand in the black hair of his lordship. With a quick jerk he pulled off a glossy black wig, beneath which there now appeared a mass of flame-colored hair.

"I present you," said the governor, "to that cunning rascal of whom we have just been talking. Lord Wyncham, I present

El Rojo. Look yonder in the long mirror to see one another, gentlemen."

He broke into laughter and sank into one of the chairs. Yet every instant, during his mirth, it was plain that he did not relax his watchfulness for a second. He kept watch out of eyes upon his companion, and the pistol was ever ready, with its two barrels presented. El Rojo rose from his chair, seemed on the verge of throwing himself at the throat of the governor, and then very slowly sat down again.

"I have been wondering when you would wake up," he said.

"Wrong . . . wrong, El Rojo. You are a clever dog, but, if you had guessed that I was actually on the trail of your identity, you would have run for the hill or the sea."

"Indeed?"

"You still face me out? I tell you, man, I was not sure, until I actually tore the wig from your head, and I half expected that I should have to pay for pulling the hair of my guest by taking the field against Lord Wyncham with my sword."

"A good guess."

"That was all . . . a guess based on a good many things."

El Rojo said nothing. He folded his hands and waited.

"And I am half tempted," said the governor, "to repeat the offer I made to you, through the late Lord Wyncham, with only a few modifications. El Rojo. . . ."

"Call me, if you please, Wyncham."

"Come, come. Do you expect me to continue that sham for your pleasure?"

"My name is Anthony Wyncham. The title was for the pleasure of Monterey, Your Excellency."

The governor could not help but laugh. "Very well," he said, "I repeat it again. Wyncham . . . since that's your true name . . . if you will be my man, I'll make your fortune."

"In what way, sir?"

"For one thing, you must help me to get Ortiza. You understand? I saw this evening that you understand how to touch her. You must teach me that. In the beginning. . . ."

"I can tell you in a single word how you may easily win her."

"Tell me, then."

"You have only to be a gentleman, Your Excellency."

"What? Are you mocking me, Wyncham?"

"I sincerely hope not."

The governor stared at him. "You are not such a fool as to defy me, Wyncham? You are not really going to do that and throw yourself back into the arms of Valdez. Think what Tarabal will do to you when he has the man who robbed him of his horses. Think of it. But, no, it is too devilish for thought."

"It is," admitted Wyncham.

"Then, my friend, let us talk business. Mark what I am giving up. I have put my administration on bad terms with the people. They put me down in their thoughts as a specimen of inefficiency. But, if I take El Rojo with my own hands, that will be another story. I would gain there, and it would be a very pleasant triumph. But I am willing to risk it all, Wyncham. I'll give up that for another thing."

"In the name of heaven, then, what is it that you want?" The eagerness of Wyncham broke for the first time into the quality of his voice.

"I want you for my friend."

"In what way?"

"As Lord Wyncham for a time . . . and afterward for other things. Let me outline my plan, Wyncham. In the first place, I absolutely require only one thing . . . that is the destruction of the Navajos. The devils have hounded me, my good fellow.

A trifling misunderstanding with them, and a dozen blood-hounds started out on my trail. They are lurking around the hills . . . they are waiting to get at me, confound them. And you know them and all their hiding places, Wyncham. In half a day, under your guidance, my soldiers would have them. Am I not right?"

"Perfectly. I could run them down in an hour from this minute."

"God bless you, Wyncham. I want the heads of the eight. And after that I have other schemes . . . great schemes, Wyncham. My friend, my friend, listen to me. There are ships sailing up and down this coast, with cargoes worth two hundred thousand *pesos* and hardly a dozen men to man them. What could a score of valiant fellows led by one brave heart like El Rojo do? And when the soldiers rode out in pursuit of the villainous pirates, there would be the honest governor to send them just a little bit astray . . . you understand, Wyncham? And the profits would be a third to you, a third to me, and a third to the hearty crew."

"A glorious idea!" cried Wyncham.

"I knew you'd see it. Now for the Indians, first."

"The Navajos first and then our partnership, Pyndero?"

"Exactly. Only one thing before we begin. I must have your word to play fairly with me, Wyncham."

"Would you trust to my word?" asked Wyncham.

"I would," said the governor slowly. "I'd trust to your word, of course."

The slave looked down to the floor, then up. "The devil has failed to teach me that lesson," he said. "I can't break my word of honor."

"You mean to say that you won't swear to be true to me, Wyncham?"

"I mean that."

"But, you fool, the other thing . . . ?"

"I know it, and I'll have to face it."

"Valdez and Tarabal?"

"Those two."

Chapter Thirty-One

PYNDERO PAYS

For a moment, the governor could not fully understand that he had been denied, and he was forced to ask: "But what the devil is in your head, Wyncham?"

"I can't play with loaded dice," Wyncham replied. "I don't like your game, Your Excellency."

José Pyndero went black of face in his fury. "I have dreamed this," he said. "This is no fact, but a dream. But I have thought of a new thing, Wyncham. Instead of giving back a slave to Valdez and Tarabal, I shall put him back in prison. I shall put him back into such a cell as Darnay occupied."

"The thought is worthy of you."

"Be silent," gasped Pyndero. He shook with his fury. He seemed on the verge of striking the other with his balled fist. But he controlled himself. "Five or six days in the slime of the prison . . . I can promise you that, Wyncham."

"You are wrong," said Wyncham.

"Ah?"

"You are wrong. I shall walk freely out of your house."

"Explain, my dear Wyncham."

"Your anger is very strong, Your Excellency, but your vanity is stronger. Through your vanity I shall escape."

"You generously warn me beforehand."

"You are a thousand times welcome, Excellency."

"Since you are so frank, free yourself."

"I shall wager a hundred *pesos* . . . I have them in my purse, which is here at your service . . . that within one minute I shall

234

stand freely before you, with a drawn sword in my hand."

"A wager like that is worthy of a madman."

"You are wrong. It is worthy of a Pyndero. I need only to recall to you one fact. You have never been beaten in a bout with foils or with naked swords."

"I thank heaven, never," sighed the governor.

"And yet," said Wyncham, "in this very house you might have been beaten."

"Might have been? You refer to the time when you fenced with me? The first touch was yours, while I deciphered your system. But remember that the next two were mine. No, no, Wyncham. You fenced strangely well to begin with . . . but after that first bout I won almost every touch in all the times we have fenced. Is that not true?"

"Listen to me . . . and believe me . . . Mortier was in the patio, as we took our exercise."

"I remember it well. His eyes stood out from his head in wonder, as he watched our play."

"As he watched *mine*, Your Excellency."

"You are a vain fool, my friend."

"I tell you, he had fenced with me on board the *Fortune*. He was recognizing my style, and, after I had made the first touch, I saw that he was about to start up, in spite of my black hair and my new name, and proclaim me as El Rojo. So I immediately changed my style. Although you were winded, and I was comparatively fresh when I engaged again, I let you touch me twice and win the bout."

"*Let* me? That is a high-sounding lie, Wyncham."

"I give you that lie back in your throat."

The rapier of the governor leaped halfway out of its scabbard. "Wyncham, if I did not remember that you were tricking me for the sake of that wager, I'd. . . ."

The governor groaned with an anguish of rage. He made a

gesture in which the great ruby on his finger was a red flash of light. For he would rather have possessed his skill with the sword than to rule ten Californias.

"It is against judgment. I give you a chance . . . a ghost of a chance to escape justice . . . but. . . ."

"Justice?" sneered Wyncham. "A word like that in a throat like yours?"

The governor moaned, for he could not speak. With a single gesture he threw away his cloak and his pistol. With another he whipped out the rapier so violently that it whistled in the air. And, at the same time, a delicate blade sang in the air opposite him, and Wyncham stood on guard.

"You cold-blooded devil," gasped the governor. "Save your wind. You'll need it to. . . ."

His anger kept him from finishing the sentence, and he lunged venomously. For Wyncham was retreating before him, laughing in the very face of a genius with the sword — laughing! Yes, as he parried and slipped to one side or the other, he still mocked the governor. And, as he laughed and fought, he talked.

"Draw back for a breath, Your Excellency," he said. "Draw back for a breathing space and look down to the bay. They are making sail on the good brig, *Fortune*. My dear friend, when they weigh anchor and away, I shall be on board."

The governor cursed him through his teeth and, as a rejoinder, flung at him a volley of strokes that hemmed Wyncham in a corner. It seemed that the next thrust would pin him to the wall. But mysteriously he glided away. There was something shadowy — something less and more than fleshly in his actions, and the point of Pyndero's rapier pricked only through the shoulder of his shirt. Still, as he stepped away, he was talking.

"I shall not go down to the brig alone. The lady, Ortiza, is waiting for me at her window, I am sure. Remember that, Excellency. As you die . . . as you suck the fog into your throat, and the darkness rolls over your eyes, remember that I am galloping on the back of the good horse, Sanduval, down to the beach where the boat waits for us. And then think of us on the deck of the *Fortune*. Is it not a happy name, my friend?"

"The devil fly off with you!"

"The worthy captain, having received enough money to pay for five passages, shall receive us without a word of question, and, having brought me out as a slave, he shall take me back as a master."

"And that you may take with you!" exclaimed the governor, lunging for his heart.

Wyncham pivoted on the balls of his feet, then thrust in return, and it seemed that the glittering blade would surely be buried in the body of the governor. But Wyncham suspended the stroke, and the governor staggered back, gasping, trembling with weariness and sick with the knowledge that he had been mastered at last.

There was no surrender. He still fought with all his skill, but this invincible warrior drove him back, and still he talked, as he fought.

"As for the sword, it is one of the presents of Valdez to me. You may notice the music it makes in the air and against your blade. Its name is *La Cantante*, my dear friend. Think of The Singer, also, as you squirm on the floor, here, like a hen on a spit. Will you do that for me, Pyndero, or . . . ?"

He got no farther. In his shadowy advance he had driven the governor back to the wall and along the wall, until the hips of Pyndero struck against the edge of a table, and, to avoid the next thrust, he was forced to bend far back and make a desperate parry. But, as he did so, his right hand closed upon a heavy bowl. He did not pause to think, but he hurled it straight at the head of Wyncham, and he saw the latter, stag-

237

gering under a glancing blow, give far back and then drop to one knee, while the sword dropped from his nerveless hand and rattled upon the floor.

There was another sound at the same time, a soft and muffled fall, like that of a bare foot on the floor. But the governor did not heed. He only saw the disarmed man before him and the sword upon the floor. If that man lived to tell the story, the whole world must know that José Bernardo Pyndero had once been beaten in fair battle, sword to sword. And he could not endure the thought. He kicked the sword far out of reach, and with his trusty weapon he ran in.

He saw Wyncham rising with difficulty to his feet. Blood was trickling down one side of his head where the bowl had grazed him. He reeled, as though he were drunk, but the governor had no more fear that he should escape than that the lightning flash will somewhere strike the earth. But Wyncham, reeling heavily away, pointed past him.

"In heaven's name," he cried, "beware of Bulé! Look behind you!"

But that was too old and childish an invention to take the attention of the governor for a single instant. He could hear voices and footfalls gathering toward the room in answer to sounds they had heard and the crash of the bowl, as it had whirled past Wyncham and smashed against the wall. Then there must have been the voices of swords on swords. But he would finish this little job before outside help came to him. He poised his sword and leaped in at Wyncham.

He missed. For Wyncham had dropped prone on the floor, and, before the governor could strike again, he was caught by the hair of the head and jerked back. And, as he fell, a knife was driven home into the hollow of his throat. So that all Pyndero saw was not the vision of Wyncham fleeing — that the latter had painted for him — but the face of Bulé, cruelly

238

triumphant, that faded instantly in the dark.

It was very little more than ten minutes after this — it was at the same time that the town was suddenly awakened by the news that the governor had been murdered in his own house — that the boat's crew that waited on the beach saw their employer rush out of the night across the white beach on a shining black stallion. They saw Lord Wyncham throw himself from the saddle and help down to the sands a lady who had been riding behind him. She was masked, but, as he whisked her into his arms and ran through the water toward the boat, a few locks of glistening golden hair streamed out from beneath her hood and shone in the light of the torch the steersman held.

"Out with the light," gasped Wyncham. "And now, give way heartily, my friends. Five *pesos* for each, if you get swiftly out from the shore."

They gave way with a will. Other hoofbeats were sounding in the distance, but they were already gliding smoothly and rapidly out onto the black face of the water and pointing toward the *Fortune*, half skeleton and half outlined with snowy canvas. They would reach it easily before it got under way.

"But look," whispered Ortiza, "the great black horse is trying to follow."

Sanduval had run into the water until it boiled around his shoulders. Now he paused and sent his great neigh ringing after his master. Darkness rolled across him, but he neighed again, and yet again. That was all. After this, there was only a faint murmur of human voices, from the beach and nearer at hand, the cheery calling of the boatswain on the brig. A little more, and they stood on the deck at the side of old South Wind.

THE END